Demon for Rent

S.M. Caulfield

Copyright October 2022

by S.M. Caulfield

All rights reserved.
Published in the United States
by the Amazon Publishing Platform

This book cannot be reproduced in any form
without explicit permission from the author.

ISBN-13: 979-8-888-62610-8

1st Print & E-Book Edition

DEMON FOR RENT

September

"Hey FATSO!! Get outta my seat!"

That was the voice of Gary the Schmuck reverberating through the school bus all the way to the back bench where I was sitting. And yes, I'm the fatso that the schmuck was referring to.

"I'm not moving, Gary."

I knew what was going to happen. It had happened before more times than not. I wasn't going to move and so, unfortunately for me, something bad would happen and Gary was the one where the bad would come from. Today it was my lunch.

Ripping the paper bag from my hands, Gary slammed it on the floor and squished it flat, using the heel of his boot to crush everything that hadn't broken when it hit the ground.

"Thanks Gary. I really love flattened sandwiches. Thanks for doing that for me."

Of course, it enraged him and he now picked up the bag and threw it out the window.

"CREEP!!! Get outta my seat!"

I wasn't going to budge. Gary's harassment had started two weeks ago after the bus I took to school changed to Gary's. At first, I was scared when he yelled at me. I would move when he screamed, because I didn't want any trouble.

2 - Demon for Rent

I don't know what happened, but one day, I just decided not to take it any more...no matter what. I mean, what was the worst that would happen to me? It was kind of strange, but Gary didn't hit. He would break your glasses, ruin your lunch, rip up your homework, and a lot of other nasty things. But, strangely, he didn't hit. Maybe that's why I decided to stand up to him.

"Find another seat, Gary. I'm not moving."

Grabbing my homework, Gary crumbled it and threw it out the window. That was ok because I had made 2 copies in anticipation of Gary destroying one of them. I was about to make another Gary-annoying comment when the voice of Mr. Grossman interrupted.

"Gary, please go to the front of the bus and sit in the seat by the door."

"Yes sir, Mr. Grossman."

Gary turned and walked quietly back to the front of the bus.

"David? Are you ok?"

Mr. Grossman was the kind of person that really cared about everybody, including me, and, of course, Gary. He was a retired policeman and had taken on driving a school bus because he wanted something to do.

"Yes sir. I'm fine. You know, Mr. Grossman, Gary never hits anybody. He just does stuff to your property."

"Gary's life has been pretty tough recently, David. I know that's no excuse, but when someone acts like he does, there's usually a reason."

With that, Mr. Grossman went back to the front and finished driving us to school. It left me wondering what he meant.

I had heard some stuff about Gary, but to me, it didn't matter. He was just a bully, that's all. Today was Friday and I was done being harassed for the rest of the weekend. After school I headed downtown to pick up a couple things for my mom. That was when I saw the shop. Tucked snugly between Elly's Knit & Notions and the Gastronibeak Bird Center was a dusty looking window with a small sign pushed up against the glass.

Demon for Rent was written in crayon on the sign.

September - 3

Peeking in the window, I could only make out a counter and a couple of folding chairs. Really, there was nothing demonic about any of that. Although the sign was curious, the rest of the place didn't seem evil or dangerous at all. Letting it go, I headed to Frank's hardware to pick up the screwdriver my mom needed. When I started back to the bus to get home, I had to pass the shop again. I couldn't help but wonder what the sign actually meant.

I guess the old saying that curiosity got the kid held. I decided to go in and check the shop out.

An old-fashioned bell tinkled as I opened the door. Entering the room, I could smell cinnamon. It wasn't like an incense smell—it was more like a cookie smell and it smelled really good. There wasn't a lot of furniture and there was almost nothing on the walls except a large brassy looking sun clock. A small wooden table with two folding chairs sat in one corner and other than that and the counter, there wasn't much else. Some papers that looked like brochures were loosely stacked on the table and just as I was about to pick one up to see what they were, I heard a door open toward the back of the room.

I turned in time to see a middle-aged woman come around the corner. Now, looking at the shop, I would have thought that she would be kind of dusty herself, with a long gypsy-like skirt and Bohemian-styled top in multiple colors and patterns. Well, that just wasn't the case. The woman, whose name I later found out was Aggie (short for Agnes) was dressed in a white t-shirt tucked neatly into relatively tight straight-legged Levi's with a worn brown leather belt clasped with a turquoise and silver buckle. She carried a blue floral-patterned plate piled with cookies and she was looking directly at me and smiling.

"Hello David. It's about time you stopped in. Have a cookie." With that she placed the plate on the counter and walked over to where I was standing.

"How do you know who I am?" I glanced toward the sign and figured she was doing some hocus pocus on my brain.

Seeing me glance at her sign, she laughed. "Oh, it's not magic,

4 - Demon for Rent

David. My daughter Lori rides your bus. She told me about you and all the problems you've had with Gary Morgan. She usually sits a couple rows up from you. Blonde hair and glasses? Pretty much only wears jeans?"

Of course, I knew her. Lori Czech. She had smiled at me a couple of times, but I had never gotten up enough nerve to even smile back. She was very pretty...too pretty for someone as nerdy as me. Her mom did look kind of like an older version of her.

"Sorry, Mrs. Czech. I just thought...well, I mean, the sign in your window kind of made me think you were...well, like a...a..."

Mrs. Czech interrupted. "Call me Aggie, David. Have a cookie and let me explain the sign.

So, there was an explanation and it was kind of a bummer when I heard it. I mean, it sounded so mystical and I guess I thought it meant you could come in and hire some creature to do your bidding and something good or bad would happen, depending on what you wanted. Well, ya, if you must know... I was thinking of Gary when I decided to go in and find out what it meant and how I could use it. It turned out to be nothing like that, or at least, I didn't think it was.

Mrs. Czech continued...

"So, David, why did you decide to come in? Was it because you thought you could do something to get Gary to stop bugging you? And yes, I know about the problems. Lori told me all about the stuff on the bus.

"I guess you're right, Mrs. Czech. I saw the sign and it crossed my mind that maybe I could scare him into leaving me alone. I mean, is the demon friendly enough to just scare Gary and not hurt him?"

Aggie Czech snickered, smiled and glanced at the sign before she spoke. "I'm a child psychologist, David. I'm doing a study on the physical and mental effects of stress on teens and other kids. I put that sign in the window because I wanted to see if anyone...any kid that is, would come in and want to hire a demon to take care of a problem."

"Has anybody come in, I mean, other than me?" I was surprised at her answer.

September - 5

"23 people so far and of those, 14 of them were 17 and under. The others ranged in age from 24 to 72. They all had a problem they needed to get fixed and they all wanted to hire a demon. Wasn't that why you came in, David? You have a problem and you were trying to find a solution?"

I nodded feeling completely stupid. I knew there really were no demons, but maybe I was hoping I was wrong.

"I'm sorry to have bothered you, Mrs. Czech…ah, I mean Aggie. I have to get home now or my mom will worry."

Mrs. Czech had told me to take a cookie, so I grabbed a couple and headed for the door.

"David, wait a minute." Pulling out a little white paper bag from behind the counter, Aggie stuck two cookies in the bag and walked over to where I was standing.

"Here, give this to Gary on Monday when he bothers you on the bus. OK?"

I nodded, took the bag and headed to the bus. On the ride home I ate the cookies she had given me and tucked the little bag with the other cookies into my backpack. I really wondered why she wanted Gary to have them, but who was I to question an adult, especially one who was a psychologist?

— •••—

By Monday, I had forgotten all about the cookies that Aggie…Mrs. Czech had given me to give Gary. Getting on the bus I went back to my usual seat and waited for the inevitable. Gary would get on in 2 more stops. He would stomp back to my seat, demand I move, and then break something of mine.

But today was different. When Gary got on the bus, he sat down in the first row nearest the driver. He wasn't talking or anything; he just stared out the window and looked like he was deep in thought. For the first day in a long time, my bus ride was uneventful.

6 – Demon for Rent

Because I was in different classes, I didn't see him again until lunchtime. He was sitting by himself at a table in a corner of the cafeteria nearest the windows. It looked like he didn't have a lunch or anything. I knew how that felt since Gary had destroyed mine many times before and I had either not eaten or shared part of a sandwich or some chips with a friend. The school did have for-pay food, but it was usually yucky and I was never so hungry that I would break down and buy it. I couldn't tell whether Gary looked hungry or not.

I then remembered the cookies that Mrs. Czech had given me for Gary. I wasn't particularly crazy about giving him anything, but I had promised her I would. Pulling the bag out of my backpack, I walked over to where he was sitting. I was kind of afraid of what he might do. I had already eaten, so he couldn't squish my lunch, but there was always my glasses and my books or backpack. I approached with some concern.

"Hey Gary, Mrs. Czech, Lori Czech's mom, asked me to give you these cookies." Gary was staring out the window and didn't even look toward me as I laid the bag down on the table.

"Well, hope you like the cookies. See you on the bus."

What was I thinking?? I guess people say whatever when they're nervous and boy, I sure was. I just had to remind him that I'd be on the bus when school let out. I knew that Gary would come out of his haze and attack my stuff. It crossed my mind that he might even start hitting if he got mad enough.

The thought bothered me all afternoon. When school was over, I hung back so I'd be the last to get on the bus because that's when Mr. Grossman also got on. Gary was already there and sitting in the front row. He didn't even look up when I passed him to go back to where I sat. There, on his lap, was the little bag with the cookies Mrs. Czech had made. I wondered why he hadn't eaten them. I mean, he didn't have a lunch, so why hadn't he eaten them?

The bus route was the same as in the morning, except backward. Gary got off the bus first. I watched as he walked down the street and then turned down a little path that ran between the houses and back towards a wooded area. I wondered where he actually lived. I had never been down there because my mom had told me I wasn't supposed to go there. I wasn't sure why. I decided to ask when I got home.

— ••• —

My house is nothing special. It's kind of middle size and comfortable. The only thing really neat was the front yard. Mom likes to garden and there were all sorts of beautiful flowers that she had planted. Sure enough, as I got off the bus, I could see Mom working away planting something near the front door. Even though it was almost the beginning of October, she still planted things that would grow and bloom in the spring. She turned when she heard me coming up the sidewalk. Smiling, she got up off her knees so she could give me a hug when I reached her.

"So, what's new David? How was your day?"

Mom always asked as she hugged and I always told her everything was great. I never mentioned the problems I had with Gary. Today was no different, but I did have that question.

"Hey Mom. Everything's good. Nothing special, but I have to ask you something."

"Ok? Anything wrong?"

Mom looked a little concerned. She always had my back, always understood even when it was something bad that I had to tell her.

"Don't worry, Mom. It's nothing. I just wanted to ask you about that place you told me to stay out of. You know, that wooded area that's back behind the houses a few blocks away?"

"Oh, sure David. What do you want to know?"

"Well, what's back there? You told me to never go into that area and I wanted to know why. I think one of the kids that rides my bus might live somewhere near those woods."

Mom looked a little pensive. You're probably wondering why I'm using a word like pensive. Well, I just learned it in my language class

8 - Demon for Rent

today and had to try it out. Mom did look that way—thoughtful, but a little sad.

"A lot of homeless and low-income people live back there David, back in the woods or near there. Don't get me wrong. I wasn't saying anything about the character of the people when I told you to stay out of the woods. No. Kids should not go into places they're not familiar with, especially wooded areas. You mentioned your friend goes back there?"

Friend...hmm. I wasn't going to tell Mom that Gary wasn't my friend.

"Yup. He gets off our bus and walks down a path between the houses that goes into that area. I thought maybe there were houses back there."

"Well, there might be. I haven't been back there for a long time, so it's possible. "

I thought about what Mr. Grossman had said about Gary having a tough life and it made me want to find out more.

"So, is there a road back there? I'd like to find out where he goes every day."

There were more pensive looks from Mom.

"Are you suggesting we drive back there and check out the area?"

"Well, if you want to. Maybe you would want Dad to go along if you think it isn't safe?"

Mom laughed.

"No, that won't be necessary. We can go Saturday."

Well, I did want to...wanted to find out more about Gary, where he lived, and maybe figure out why he was so angry all the time...at least when he was around me. So, I said yes, of course, and mom said we would drive back there and check out the area around noon. I couldn't wait.

— ••• —

I was up early on Saturday to get my chores done before Mom and I went on our little adventure. Ok, it wasn't anything really special, but I was excited anyway. Mom had to do the grocery shopping and of course, I worried that she wouldn't make it home in enough time for us to take our drive. But, right at 11, she pulled into the driveway and yelled at me to come help with the groceries. I always helped when she asked. She never asked for a lot and I never had to do so many chores that I wouldn't have any time for fun. Well, there was that time last Thanksgiving when Gramma Sis came to visit. I think I ended up cleaning for a whole weekend. Don't get me wrong here. Mom and Dad cleaned too. It just seemed weird to me that we had to do that much cleaning just so somebody visiting for a few hours would think we were really neat. I mean clean neat.

Anyway, right before noon Mom came to my room and reminded me that we were going to take a drive. Excuse me? I had not forgotten. It was a beautiful day and I wanted to take Dad's jeep so we could take the roof off because it was always really neat to do that. And this time, I didn't mean clean, I meant really, really neat.

Mom had looked at a map and figured out the best way to go back into that area. There were a couple of ways and she decided on the one that took us straight through the forest, the place she didn't want me going by myself. You know, thinking about Gary, I realized he went back that way every day after school. Nothing bad ever happened to him…at least I didn't think it had.

It didn't take us too long to get to the turnoff that would take us through the woods. At first, nothing was there but trees, but then, the area started looking more like the street where I live except pretty run down. There were smallish houses on both sides of the road with a lot of junk just sitting around. We passed an old rusted-out bus that looked like maybe someone lived there. Then, there was this truck with no tires propped up on concrete blocks right in front of a house that someone was definitely living in. I mean, there were curtains in the windows and a rocking chair on a covered porch. Definitely, or at least to me, the house was occupied. Some of the houses were boarded up, but I really think that people lived in those as well.

10 – Demon for Rent

We hadn't seen anyone yet, but as the road curved back toward the area where I thought Gary must live, we spotted a couple of girls walking a dog alongside the road. I thought I recognized one of them as someone who went to my school. I'm in 7th and the girl was probably in 8th. Staring at us as we drove slowly by, they were probably wondering who we were, just like I was wondering who they were.

A little further down the road we passed a gas station and what looked like a little market. There were some people there that were getting gas and shopping, I guess. I was surprised, because I hadn't expected anyone but the homeless people Mom had mentioned.

We had gone further than where I thought Gary lived, but when we came up on a cross street, Mom turned and headed back in the direction of the path between the houses.

And suddenly, there he was. He was sitting in front of a tiny trailer that didn't look much bigger than the pop-up RV that my family uses when we go camping. He was slouched over, head in hands and it looked like something was wrong.

Mom noticed him as well and pulled over to the side of the road. Turning the car off, she unsnapped her seatbelt and started getting out.

"Wait, Mom...what are you doing?" I grabbed her arm which stopped her for a minute. But, when my Mom wants to do something... well, you know.

"David, you see that child over there? Something's wrong and I'm going to find out what."

"Mom, that's Gary, the kid who I told you lives up here."

"Well, come on then. Let's find out what's wrong with your friend." Oh well. I either had to tell Mom about all the problems or get out of the car with her and see what Gary was up to. It was silly, but I just didn't want to tell her. She would get involved, talking to the school and his parents. She would make a stink and I really didn't want to go through that. So, I got out of the car.

Gary was sitting on an old rusty step that led up into the trailer. He was slumped over and didn't move until Mom spoke.

"Gary?"

Gary looked up and of course, the first thing he saw was a person... I mean...was me. He looked genuinely surprised and was about to say something when he spotted my Mom.

Mom made the first move.

"Hi Gary, my name's Mrs. Allen. I'm David's Mom. We were just passing through your neighborhood and saw you sitting there. Is everything ok? You look kind of down.

"My Mom's sick. I don't know what to do."

He sounded really sad and of course, Mom became concerned.

"So, Gary, where's your mom?"

"In our house."

"Where's your house?" Mom asked.

He pointed at the trailer.

Mom didn't ask. She just brushed passed Gary and went right in. I forgot to tell you that Mom is a nurse and works part time at one of the emergency centers in our town.

And now, here I was, standing alone, face to face with the bus bully and he was doing nothing. I decided to take a chance and talk.

"So, what's going on, Gary? What's the matter with your Mom?"

Gary slumped down again.

"Don't know. She's been sick for a while."

Just then, Mom came out of the trailer. She was on her phone talking to someone at her job, I think. Getting off the phone she spoke to Gary.

"Listen, Gary, your Mom is pretty sick. I've called emergency and they'll be here shortly. She was worried about money, but I told her not to be. My clinic doesn't worry about that. We just want to make sure people are ok, that your Mom will be ok. Oh yes, your Mom said you don't have anyone you can stay with, so, you're coming home with us."

OH MY GOSH. Gary the bully was coming to my house. I didn't think it could get any worse than that, but it did. Gary didn't have any clean clothes to take along, so Mom offered mine. My clothes on Gary.

12 - Demon for Rent

Dang! I would never wear that stuff again.

It was about 10 minutes until I heard the emergency siren and saw the ambulance turn on to the dirt driveway where Gary lived. Two men got out of the truck and Mom walked up to meet them. She addressed them by name and pointed to the trailer. One of the men got a stretcher from the back and the two entered Gary's home. It felt like forever, but maybe it was only 10 or 15 minutes before they came out with his Mom. She looked very pale and her arms were skinny…almost boney. Mom walked along by her side and as the EMT's were getting the stretcher with her on it into the truck, she reached over and touched Mom's arm. Mom leaned over and nodded as if agreeing to something she was saying. Then, it was over. The back door shut and the ambulance, sirens blaring, drove off toward town.

And there we were…me, Mom, and Gary. Just us, getting into my Dad's Jeep. Just us, heading to my home.

Could it get any worse than that?

—•••—

October 2

My home is comfortable. It's not that big, but big enough to have three bedrooms and that, right now, made me very, very happy. Our guest room was where Gary was going to stay and he wouldn't have to spend the night in my room with me.

I had never paid much attention to him except for when he was harassing me on the bus. He always wore an army shirt that was way too big for him, or for any kid for that matter, so I never really saw what he looked like. I mean, I barely ever looked at him in school and then, I always kept my head down and never made eye contact because I didn't want anything bad to happen.

Mom had given Gary some of my clothes to wear. Now, I'm not really fat, even though he calls me fatso all the time, but I may be a teeny bit bigger than most kids my age. At first, I thought Mom was giving him some of the clothes I wear now, but instead she had found stuff that didn't fit me anymore and gave that to him.

I had to set the table and I didn't see him until dinnertime. We weren't having anything special, just burgers and tots and some green salad that Mom insisted we always eat. I wasn't big on greens, but eating a little did keep Mom happy.

Gary stayed in our guest room until Mom called him to eat. Because he seemed pretty dirty, Mom had told him to take a shower and change to clean clothes. When he came to the table, he was in my old Avengers T-shirt and Jeans. I was surprised at how the clothes just hung on him. He was a lot smaller than me even though he was taller. He kind of looked boney like his Mom looked.

Dad had finished grilling the burgers and we all sat down at the table. Each of us got one and we could take as many tots and as much salad as we wanted. When I passed the tots to Gary, he only took a couple. He didn't take much salad either. I could tell he was really hungry because of how fast he ate his sandwich and drank the soda Mom had given him. Even after he finished the food on his plate, he still looked hungry, but when Dad asked him if he wanted another sandwich, Gary shook his head no.

He stayed pretty quiet during dinner and only spoke when Mom or Dad asked him something. The only time he actually said anything was when Mom mentioned that she was going to the clinic tomorrow to check on his Mom.

"Mrs. Allen? Can I go with you? I'd like to see my Mom."

Gary looked concerned and Mom, of course, agreed he could go with her.

After dinner, I loaded the dishwasher. Gary actually helped me. He didn't say a word but handed me the dishes from the table as I rinsed and loaded. After that, he went back to his room. There's a tv in there and I figured he was just going to watch something, but I didn't hear anything at all when I went to my room which is right next to his. I wasn't worried about it or anything. I mean, after all, it was Gary.

Why should I worry about someone who was always mean to me? This was getting difficult. I really needed to find out what was going on with him.

— •••—

Sunday is a quiet day at my house. I never have to do any chores… well, except homework if I haven't finished it. Mom always wants us

October - 15

to go to church in the morning, but with Gary here, not knowing if he was religious or not, she decided we would miss this week. Mom never forces me to go, but I always do. I kind of like listening to the minister, Reverend John Thomas. He doesn't preach fire and brimstone. Instead, he talks about how we all should be good neighbors and lend helping hands to those in need.

Mom always practices what the Reverend preaches. She's always doing something to help people who need it. Sometimes Mom has me mow a lawn or help clean up a yard or run an errand for someone. Dad gets to do stuff, too. He's an electrician by trade and can fix lights that aren't working and other stuff. Actually, Dad is really good at just about everything around the house.

Anyway, after breakfast, Mom and Gary left for the clinic and because Dad needed to get parts to repair a lamp, we headed over to the hardware store a few minutes later. I knew that Dad liked to chat with the owner, Frank de Marco and that was ok with me. I planned to take that time and walk over to Aggie Czech's store so I could talk to her about the whole Gary thing. I needed to know what she thought. After all, she was trained to figure out stuff like that.

As soon as we got to Frank's store, I told Dad I was going to walk over and see Lori Czech's Mom. I thought maybe he would ask me why, but he didn't. He had already spotted his friend, so he reminded me to be back in an hour when we would head home. I promised and took off to the store. It was only a 10-minute walk, so I knew I had plenty of time to get there and back by the time my Dad was ready to go home.

I wasn't sure she would be there, because it was Sunday, but if she wasn't, I figured I would drop into the bird center next door. I liked looking at all the different birds. When I got to the store front, however, I saw that a light was on inside. I could see Aggie at the counter doing something on her laptop. I tried to open the door, but it was locked. Aggie must have heard me, because looking up from what she was doing, she smiled, waved at me, then walked over and let me in.

"Hi David. How's it going? You do know my daughter, Lori, don't

16 - Demon for Rent

you?"

What? Lori was here?

Lori looked up from the little table in the corner and spoke to me as if we were old friends.

"Hi David. Nice to see you someplace other than on the bus. So, how come you stopped in? To see me?"

Oh no. I felt my face get red. I didn't want Lori to know that I had come in before to rent a demon to help me with the Gary problem. Plus, I didn't want to say that I didn't come to see her. Dang!

"I, ah, I...I..."

Aggie Czech must have heard me trying to tell her daughter why I was here because she interrupted my ridiculous stutter.

"David stopped by to get my recipe for Oatmeal Chocolate Chip Cookies to give to his mom. You know, I forgot to copy it, David. Just give me a second and I'll have it for you. Lori, why don't you show David what you're working on?"

Relief.

"Sure Mom. So, come sit down over here David and I'll show you."

I walked over and sat down next to her, noticing how pretty she was. Her long blonde hair was tied back in a ponytail and she was wearing her usual jeans, t-shirt, and a denim jacket that was trimmed with rhinestones.

There were markers on the table and some black and white pages that her Mom must have printed out for her. The top page read ***Schwab Middle School Food Drive. Donate a non-perishable item or two...or more and get into the Halloween Dance Free.***

"So, David," Lori began, "I'm the 7th grade organizer for the food drive the school decided to do. I'm looking for some kids the Thursday before the dance to help manage the food and get it out to needy families and to a couple of the shelters. Would you like to help?" I mean, maybe you and your Dad would like to help?"

Yes, it was October and we were coming up on my first Middle School Dance ever. I mean, I was thinking of going with a couple friends, but never thought of going with a girl...until now. I started wondering if she would even go with me if I asked. Well, I certainly didn't want to hear no, so it was better to get that thought out of my mind and just go with the guys I hang around with. Now, here was Lori asking me to hang out with her...well not really hang out...help her with something very meaningful. Mom would approve and Dad...well if Mom wanted him to help, he would. Then I remembered Gary and wondered if I should offer him as a helper too.

"How much time would you need, Lori? Right now, we have a house guest."

"Oh." Lori looked a little disappointed. "Don't worry about it. I can always get some other kids."

I felt my face go red again.

"No, no, that's not what I meant. I meant that maybe the kid that's staying with us would want to help as well."

Oh, oh. I knew what was coming next.

"So, who's staying with you, David?

I mumbled his name.

"Who? Wait, I think you said Gary. Is that what you said?" Lori looked at me as if she had misunderstood.

"No, you heard me right. Gary from the bus is staying at my house."

Lori snickered. "So, tell me all about it, David. How, in the entire world would you have Gary staying at your house?"

"It's a long story, Lori, but the short of it is that his mother is sick and in the hospital and Gary didn't have anybody to take care of him, so my Mom offered. I mean, he hasn't done anything bad so far."

"How long has he been staying with you?" Lori looked interested.

"Since yesterday afternoon."

Lori snickered again. "Well, good luck, David."

Just then, Aggie Czech came over to the table holding a piece of paper and handed it to me. It was the recipe.

"Give this to your Mom, David. It makes 4 dozen really good cookies."

"I will. Listen, I have to get back to the hardware store. I told my Dad I would meet him in an hour and it's pretty close to that now."

With that, I said goodbye and left the shop. Walking back to the hardware store I thought about Gary. You were probably thinking I was going to say Lori. Well, I thought about her, too, but I was wondering about him and his Mom and what was wrong with her and why they were living where they were and...

"David! You're late."

Dad was standing by the Jeep waiting for me.

"Sorry, Dad. Lori Czech was there and I was talking to her about some charity work she's doing at the school...for the school's Halloween dance."

Dad laughed. "So, didn't you tell me you were going to see Aggie?"

"Do you know Aggie...Mrs. Czech I mean?"

"Aggie went to school with your mother."

Wow, I never expected that. I never thought that she would know my Mom. Thinking about it, she was about the same age and her daughter was my age in the same grade. Dang! She might end up telling Mom why I came into her shop and I didn't want that to happen. I needed to tell her not to say anything. I mean, me trying to hire a demon could get me grounded for a really long time...maybe for life even.

I decided I'd go see her after school tomorrow, but then, I remembered Gary. He would be coming home with me on the bus. Maybe I could ask Lori whether her Mom told the kids' parents why they came to see her. You know...rent a demon to do something to someone. Yes, that had to be the plan. I would talk to Lori tomorrow.

Mom's car was in the driveway when Dad and I got home. Going into the house I saw her and Gary in the kitchen. It looked like they were getting ready to make cookies. I had the recipe from Aggie and what the heck, maybe they could make some of those cookies that she had made in her store.

"Hey Mom, what's going on? It looks like you guys are making cookies. So, here."

I handed the paper to my Mom.

"Aggie Czech...Mrs. Czech, I mean, she gave me this recipe and I was wondering...maybe you'd like to make some of those cookies? They were really good. I mean, ask Gary."

I turned and looked at Gary, who just shrugged his shoulders.

"I didn't eat those cookies."

"What do you mean you didn't eat them? Mrs. Czech told me to give them to you. What did you do with them...throw them away?"

Typical Gary behavior. Somebody does something nice for him and he still acts like a jerk.

"I gave them to my Mom."

What? He gave them to his Mom?

"Why'd you do that Gary? Mrs. Czech said they were for you."

When I said that Gary turned and walked out of the kitchen and down the hall. I heard a door close and I knew he had gone into his bedroom. I turned to Mom. She was just standing there looking at me in that kind of annoyed way she would look when I did something she wasn't particularly happy with.

"What? You're not upset with me for saying that, are you? I just wanted to know why he didn't eat those cookies himself. I mean, it was ok he gave them to his Mom, but Mrs. Czech said they were for him. I just wondered why."

Mom was pensive (there's that word again).

"Oh David. Someday when you're older you'll understand better.

"Why did you say that, Mom? I hate it when you say stuff like that."

And then, she laid it on me.

"So, Gary's Mom, Anna Morgan, is very, very sick. She has pneumonia and there are some complications. She's extremely weak and is having trouble fighting it. She has no insurance and there wasn't enough money for a doctor visit. If we hadn't stopped by when we did, well, who knows what would have happened. She could have died."

"So, she couldn't go to a doctor because they didn't have any money? Did she say anything else? Maybe about why they were living

20 - Demon for Rent

there? I mean, that trailer was so tiny. I think it's smaller than our camper. How could anybody live in something like that?"

"She didn't tell me David. Gary did. They lost their house a year ago and they had nowhere to live. They found this old trailer back where all the homeless people are. That's where they've been staying for the last few months. "

Mom continued...

"You know, David, Gary's been very concerned about his Mom for a long time. I guess they didn't have much money for food, either. You asked why he gave the cookies to his Mom? Well, she would always feed him first and then tell him she would eat later, when really, there wasn't enough for both of them every day. He thought maybe the cookies would make her stronger...help her get her strength up and get better."

I had noticed how skinny Gary was, but never thought it was because he didn't have enough to eat. I don't know what I thought. His Mom looked the same and I guess I just thought it was because she was sick. So, maybe this was why Gary was so mean to me. Maybe not. Still...

Mom left the kitchen but came back a few minutes later and started making the cookies. She said that Gary had decided to stay in his room until dinner. I felt kind of bad. I wasn't trying to be annoying like I was on the bus. I hadn't really thought that anybody I knew, including Gary, could be so poor that they were starving. I guess I was wrong.

— ••• —

Dinner was very quiet. Gary didn't say anything at all and Mom and Dad were not as talkative as they usually were. I guess Dad hadn't told Mom that I had gone to see Aggie Czech and I was happy about that. I didn't really want to have to answer questions about why I went to see her. I figured Dad just thought it was to see Lori and that was ok.

After dinner I loaded the dishwasher and Gary helped. He didn't say a word. When we were done, he went back to his room and closed the door. After that, I did my homework and watched TV with Dad for a while, then went to bed. I was thinking about the bus and talking to Lori tomorrow as I drifted off. Maybe I should ask her to the dance. Maybe not. Well…maybe.

— ••• —

You're probably wondering what I look like. I'm nothing special. My best feature is covered up with glasses. Other than blue eyes, I look like everybody my age—normal height, weight, and plain brown hair. Well, I guess I'm just a teeny bit heavier than other kids. I mean, I'm not fat—I'm just bigger, kind of. Except for Gary, nobody has ever said anything bad and even if they did, I could care less. At least, it didn't matter until now…until I started thinking about Lori and asking her to the dance.

I was really looking forward to seeing her on the bus. She got on a few stops before me, so I got it in my head that I would get on, smile, say hi and sit down next to her. Then, I would get the business stuff out of the way. You know…asking her to ask her Mom to please not mention why I was at her shop. You remember…the demon for rent stuff? She would say sure and then, I would make small talk, mention her charity work, and then, casually, ask if she was going to the dance with anybody. If she said no…wait… I mean WHEN she said no, I would say that maybe it would be fun if we went together. What a plan! For the first time in a long time I was looking forward to going to school.

— ••• —

Mom is one of these people who hates being late and because she hates it so much, everyone in the family has to be early for everything. Monday was one of her extra special early days, probably because the weekends were "early free". Because of this Gary and I were out waiting for the bus a whole 30 minutes before it would even get here.

22 - Demon for Rent

Gary was still not talking so I decided to take a chance and say something.

"So, Gary, are you going to go see your Mom after school?"

"I can't."

"Why not?"

"The doctor said they're doing some tests and she probably won't be awake for a while. I guess they wanted her to rest afterwards. Your Mom said she would check to make sure she was going to be ok and then she told me we would go tomorrow and visit her."

"When your Mom gets out of the hospital, what are you going to do? I mean, Gary, you can't go back to that trailer. It won't be healthy for her."

Gary sighed heavily. I could tell what I said upset him. I didn't want to get him so upset that he would yell at me...or worse. I had to think fast.

"I'll talk to my Mom, Gary. She'll know what to do. Maybe you guys can stay with us for a while. You don't have to worry."

Gary sighed again and he was about to say something when the bus came around the corner...and that was that. Gary just got on the bus without saying whatever he was going to say. He sat down in the front where Mr. Grossman usually made him sit.

I was really excited that I would be seeing Lori, but when I looked for her on the bus, she wasn't there. She wasn't in school either. I decided I would stop by her Mom's shop after school and see if she was ok. I didn't want it to look too obvious, so I decided to take Gary along. When I mentioned it to him, he just nodded ok. No words...just a nod. This not talking much was bothering me a lot. And no yelling? Was I missing the yelling?

Anyway, after school I called Mom on the school pay phone and let her know we would be a touch late, but not so late we would miss dinner. She reminded me she was taking Gary to the hospital after we ate.

After school, Gary and I grabbed the bus that would take us down to Aggie's shop. I had to pay for Gary because he didn't have any money.

That was ok, except it made me feel worse about what he and he and his Mom were going through.

The shop was a couple blocks from the bus stop and we walked (silently, of course) to Aggie's place. It was October and it was windy and getting cold. I had a super nice Levi's jacket that kept me comfortable when it was like this. Gary didn't have a jacket and he kind of scrunched his arms up tightly against his body, trying to stay warm. I made a mental note to ask mom if she could dig up a coat for him to wear.

When we got to the shop I could see Aggie at the counter on her computer. I didn't see Lori. I didn't see the Demon for Hire sign either. As we opened the door, she saw us, smiled and came around the counter to meet us.

"Hi David, what's going on? Who's your friend?"

"Hi Mrs. Czech…Aggie I mean. This is Gary Morgan."

"Gary?", Aggie smiled, "Well, nice to meet you, Gary. Hey, no coat? It's a little chilly out there.

Before Gary could say anything, Aggie spoke again.

"So, Gary, what size are you? Oh, never mind. Just wait a second."

Aggie walked back around the counter, reached down and pulled out a large Macy's bag.

"When I rented the space here, I found this bag stuck down behind the counter. No one ever claimed it and I just never got around to doing anything with it. Why don't you try this on?"

And with that, Mrs. Czech pulled a jacket from the bag and handed it to Gary. It was a brown suede bomber jacket and it looked really, really neat.

Gary just stood there staring at it.

"Go ahead Gary. Try it on. Let's see if it fits."

Gary slipped it on and it was a perfect fit.

"Gee Mrs. Czech, thanks."

Gary actually sounded grateful, and the jacket…well it fit him so well it was like he shopped for it himself.

24 - Demon for Rent

I was wondering where Lori was, so I decided to ask.

"Mrs. Czech…Aggie, so, I was wondering where Lori was today. She wasn't on the bus and wasn't in school either. I was supposed to help her with the food distribution and just wanted to know when she would need me…oh, and Gary, too."

Aggie Czech laughed. She knew. I don't think I could have felt any lower and was about to try and mumble something that sounded halfway intelligent when she interrupted my self-pity.

"Lori had some business to take care of for the charity, so she didn't have to go to school. She did her school work early so she wouldn't miss anything or get behind. She said if you stopped by to give you this."

There was a folder on the counter and she picked it up and handed it to me.

"What is this, Mrs. Czech?"

"It's just a schedule of what needs to be done for the food drive. If you and Gary can commit to a few hours on the Thursday before the dance, Lori would really appreciate it. She can get you both excused from school if you help. You did say you would, didn't you?"

Gary and I both nodded yes.

"Well, great then. Pick out what you want to do from the list. It shows how many hours you will have to work. Oh, and don't forget your Dad. We need a couple of drivers and I believe you told Lori he could help?"

Dang. I had told Lori my Dad would help and I had forgotten to ask him. I shook my head yes and crossed my fingers that he would agree. I mean, work wasn't a big deal because he had his own business. What was a big deal was that I hadn't asked.

"Can we get back to you on the times, Aggie?"

"Certainly, and I'll give your Dad a buzz and see if we can use one of his trucks."

What? She was going to call Dad? This was not good. This was me in trouble. I had to think fast.

"Well, he's on a job right now. Can I have him call you tomorrow?"

October - 25

"Sure, David. I just need to know by Friday, because we have to get the transportation settled before then."

I agreed to have Dad call tomorrow. That would at least give me enough time to talk to him tonight. We had to get back so we wouldn't be late. Gary thanked Aggie again for the coat and we left. We ran to catch the bus and I got on first and walked to the back where I usually sit. Instead of sitting down in the front like he usually does, Gary walked to the back and sat down right next to me. For some reason, I wasn't surprised. He had been pretty mellow since his Mom went to the hospital. As he sat there he held his arms out looking at the jacket. And then...

"That was really nice of Mrs. Czech to give me this coat. It was so cool and weird, too."

"So, Gary, what's so weird about someone doing something nice for you?"

"No, that was really nice. The weird part is that I was looking at a magazine yesterday and saw one just like it and I was thinking how great it would be to get it. I can't believe I actually did. Weird, huh?"

It was weird. And now, of course, my mind went back to the DFR stuff (you know). I mean, first I go into the shop to get help from a demon and now, Gary's staying at my house. That was even weirder than the coat. Could Aggie Czech be more than just a psychologist? I would have to investigate.

— ••• —

Dad doesn't get mad too often and he wasn't mad when I told him how I had promised his help and the use of one of his trucks for the charity stuff Lori was working on. No, he wasn't mad, but he was annoyed. I got a lecture about responsibility and how I was old enough to be taking it. But, even after my lecture, he agreed to everything they needed. My Dad...the best.

Anyway, Dad was going to call Aggie tomorrow and get all the

26 - Demon for Rent

details. Gary and I had to go over the schedule and figure out what we each wanted to do. We then had to commit to at least 4 hours. I picked distribution because I thought it would be neat to help pass the food out. Gary said he wanted to work getting the boxes ready. It was strange. I never thought of Gary as a helper, but he was. Every time my Mom asked him for help, he did it without any complaining.

After we had gotten back from our little trip to Aggie's shop and after dinner, Mom took him to the hospital for a visit with Anna. That's his Mom's name, if you don't remember. Dr. Schwab (his Dad was who our school was named after), who was assigned to take care of her told Mom she was getting a little better, but still had to stay in the hospital for a while. That was ok. I was actually starting to get used to Gary being around. When he wasn't yelling or squishing something, he was pretty mellow, polite even, at least to adults.

Mom and Gary got home a little after 8. I had already finished my homework and was watching tv with Dad when Mom called me into the kitchen.

"So, David, how come you didn't tell me you knew Aggie Czech? What were you doing over at her shop?"

Oh no. this was not good. What was I supposed to say now?

Just as I was about to fumble through some lame excuse as to why I was there, I heard a noise behind me. Turning, I saw Gary standing in the door.

Stepping forward, he spoke to Mom. "David and I stopped in to see Mrs. Czech's daughter, Lori. Your husband, Mr. Allen and Davey and me are helping her with a food drive."

Mom laughed. "Oh, you stopped in to see Lori, did you? Very pretty, isn't she?"

Gary spoke up. "Yes, ma'am, she is, but we were supposed to get the food drive information from her and she wasn't in school. So, Davey and I went over to Mrs. Czech's shop to see if she was ok."

"Well, that's great, guys. And don't forget, there's another person in this house who is more than happy to help. The next time you see

Lori or Aggie, please let them know that Kim Allen will be happy to contribute some of her time as well for a worthwhile cause. Oh yes, and before I forget, are either of you thinking of asking Lori to the school's Halloween dance?"

Gary spoke right up. "I think Davey wants to."

I could feel my face go red as I tried to speak.

"I…ah…no…ah…ah.."

I just couldn't get any words out.

Mom started to laugh. "It's ok, but if you really are wanting to ask a girl out, I think your dad will want to have the talk with you."

The Talk? Oh God, what did she mean? Did she mean the "sex" talk? Oh God. That was one talk I did not want to have.

"NO. I just wanted to get the charity stuff from her. Gary and I are going with a few of my other friends and they're not girls."

Gary looked surprised.

"Well, ok then, but eventually, you will have to talk to your Dad about stuff. You understand?"

I was embarrassed, but nodded to let her know I did understand. And, any thought of asking a girl to a dance disappeared from my head completely. Maybe in another 50 or 100 years. Maybe then and ONLY then would I be ready for "The Talk."

That was all I could take. Mom was still smiling when I said good night and went to my room. Gary stayed behind. He talked to Mom a lot. That was OK. I guess he really did need to talk to someone.

— ••• —

It was Tuesday and I had to get up early to study my language lessons because my teacher, Miss Montgomery was going to have a surprise quiz today. I mean, they aren't always on Tuesday, but she kind of has a pattern that I figured out a couple tests ago. The day before the quiz she always ends the class with the same words. She says how important it is that we speak well and understand what we are saying. She tells us

28 – Demon for Rent

to study hard, because the more we know, the farther we'll go. The day after she says those words, we have a quiz.

Now, I haven't told anybody else that I know there's a pattern. I guess that's because I always want to do better than the other kids in my class. Gary has Miss Montgomery too, but at a different time, so I decided I would let him know that I thought there was going to be a surprise test.

After getting settled in on the bus, with Gary sitting beside me, I told him.

"So, Gary, I think Miss Montgomery might be having a quiz today. You have her class after lunch, right? I just thought I'd let you know so you could study a little after you eat."

"That's ok. I know the lesson already."

Well, that was surprising. I thought Gary wouldn't know the lesson and would be happy I told him.

"So, how are you doing in that class? I'm getting a B, maybe even a B+."

"A."

What? Gary was getting an A? How could that possibly be?

"Wow, Gary, that's great. No matter how hard I've studied, I never do any better than a B."

Gary laughed.

"My Mom was…is a teacher. She always makes me study, always makes sure I know all the stuff I'm supposed to know."

I had never heard him laugh before and I'd only seen him smile a couple of times, once when Aggie Czech gave him the jacket and a few times when he was talking to my mom.

"So, how are you doing in your other classes, Gary?"

"A's."

"All A's?"

"Yes."

I was shocked. I never thought Gary could be smarter than me. I mean, he'd been so nasty I never would have thought he was even doing well in school. Mom and Dad have always told me not to judge somebody before I know all the facts. I did with Gary.

I was right about the test. As usual, I got a B and as usual, now that I know, Gary got an A.

— ••• —

The rest of the week went fast. On Saturday, the doctors told Mom that Gary's Mom was doing better and she would probably be released the following Wednesday if she continued to improve. That was the day before we were helping Lori with the food drive.

Gary was worried about what they were going to do, but Mom reassured him that everything would be ok. She had a plan. We have a really large attic area that we only use to store stuff like Christmas decorations. I guess it was a week ago that Mom started cleaning it out. By today, Saturday, Mom had cleaned and organized the space. Dad put in a wall so that what was left in the attic was separated from a nice open space near the attic window. It was big enough for a single bed and a dresser and a small desk.

Later in the day Mom informed me that Gary was going to move up into that room and his Mom would stay in our guest room. Mom had talked to Gary about this before she told me. I kind of suspected that was what was happening and I guess I didn't mind. Gary was ok…now. He still barely talked to me, but he was starting to open up a little. All that bully stuff was probably just because he was scared and angry at the same time.

We had to go back to the trailer to get the few things that Gary and his Mom did have. When we got there we found the door open and it looked like someone had gone through their stuff. Gary looked around but didn't think they took anything and that was probably because there wasn't much to take, just clothes and pictures mostly. We packed up all that. There were some dishes, too, but the only pieces Gary wanted were two mugs—one that was his mom's and one that was his. A few books had been dumped from a box and lay on the floor. We repacked them to take along. There was one last thing that Gary took. Hidden away behind the couch cushion was a screwed in panel. Gary used a dime to remove the 4 screws and take the plate off. He pulled a small cigar box out of the hole, looked inside it, then tucked it under his arm and indicated to Mom that there was nothing else to take.

I wondered what was in the box and I'm pretty sure Mom was wondering too, but she never said a word about it and I sure wasn't going to say anything.

When we got home, Gary had Mom put the books in the guest room for his mom. He put that box in there as well. Mom took all the clothes to wash and Gary headed up to the attic to arrange stuff the way he liked it. I think he was excited about it, about having a place to stay with his Mom, I mean.

Mom mentioned that he still needed a lamp and I had an extra one, so I took it up. The door was open to the attic and I saw Gary just sitting on the edge of the bed, So I knocked. He looked up and motioned for me to come in.

"Hey Gary. Mom said you needed a lamp and I had this extra one."

I put the lamp on the desk and turned to leave, but Gary reached out and touched my arm.

"Wait, Davey, can you talk a little?"

"Sure. What's up, Gary?"

I sat down on the desk chair and wondered what Gary wanted. I mean, he never started conversations with me, so this was not expected.

"I just want to know why your family is so nice to my Mom and me. I don't understand."

I laughed.

"This is what my Mom does. She helps people. I think she was born to help people. Mom saw that you guys needed help and well…that was that."

Gary looked a little confused.

"So, how did you guys know we needed help? How'd you guys end up coming up to where my Mom and I were living?"

I could have lied, could have told him we were just taking a drive, but I decided, what the heck, I might as well tell him the whole story. So, I did…everything, from the bus problems to the demon for rent to the drive to find out a little bit more about him and where he lived. He just sat there and listened, but when I was done rambling on, he said something I wasn't expecting at all.

"So, it worked."

"What? What worked? What are you talking about, Gary?"

"I tried to get help for my Mom and me before. I talked to the counselor at the school, but when my Mom found out, she made me promise not to say anything more about what was going on with us. She's very proud and she has never ever wanted to take help. I swore I wouldn't say anything, but I had to do something. So, I figured that if I caused a lot of trouble, someone would eventually go up to where we were living to talk to her about all the bad stuff I was doing. That way, I wouldn't be breaking my promise to her. I thought it would be someone from the school that would end up coming to our house, our trailer. It was you and your Mom instead."

I just sat there with my mouth hanging open. Gary shut up and just sat there staring at me. I wasn't sure what I was supposed to say, but I managed.

"Why me?"

Gary smiled.

"Because you always sat by yourself at the back of the bus. I could bother you without bothering anybody else. I stopped when my plan didn't seem to be working. Nobody was coming up. Nobody seemed to care enough to go talk to my mom."

"Why didn't you just ask me for help? I could have talked to my Mom."

"I had promised not to say anything to anybody about our situation. I never lie to my Mom. If I had told you I would have broken my promise. The only thing I could do was cause a real stink, so I did. It worked, but not how I thought it would."

"You squished my lunches, Gary. You threw my homework out the window. Worst of all, you broke my glasses and my family had to get them replaced."

Gary sighed and looked down.

"Yes, and I'm sorry about that. I didn't mean to break them. I promise I'll pay your parents back for the glasses…for everything."

"I think you should tell my Mom about all this."

"I already did. I asked her if she wanted me to talk to you and she said no, not until you said something. I was hoping that asking you some questions about stuff would make you talk to me. Finally, you did."

My Mom knew and she never said anything. That was typical of her. She was always thinking of the best ways for me to learn stuff. I guess she wanted me to start talking openly to Gary about our problems rather than have her step in. I gotta give it to her—she is a smart lady… but I really think she should have told me.

I was pretty annoyed about all this crap. I told Gary I was going to talk to my Mom and that it would probably take a while for me to deal with all this. With that, I got up and went down to my room, closed the door and stayed there until dinner. Gary must have said something to Mom about our talk because she didn't call me to set the table. It was Dad who came to my room and knocked, then opened the door.

"Hey sport, you doing ok? Your Mom told me what was going on. You want to talk about it?"

"Not particularly, Dad. I'm kind of pissed at Mom for not telling me about Gary. Did she tell you?"

Dad nodded and then continued.

"You know, Mom talked to Aggie Czech about how to handle the situation. Aggie thought it was better for you to deal with all this directly with Gary. So, your Mom did what she recommended."

Now, I got really nervous. I didn't want them to find out about the hire a demon stuff.

"Did Aggie, Mrs. Czech, I mean, say anything else?"

"Nope."

That was all Dad said…just Nope.

"Come on for dinner now, David. We can talk more about all this after you think about it for a while…maybe tomorrow or the next day?"

I nodded ok and followed Dad to the dining room. Gary and Mom were already sitting there, waiting for us to eat.

Dinner was pretty quiet. I wasn't planning on saying anything and Gary didn't either, except when Mom said something about his Mom getting out of the hospital in a few days. When Mom mentioned it, Gary had a question.

"So, Mrs. Allen, when my Mom gets out of the hospital, she'll want to work. Will she be able to? I mean, she's a teacher. Do you think she'll be able to get a job?"

I could hear the concern in his voice and I started feeling kind of bad that I was so mad about the bus and all the nasty stuff.

Mom came back with the right response.

"So, Gary, first we have to make sure your mom is strong enough to work. The doctor is probably releasing her from the hospital because they've managed to take care of the pneumonia. She is still going to be weak and that means she will need to rest for a while to get her strength back."

Mom paused.

"But, when she's ready, we'll start a job search for her. In the meantime, you guys will stay with us. I did go over and talk to your mother about it, so there won't be any surprises or concerns. You know, she's qualified to teach 1st through 7th grades. I'm positive that we'll be able to find a good job for her, especially because of the new elementary school they're building on the west side of town. That won't be ready until the next school year. Still, I think we can find other work for your Mom before then.

Gary sighed heavily.

I couldn't tell if the sigh was concern or what. Maybe it was just relief that his Mom and him wouldn't have to worry any more.

34 - Demon for Rent

The rest of dinner was pretty quiet and afterwards Gary and I cleaned up the table and loaded the dishwasher. Like usual, he wasn't talking, but I decided that would have to change.

"So, Gary, me and a couple of my friends are going to go to the Halloween dance and hang out. I figured you should come along. I mean, you are staying with us and we're going to be working the charity stuff together. Your Mom won't mind, will she?"

Gary just kind of stood there looking at me. I think he was surprised that I was even asking him to hang out.

"Why would you want to hang out with me, Davey? I treated you pretty bad."

"Look, Gary, I'm not happy about all the bus stuff, but I understand. I know now that what you did was to help your mom. I'm not going to hold a grudge. I mean, if I had been able to hire a demon like I tried to, maybe things would be different.

I laughed and so did Gary.

"Please don't tell my mom about what I tried to do, ok? I'll be grounded forever if you do."

"I won't Davey. I promise."

Just then, Mom came into the kitchen. I was worried she had heard me say the demon stuff, but I guess she hadn't. She just got a few cookies and went back to watch tv with Dad.

Gary and I finished the dishes and I went to my room to do my homework. I guess Gary had already done his because he went in to watch tv with my parents. He seemed comfortable here. I didn't mind either. I guess it was nice to have another kid in the house, including Gary.

— ••• —

Wednesday came up really fast and after school Mom and Gary went to pick up his Mom. Although Anna was still very weak, the doctor felt she would recover quicker at home.

Anna needed help getting out of the car. Dad was right there to get her into the house and situated in the guest room. The doctor said she could walk a few steps, but that she should not do any more than that. They had given her a cane to help her stay stable when she did have to move around, like getting to the bathroom

Mom had put a small bookcase in the guest room and Gary organized her books. She had some pretty nifty items, at least that's what Mom told me. I'm not sure Gary's Mom knew what she had, because she kept the books just sitting in a box on the floor of the trailer. Whoever had broken in didn't realize they were worth anything either, because they were just dumped after the break-in. I mean, they probably weren't so valuable that they would buy a house or anything, but Mom thought that a couple would bring enough for them to live on, at least for a few months. Mom said not to talk about how valuable she thought the books were. She didn't want Anna to feel any unnecessary pressure to try and get money from some of the only things that they still had.

That made me wonder what was in the box Gary had pulled from behind the panel in the trailer. I decided to ask him, now that we were kind of talking.

"So, Gary, that box you got out of the trailer...not the book box, but that little box...was there something important in that box?"

"Mom had our birth certificates in there and our social security cards. There were also a few pictures of my Grandma and Grandpa, plus Grandpa's gold watch."

"What about your Dad, Gary? Is he around at all?"

Gary looked angry, but it wasn't toward me, thank heavens.

"Dad is what got us into this mess in the first place. He split. We don't know where he went. Mom couldn't pay the mortgage by herself and then...well...there were cuts at the school she worked at and she lost her job. We hung on as long as we could, staying in cheap motel rooms, but Mom started to get sick and the small jobs she took to make a little for us to live on pretty much went away. We ended up staying in that trailer."

36 – Demon for Rent

I kind of wished I had never asked because I was feeling really crappy about all they had gone through. In a way, I guess, it was also kind of good that Gary was now talking a lot more to me. Mom would probably say we were starting to bond, but I don't think there's been enough better times between us for that to be happening yet.

"Look Gary, things are gonna get a lot better for you guys. There won't be any living in a little trailer anymore. Never again. You can stay with us as long as you need to. And your Dad? Well, he's not even worth thinking about anymore…so don't!"

Gary smiled. He didn't have to say anything for me to know he really appreciated what I had said. I started thinking about how all this started happening and other than the bus crap, the only thing I could connect to everything was Abby and her demon stuff. Was there a connection? I wasn't sure, but I really did want to find out more.

— ••• —

Anna Morgan insisted on coming to the dinner table that first night she stayed at our house. Gary helped her stand and using the cane, she walked very slowly to the dining room. The doctor had wanted her to eat stuff like soup and a little bread until she got her strength up, so Mom made homemade chicken noodle and sandwiches for dinner. Mom thought the sandwiches would be a little too heavy for Anna, so she had bread and crackers for her and a little butter. She ate the soup, but then asked if she could be excused to go lie down. Gary helped her back to her room and came back to finish dinner.

Mom started talking about the charity stuff we were going to do tomorrow. She had decided to pass on helping so she could stay home with Gary's Mom, just in case she needed something. Gary and I were actually looking forward to helping. I know Gary had already done all the school stuff he had to do to make up for the time we would be out. I was still working on mine and figured that if I didn't get completely done I could do it after we got back.

After dinner, like usual now, Gary and I loaded the dishwasher and then I went back to my room to try and finish my homework. Because Gary had already finished his, he went to watch tv with Dad. Mom had gone in to chat with Anna for a while. I know that she didn't want her to feel all alone in a strange house and everything. Mom had taken a little time off from her part time work at the clinic to stay home. I think she liked another woman around to talk to. After all, she only had me and Dad and then Gary before that.

Just as I was finishing up my math, there was a knock on my door. It was Dad reminding me that we were leaving around 7 and to be up and ready before then. I said fine. I was looking forward to helping and maybe seeing Lori tomorrow.

Don't take that the wrong way. Like I said before, I'm not interested in girls and won't be for a zillion or so years. All the junk that you have to do when you like a girl is just not worth it. But, Lori's my friend. I just want to make sure everything is cool with her. You understand, right?

— ••• —

Thursday was going to be a busy day. Gary and I were up and ready by 6:30. We snarfed down a little cereal and some juice while we waited for Dad. All the workers had been given a t-shirt with the food drive info on the front so when we went to pass everything out, people would know that we were supposed to be doing that and we weren't some creeps trying to bother them.

It took us 25 minutes to get to the warehouse. Some of the helpers were already there, including Aggie and Lori. When Lori saw us drive up she smiled and waved. Dad parked the truck and Aggie came up to greet us when we all got out. She went right up to Dad and gave him a hug.

"Keith, I am so happy to see you. Thanks for taking the time to do this. It is for a really good cause."

I was kind of surprised by all this. I didn't realize that they person-

38 - Demon for Rent

ally knew each other that well.

Aggie continued.

"So, Gary will be working with me in the warehouse. Keith, you'll drive the Northeast route with your son, David. My daughter Lori will go with you. She'll be the contact with the recipients of the food. You'll also get the boxes out and make sure they're marked for the house they're being dropped off at. Of course, you'll also keep the kids safe just in case there are any issues."

Wow! This charity stuff was getting even better. I was going to be working with Lori. NOT that I really cared that it was Lori. I mean, it could have been any other kid. But, she is my friend, you know, and it's always great to work with a friend. Right?

Anyway, a couple of the other Dads loaded the truck for our first run. This would be our first trip of the 6 planned trips we would make. The first 4 stops would be taking boxes to families in need. The last 2 would be dropping off at some of the homeless shelters around town.

The truck was packed and ready to go. Lori had the distribution list and hopped into the back seat. I would have let her sit in the front, but she didn't seem to care. The places where we were going to give out the food were in the area that Gary and his Mom were living. I could see that the neighborhood looked poor.

Lori gave Dad the first address—Mrs. Mary Skriver, 2702 Trail Road South. That was one of the roads Mom and I drove when we went up to see where Gary lived. The house was one of the first coming out of the forest. It was tiny and set back from the road so you wouldn't really see it unless you were actually looking for it. We turned down a little dirt road that ended directly in front of a run-down porch with an old rocking chair.

We all got out of the truck and Dad went to the back and stood waiting while Lori and I went up and knocked. After a minute a very frail older lady came to the door. She looked like she was in her 70s or 80s.

Lori spoke right up.

"Hi Mrs. Skriver. My name's Lori Czech and I'm part of the Schwab

Middle School food drive. Your name was given to us by the City of Mercy Community Services Center as someone who maybe would benefit from a little help? We have a few things we would like to give you. Can we bring them inside?"

Mrs. Skriver nodded and held the screen open while Dad and I brought the boxes in. As Lori was telling her what was in the boxes, I saw Mrs. Skriver take a Kleenex and start wiping tears away. Lori had some documents for her and explained that there was more help for her at the center. She also gave her a $100 gift card so she could purchase other things that she needed.

I could see Mrs. Skriver was grateful. She must have been lonely, too, because she asked if we could sit and talk for a while. We couldn't because we had to do the other deliveries, but Dad spoke up and told her that someone could come by and visit in a couple of days. That was probably going to be Mom and since Mom was a nurse, she could check on her health as well.

The next couple of stops were kind of the same as Mrs. Skriver—an old couple living on a tiny social security check and a young mother with a baby who just needed a little help to get through the next few months. They were just as grateful as Mrs. Skriver.

Our 4th and last stop before we went back to the warehouse to get more stuff was a little more interesting than the others. There was no address to go to, just a general location and the description of a couple of tents set up back at the edge of the forest. It took us a little time to actually find the location, but when we did, Dad decided that he would make contact with the man that lived there before letting Lori and me do our stuff.

As we drove up we could see him sitting by a fire with 2 scruffy-looking dogs lying next to him. Dad told us to stay in the truck until he was sure it was safe to get out. He got out and started walking toward the man. The dogs got up growling, but the man spoke to them and they laid back down.

Dad started to talk to the man and after a few minutes, they shook hands. Turning toward the truck, he motioned that Lori and I could get out. As we walked toward them, Dad spoke.

"Lori and David, this is Sergeant Jimmy Hughes."

He was an Army guy and so was my Dad; whatever Dad had said to him made everything cool for Lori and me. I could see he had been injured. It looked like he was missing a leg or part of one. His hair had grown longer and he had not shaved in a while, I don't think.

Jimmy Hughes smiled and it made me think he was a nice guy who was just kind of down on his luck.

"Nice to meet you guys. And these fine animals here are my friends, Hank and Wiggles."

I laughed. Lori didn't wait for me to say anything before she started her speech.

"Sergeant? We're with the Schwab Middle School food drive. We received your name from the City of Mercy Community Services Center. They believed you could benefit from a little help. We brought some staples for you...and your doggies, of course. We have both dry and wet dog food for Hank and Wiggles."

"Little lady? I really don't need much help, but I do appreciate the meals for my friends. Thanks."

"Sergeant? Sir? You're welcome, but we're going to leave the other stuff for you anyway. We also have a gift card for you for other things you might need and I want you to take it."

She reached out and handed it to the man.

I was kind of surprised that she was so direct. It was cool. She probably got that from her Mom. We stayed a few more minutes while Dad chatted with the Sergeant. Like Mrs. Skriver, he seemed kind of lonely and Dad told him, like we told her, that we would stop by and visit in a few days.

The Sergeant thanked us and Dad shook his hand again. When we got into the truck, I did have questions. As we were driving back to the warehouse I made it a point to ask them.

"So, Dad, what's with the Sergeant? I mean, he seems like a nice guy. How did he end up living in a tent homeless?"

Dad looked serious when he answered.

"You know, David, war does something to the people who participate in it. Nobody ever comes back the same. But for some, well...some like the Sergeant for example...they come back and they're lost. War kind of hangs on to their minds and affects how they live, what they do, and how they interact with people in everyday life."

Lori was listening, too.

"Mr. Allen? What do you think really happened with him?"

"I don't know, Lori. Do you know what PTSD is?"

Lori shook her head no.

"Well, it stands for post traumatic stress disorder and it's just what I said—it means that war still has a grip on you and on your life. Some, like the Sergeant, find it really hard to shake that grip."

"What about you, Dad? How come it hasn't affected you?"

Dad smiled.

"Your wrong, David. I was affected. Everybody that goes to war is affected. I was luckier than a lot of soldiers. I had a ton of support. Your mom? Well, you know what she's like. She made sure I got the services I needed to be a productive member of society again."

Lori had been listening to everything Dad had said.

"Listen, Mr. Allen. I'm going to talk to my Mom and see what we can do for the Sergeant. My Mom has a lot of connections. I know she'll be able to help him."

"Well, Lori, you can only be helped if you actually want it. I'm not entirely sure that Sergeant Hughes wants our help...yet. Let me think about this for a few days. For now, let's get back to the task at hand."

That was all Dad said. We headed back to the warehouse, reloaded the truck 2 more times, and finished our deliveries by 7:00 in the evening. There was supposed to be a pizza party after all the deliveries, but Dad was tired and when we met up with Gary, he was wanting to get home to see how his Mom was doing.

I knew she was doing good because she was with my Mom and Mom wouldn't let anything bad happen. I understood though. We made sure Lori was back with Aggie, then said goodbye and that we'd see her in school tomorrow.

Driving home, Gary asked how the deliveries went and I told him about the people we had met and how good it felt to be helping them. I didn't mention the Sergeant, at least not in front of Dad. I wasn't sure how he'd react if I talked about his problems.

We pulled up in the driveway just a little before 8. Gary started toward his Mom's room as soon as we got inside but stopped as he passed the hall that was open to our living room. I could hear laughing. Looking in I saw Mom and Anna watching a show on tv. Mom looked toward us first and smiled.

"Gary and David, you're home. So, how'd it go? Good? You must be hungry. There are sandwiches in the fridge. Grab a couple and come in here and watch some tv with us. We're watching a really funny show about some nerdy scientists trying to get girlfriends."

Gary spoke up.

"You mean Big Bang Theory Mrs. Allen? I like that one, too, but I'm a little tired, so I think I'll just grab a sandwich and call it a night. How're you doing, Mom?"

Anna looked up and smiled, telling him she was fine. She seemed better. She still looked awfully skinny and pale, but she seemed relaxed and kind of happy. I was glad she was doing better.

Anyway, I wasn't really up for watching tv and I wasn't hungry either, so I said goodnight and went to my room to relax. Tomorrow was going to be another big day—my first school dance.

— ••• —

I guess all the stuff we did yesterday wore me out, because I slept through my alarm and Mom had to wake me up. I rushed to shower and dress and when I came to the kitchen, Gary was already there eating some cereal. I was kind of excited about the dance. Gary and I were going to go over to one of my friends after school and hang out there until it was time to go to the gym. Although the school said we could wear costumes during class, we decided to wait until the evening.

I was going to go as Batman and Gary was going to be Robin, but Mom thought that because Gary was taller, he should be the caped crusader and me the sidekick. I guess that was ok. I kind of liked how Robin dressed.

After classes my friend Eddie Anderson's Dad picked us up in a limo. This is not what you're thinking. They're not rich or anything. Eddie's family owns a limo service and Eddie thought it would be totally cool to get his Dad to drive a bunch of us to the dance in one of their vehicles. I liked it. I had never been in a limo and neither had Gary.

There were 7 of us going together— me and Gary, Eddie and his sister Meg, Scott and Steve Cooper, and Abby Davis. Scott had a thing for Abby which is why she was going with us. And of course, Meg had to go because she was related. I thought it was just going to be us guys, but you know how that goes, especially when parents and girlfriends get involved.

I wondered whether Mr. Cooper had the "talk" with the guys. Maybe they would say something about it. I wasn't going to ask, but it sure would be interesting to find out what his Dad said. That would give me an idea of what my Dad was going to say to me…40 or 50 years from now, that is.

Mrs. Anderson had Pizza and soda for us. They had a really neat family room and we all hung out in there until it was time to leave. Eddie was going as Thor and it was kind of funny since he was smallest guy in our group. His sister was going as Captain Marvel. Scott and Steve abandoned the superhero stuff completely. They decided to go as the Lone Ranger and Tonto. Abby didn't particularly like dressing up, so she was going as a doctor, with a white lab-type coat and a stethoscope draped over her shoulder. That was about it.

At 7 we all piled into the limo and Eddie's Dad drove us to the gym.

44 - Demon for Rent

The dance was going to start at 7:30 and everybody was kind of milling around waiting to get in.

We were all feeling pretty good about the limo and stuff. Everybody stared as we got out. I mean, we're not the most popular kids in school and most everybody ignores us most of the time...but not tonight.

The gatekeeper (our principal) was dressed as the Grim Reaper, with a long black cloak and a sickle thingy that looked like it was made out of paper mâché. Right at 7:30, he unlocked the gym and all the kids poured in. I looked for Lori, but didn't see her. Meg and Abby went to hang with a bunch of girls and the rest of us guys headed for the snacks and drinks.

The school had hired a local band called the Last Band Standing. I thought it was a lame name, but the group sounded pretty good. They played mostly oldies and a few newer songs. They started out with a lot of rock at first, but a little later in the evening their music slowed way down. A lot of the kids started pairing up. Even Gary decided to ask someone to dance—Debbie Mackenzie. I think he asked her to dance because she was taller than most of the guys in our class and nobody was going to ask her.

But then, there was Gary, who was also taller than most of the guys in our class. I think he saw her standing all by herself watching her friends get asked to dance and, well, that just didn't seem to fly with Gary, so over he went and asked. They didn't tower over all the other kids, but it almost felt like they did. They were kind of in the middle of the dance floor and I could easily see their heads over everybody else.

I was still standing by the snack table with a few other guys when I spotted Lori. She was over on the far side of the gym with some of the chaperones and that was probably because one of them was her Mom.

I wanted to go over and ask her to dance, but something kept me from doing it, probably the talk fear...or maybe just general girl fear. I mean, thinking about the asking is one thing, doing it is a lot tougher.

Just as I was getting up the nerve to go over there, I saw one of the 9th graders walking her out to the dance floor. A 9th grader—can you believe it? I was getting depressed as I watched. She was looking up at him smiling. It could have been me and it wasn't because I was a chicken. I felt crappy.

Lori danced with him all evening. When it was time for the dance to end, he walked her over to Aggie and gave her a little hug before walking out to find his parent and go home.

Eddie and Gary found me moping over by the food. We all waited there for the rest of the kids and when we were all together, we went out to wait for our limo ride home.

Gary and I got dropped off right before 11 and I went right to my room so I could continue moping. Maybe I would feel better in the morning. Well, maybe not. At least Gary had a good time.

— ••• —

It was Saturday, the dance was over, I felt miserable, and life was going on. I didn't really want to leave my room, but Mom knocked on my door and reminded me that there were chores to be done and I should get dressed and get moving. Ok, fine.

As I came into the kitchen, I saw Gary's Mom sitting at the table drinking a cup of coffee. She smiled at me and spoke.

"Good morning, David. How are you today?"

I was feeling pretty grouchy, but I didn't want to upset her because she'd been through a lot. So, I choked down all the depressed stuff and smiled back.

"Hi Mrs. Morgan. I'm fine. How's it going for you today? Are you feeling better?"

"Much better and good enough for this cup of coffee. And David, I want to thank you very much for helping me and Gary. I don't know how we can ever repay you."

"I didn't do anything, Mrs. Morgan. It was my Mom."

"It was both of you, David."

Just then Gary and Mom came into the kitchen.

"Hi guys. Gary and I were just getting the garage sale items ready."

What? I didn't know anything about a garage sale.

"So, what are you selling, Mom?"

"Oh, just some of the stuff in the attic and a few other things...it's to support the City of Mercy."

"What other things?"

Mom mumbled something I couldn't understand.

"What? Mom, what exactly are you going to sell? Is it mine?"

"Well, you don't play with those things anymore and since they're in such good condition...almost unused, I thought what better way to put a little extra money together to help the City of Mercy with some of the programs they have.

"What toys, Mom?"

"Oh, that old erector set you barely played with, your chemistry set, and that set of action figures...you know the ones...Transformers?"

"What? No way! My Transformers? No way, Mom!"

Mom laughed. "Look David, if you can show me that you've even looked at those figures in the last year—no wait, the last 3 years, I'll take them off the list."

Dang! She was right. I hadn't seen those figures in years. I guess I could spare those things for a good cause, but why is it that Mom always has to take these decisions into her own hands?"

"Fine. You're right. I don't need them. Take them."

Mom could tell I was upset.

"Come on, David, it's for a good cause. Plus, some little kid is going to be really happy to get them."

"Mom, like I said...it's fine."

Maybe I was grouchy because of all the Lori stuff. I mean, I hadn't even looked at those figures for years, so there was no real reason I would want to hang on to them.

— ••• —

Dad asked me and Gary to rake the leaves, so right after breakfast we did just that. I raked and Gary bagged. It didn't take us long to finish. We had the rest of the day free and I thought it would be kind of fun to go down to Gastronibeak and look at the birds.

Gary laughed. "Are we really going there to look at the birds, Davey? Really?"

"Well, sure. I mean, they're really neat birds."

Did stopping by Mrs. Czech's business cross your mind at all?"

"Ok, fine, Gary. I was thinking maybe Lori would be around. I wanted to ask her how she enjoyed the dance."

"You know how she enjoyed the dance."

"Maybe she was faking it."

"I don't think so."

"God, Gary, do you have to be a smart know-it-all?"

"Look Davey, if you wanted to ask Lori to dance last night, you should have."

"I tried to go over there and ask her, but I was too late. That 9th grader got over there first."

"It was almost a full hour after the dance started that he asked her. You had plenty of time."

"OK, so I chickened out and it's mostly because my Mom threatened to make me have the "talk" with Dad if I wanted to ask a girl out or maybe even dance with one. You know...*THE TALK*?"

"Oh, that. I understand now. So, Davey, you know, you should probably hang back for a while. You don't want to seem like you're stalking her."

"No! No! She wouldn't think that, would she? I don't want that. I mean, I just kind of wanted to see her and try to figure out if she was interested in that kid."

"Or you?"

I felt my face go red.

48 – Demon for Rent

"Well, maybe. She's out of my league though. Still…"

"Is she worth having the "talk" for?"

"Gary, I don't know if any girl is worth that. Did your Mom have the talk with you?

Gary shook his head no. "She mentioned it once, but with all the stuff she's been through, it just kind of slipped her mind, I guess."

"Well, that was fortunate. Not the part where your Mom goes through a bunch of stuff—just the slipping the mind about the talk part. So, do you want to go look at the birds or not? We don't have to go over to Mrs. Czech's office."

Gary said sure, so I told Mom where we were going, then we took off to grab the next bus downtown. I didn't have to pay for Gary, because for help with the chores, Dad paid him just like he pays me. I think that made Gary feel pretty good. I think it had bothered him that I always had to pay for the both of us.

—•••—

It was windy and cold when we got off the bus. The weather people had said we might get an early snow and you could feel that almost-snow dampness in the air. I had worn a sweatshirt under my jacket and Gary, of course had that really neat bomber. We could have used gloves, but neither of us had any, so we kept our hands tucked away in our jacket pockets.

When we got to the bird center, I peeked over toward Aggie Czech's office and was happy to see that it was completely dark. Nobody was there and that, I decided, was a good thing. At least Gary would say it was. I could get back to the important stuff.

We spent an hour looking at the birds and then decided to walk down to the animal shelter and take a look at the dogs and cats waiting for adoption. Gary asked me why we didn't have any pets. I told him we used to—a Brittany Spaniel named Clover. Mom loved her and was heartbroken when she died. We haven't had any pets since and even though I had really wanted another dog for a while, Mom just wasn't ready.

It had been over 2 years since Clover died, so maybe Mom would consider a new friend. Gary and I decided we should go down and just take a look at what the shelter had ready for adoption. Now, that doesn't mean we would be able to get a dog. But what was the harm in looking?

It took us a half an hour to walk down to the shelter. We could actually catch a bus back home from there after we were done checking out the animals.

The shelter was pretty new. It held space for dogs and cats, plus there was an area for other pets, too—snakes, lizards, spiders, rats, rabbits…all kinds of things. Gary and I went to look at the lizards. They were totally cool. There was an Iguana that was over 3-feet long. It was friendly and the shelter allowed some of the older kids (like me and Gary) to pet it. Well, it wasn't actually like petting—it was more like just touching a scaly body. Ig seemed to like being touched. That's what Mr. Stevenson, the manager of the shelter named him. It fit, I guess. Ig the Iguana. I liked the name.

Anyway, once we got done checking out everything in that room, we went to look at the dogs. There were a lot of them. Mr. Stevenson said there were 78 ready to go. We started walking down through the pens. At the very end was where they kept the younger dogs and in one pen there were 9 of the cutest little Saint Bernard puppies you have ever seen.

I immediately wanted one and asked Mr. Stevenson what we'd need to do to adopt. Of course, it came down to paying the $175 adoption fee, parent approval, a house with a yard, and a guarantee to take care of a dog that was going to get really big.

So, the house, the yard and the care were no problem. The parent approval? Well, I wasn't sure I could convince Mom and Dad that we just had to get one. Plus, then there was the fee. I knew we could afford it and even if I had to pay it myself, I could. I had saved over $300 from my allowance and other stuff I had done for some of the neighbors.

Mr. Stevenson gave me the adoption papers and told me to have one of my parents sign them. Then, he would send someone out for a home check to make sure it was adequate as a place a really big dog could call home. I told him there was no problem to any of what we needed to do.

Gary didn't say anything until we started to the bus stop on our way home.

"Davey? Do you really think you should have told Mr. Stevenson that there was no problem adopting one of those puppies? Maybe you should have asked your parents first."

"I probably should have, but I really wanted one. I guess this is just a leap of faith."

"What? What do you mean, Davey? Leap of Faith?"

"I mean…I have faith that my Mom will want a puppy and I have faith that she'll convince Dad that it's the right thing to do."

"A puppy…that's one thing, but a puppy that grows into a giant dog…well, Davey, a leap of faith might not be high enough."

Gary didn't say any more. He was right. Maybe I did go a little too far making promises. All the way home on the bus I thought about everything. I started imagining what Dad was going to say and certain words came to mind…irresponsible…irresponsible…irresponsible. I know that's only one word, but it felt like a bunch because I could hear Dad saying it over and over again.

As soon as we got home I went directly to my room. I had to figure out which of my very understanding parents I should talk to. On one hand, Mom usually makes the decisions and Dad goes along with whatever. On the other hand, it was Dad who brought home Clover as a puppy even though Mom had insisted she didn't want pets. That was 14 years ago.

2 years is long enough without a dog, so maybe Mom would be more open now. If she went for it, I knew Dad would be fine with it as well. I just had to get up the nerve to ask.

— ••• —

Saturday night is always movie and fun food night. What that means is that we can have anything we want so long as it's food that comes from some fast food place. Today was supposed to be my turn to pick, but I let Gary do the picking. I figured it would be something I liked and I was right. He picked pizza. It was Dad's turn to pick a movie. We never knew what Dad would pick. The last one he picked was *The Great Escape*. It was an old movie and it was pretty good…but old. I was hoping that this time Dad would pick something new or at least newish. Dad thought about it for a while and picked *Beethoven*.

What? He picked a dog movie and not just a dog movie, a Saint Bernard movie? How could this be?

I looked at Dad and he was staring at me. He knew.

"Dad, you know, don't you? How did you know?"

"Come on, David, you can't tell me you don't remember my old friend Charlie Stevenson, can you?"

I had just never connected the Stevenson at the shelter with the Charlie Stevenson that was Dad's friend. Charlie Stevenson the friend had been at our house for a Christmas party last year. I hadn't paid much attention to anybody that was there, but I did remember Charlie because he was wearing one of those ugly X-Mas sweaters.

Before I could say anything, Dad continued.

"David, getting a dog is a big deal, especially for your mother. For you to make a commitment to take a puppy without talking to us first is not acceptable. Learning responsibility is important. We've talked about this before.

"I'm sorry, Dad. I just liked the puppy a lot. I told Mr. Stevenson I was going to talk to you, but I just hadn't had a chance yet. I can call him now and tell him you guys said no."

"You don't have to, David. I've already talked to Charlie."

Just then Gary's mom came into the room. She was still using her cane but seemed to be walking better.

52 - Demon for Rent

Dad got up and told her to take his lounge chair. He figured she would be more comfortable in it than on the couch because it had a footrest you could raise up. That would let Anna kind of stretch out if she wanted to.

Anna thanked him and got comfortable, then asked Dad where Mom and Gary were.

"They went to pick up the pizzas for dinner. Kim said she'd pick up some soup as well, for you Anna, just in case you didn't want all that cheese and bread."

Anna laughed. "I think I might be up for a little cheese and bread."

I was kind of surprised that they had gone out to pick up the pizzas. Usually, we just had them delivered. I figured it was so Dad could talk to me with no one around. I guess I was grateful. I really didn't want Gary hearing first-hand what he had probably thought would happen.

It was taking Mom and Gary longer than expected to get back. Dad called just to make sure everything was ok and told us Mom said there were a lot of people waiting to pick up and it would be another half hour. That was ok. The news was on and Dad and Anna were chatting as they watched it. I went back to my room to wait until dinner.

I felt crappy, not so much that I wasn't getting the puppy, but because this was the second time in 2 weeks I had made a commitment without talking to my parents. You know…the charity helping I promised Dad would do? He was not happy about me not clearing it with him first, so I suspect he was even less happy about this.

Just then I heard the door and knew they had gotten home. I came out of my room just in time to see Gary carrying 3 pizza boxes into the living room. Dad saw me and told me to grab the napkins and paper plates, which I did. Mom was still out in the garage, probably getting the soda and whatever else she had bought. I started out to help her, but Dad told me to stay put and that Gary would take care of it. Ok. I could tell Dad was still irked, but why didn't he want me helping Mom? Oh well, I guess I just don't understand parents. It was fine that Gary was helping.

Just then, I heard Mom's voice. Looking toward the kitchen I saw her carrying a big box. Dad got up and walked over to Mom and took the box from her. Walking into the living room he came over to where I was sitting and put the box down in front of me. It was the puppy, the one from the shelter, the one I liked the most.

"What? No Way!! You got the puppy? Wow! Thank you!!"

Mom smiled. "You know, David, Dad and I have been talking about getting another dog for a while now. I really don't mind that it's a Saint Bernard. I had one growing up, so I'm used to big dogs. But you have to understand, David, you and Gary will have to take care of him—make sure he's fed and watered, train him so he doesn't pee in the house, and do everything else he might need. For now, it's you and Gary, but when Gary and his Mom leave...not for a while yet, but when they do, you'll be responsible completely. Do you understand?

I nodded yes.

The puppy started whining and Dad bent down and picked him up. He was so tiny and all fur. Dad was smiling. I could see he liked the puppy, too.

"David and Gary? Tomorrow you'll come up with a name for our new friend. Plus, you'll need to figure out where he'll sleep. Puppies have a tendency to cry when they're away from their mothers, so be prepared to be awake for the first few nights. You might want to take turns watching him."

Gary's Mom was looking at the puppy and smiling. Dad was standing near her and she reached up and touched the puppy.

"Anna, do you want to hold him?"

Dad leaned over and put the puppy on Anna's lap. She lit up. Gary told me later that it was the happiest he had seen his mom in the last few months. The puppy must have known that Anna had been sick, because he didn't wiggle around or anything. He just curled up in her lap and went to sleep.

We were about ready to eat pizza and start the movie. Mom went over to take the puppy and put him back in the box, but Anna asked if it was ok that she held him for a little longer. Of course, it was. Mom set

54 - Demon for Rent

up a tray next to where Anna was sitting and put some pizza and soda there for her.

Dad had lied to us about the movie. He had rented Avengers End Game, probably because Mom told him to. Mom is a big sci fi fan; Dad prefers military stuff and Westerns.

The puppy lay on Anna's lap during the whole movie, like for 3 hours. When it was time to call it a night, Mom carefully picked up the puppy and put him back in the box. Dad helped Anna up and back to her room and Gary went upstairs. That left me, Mom and Dad. I was about to head back to my room when Dad stopped me.

"David, you understand how important it is for you to step up and take responsibility for this animal. We are not going to do it for you."

"It's a puppy Dad, NOT just an animal."

"Don't play with words, David."

"Sorry, Dad."

Dad relaxed. "Take the puppy outside and see if you can get him to pee. Make sure you keep him in the box tonight, in case of any accidents.

I agreed and nothing more was said. I took the box with the puppy out to the yard. Putting him down in the grass, he started wandering around, but then squatted and peed. We stayed out for a little longer before I popped him into the box and carried him back into the house and my room. Dad had told me to keep him in the box and I did...until midnight when he started crying like crazy.

I wasn't sure what to do. I tried to ignore him, but the crying continued, so I sat down next to the box and picked the puppy up. The crying stopped, so I put him back in the box and went back to bed. But, just a few minutes later, the puppy started crying again.

Now, I know Dad told me to leave him in the box, but I wasn't going to get any sleep if the puppy continued to cry. So, I did what he told me not to do. I picked up the puppy and put him next to me on my bed.

He must have been lonely for his Mom because as soon as I did that, he stopped crying and went to sleep. I was a little worried that he would wake up and fall, so I put a couple of extra pillows between him and the edge. I figured everything would be ok, so I went ahead and went back to sleep.

Unfortunately, I was wrong. No, the puppy didn't fall off the bed. No, I didn't roll over on him. He peed. I know, I know. Dad warned me and I didn't listen.

It was very early when I woke up and felt a large wet spot. The puppy was moving around and came up to me wagging his tail and licking my face. I had to do something right away, so I picked up the puppy, got his box and carried both up to Gary.

I knocked and went in. Gary was sleeping soundly, but the puppy was yipping now and he woke up.

"Hey, Davey, what's going on? Is everything ok?"

"NO. The puppy peed on the bed. I have to clean everything up. Can you watch him?"

Gary laughed. "Sure."

"It's not funny Gary."

"Didn't your Dad tell you to keep the puppy in the box?"

"I didn't do it and now I have a mess to clean up. And just how did you know what Dad said? You had already gone up to your room."

Gary laughed again. "I was kind of listening to see what he was going to say. Don't worry, I'll take care of the puppy. I can take him outside while you clean."

"Great. I have to do it before Mom gets up. I'll come out after I get the wash started."

On Sunday Mom usually sleeps a little later, which was good for me. It would give me enough time to do a load of laundry before she got up. I got the sheets and stuff off the bed and down to the basement where the washer and dryer were. After starting the wash, I went outside. Gary was sitting on the front step and the puppy was wandering around in the grass. Sitting down next to Gary, I watched as the puppy did his thing. The wind was blowing and the leaves that were left in the yard were moving around and as they did, the puppy would yip and jump toward the leaves, trying to catch them. It was fun just watching him.

"Gary, I think it's time we named him. What do you think?"

"Well, nothing too sissy, like Fluffy or Spot."

"No, nothing like that. How about some macho name, like Titan?"

"I don't know, Davey. It doesn't feel exactly right.

"So…Atlas?"

"No."

"So, think of something that fits, Gary."

"Hmmm…well, he's already caused you a little trouble, so how about Rascal?"

"Rascal? I like it. Rascal it is!"

We sat there watching Rascal play in the yard. After 10 minutes I had to go in and dry my sheets and blanket. Gary stayed outside. It was getting really cold and when I came back out it was just starting to snow. The puppy seemed to like it and would jump up and try to grab the flakes as they floated down to the ground. Rascal was perfect. Gary did good naming him.

— ••• —

By Sunday afternoon there was an inch of snow on the ground. Dad and Anna took care of Rascal while Mom took Gary and me to the mall to get some gloves and hats. She also decided to buy Anna a sweater because she didn't think she had anything warm enough for around the house. We then went to the pet store and picked up some things that Rascal would need. We got bowls for food and water, a bed and pee pads for training, plus a collar and a stuffed dog toy so the puppy wouldn't feel alone at night. She also bought a dog cage that Mom called a crate. This was in case we had to leave the puppy without anyone watching him. I guess it was ok. It was pretty big, especially for a little puppy.

When we got home we found Anna and Dad in the living room and Rascal curled up sleeping on Anna's lap, just like last night.

Gary and I got the pet stuff out of the car. We put the bed and the toy in my room and the rest of the junk in the kitchen. Mom had gone to talk to Dad and Anna. She gave Anna the sweater and Anna thanked her a ton of times. I know she was grateful for everything my parents were doing for her and Gary. Actually, I was grateful too. Having Gary around turned out to be really neat, fun even. This is something I would never have expected because of all the bus crap. But, it was good. I was really liking him around.

The puppy was sleeping so we didn't have to take him out yet, but Dad did ask if we could shovel the walk and the driveway, which we did. All the chores went faster with Gary helping. He started on the driveway and I did the walks. We would probably have to do it again tomorrow because it kept snowing. It was the most snow we had this early for years.

It felt good to go inside after we finished, but when we got in, Rascal woke up and we had to take him out. That was ok. You know, Saint Bernard's like the cold and we could really tell because the puppy loved playing in the snow.

After we got in, I had to talk to Mom and Anna about taking care of Rascal while Gary and I were in school. When I mentioned it, Mom just blew it off, telling me not to worry about it, that everything would be fine. Ok, I knew if Mom said that, it would be.

The rest of the day went fast. I had to do a little homework after dinner. Gary was done already and didn't want to watch tv with the parents, so he sat on my bed and played games on my x-box. When I finished it was about time for bed. Gary said goodnight and went upstairs. I went down and got Rascal, then took him out one more time in the hopes he wouldn't have to pee again until morning. I could see that the snow was coming down heavier than in the afternoon. It looked like we were having a real blizzard.

Even though we had bought a bed for Rascal, Mom said to keep him in the box until we got the peeing problem mostly resolved. I put him in the box with the fuzzy stuffed animal we bought so he would feel like he wasn't alone. Luckily, it seemed to work. He curled up and went to sleep.

As I fell asleep myself, I started wondering if there would be school tomorrow. What a bummer for Halloween.

—•••—

November 3

We woke up to almost a foot of snow and school was closed for the day. Gary and I were up early. We got the puppy out and by the time we came in, Mom and Anna were having coffee in the kitchen. They said they would watch Rascal while we started shoveling. The snow was still coming down pretty heavy, but the weather people thought it would start to clear later in the morning. We were still shoveling after 2 hours, but we got most of the heavy stuff cleared, so it wouldn't be too bad to get the rest when the snow stopped.

We were fine where we lived because the power had stayed on, but other areas weren't as lucky. Dad had already left because there were electrical problems throughout town that the storm had caused and he and his crew were out helping where they could.

The clinic called for Mom and asked her to come in. She agreed because me and Gary were staying home and could keep an eye on Anna and Rascal. When she left she took Dad's Jeep because it had better traction in the snow than her car. I was a little concerned, but Mom was a good driver, so I knew she'd make it ok.

Rascal still had to be fed, so we set up the bowls with food and water in the corner of the kitchen. The puppy was thirsty but didn't eat as much as we thought he should. We put a pee pad down kind of near his bowls. I'm not sure how they work, but it might be something called a pheromone that the puppy can smell and will cause them to pee in that area. Well, he peed in that area but missed the pad, Close enough. Gary cleaned it up and I said I would have to do the next accident.

Anna was in the living room watching the news on tv. There were all sorts of accidents. There was one on the interstate that was a multi-car crash and there were a lot of injuries. This is why Mom had to go in, I think.

When we brought Rascal into the living room, Anna lit up. She really liked the puppy. Gary put the puppy down on the floor and he immediately went to her and tried to crawl up on her lap.

Laughing as the puppy did this, she finally asked Gary to lift him up. When he did, Rascal got up on his hind legs and starting licking Anna's face. She laughed and pulled the puppy down, situating him on her lap. And, just like before, Rascal calmed down and went to sleep.

— ••• —

With Rascal behaving, Gary and I got some cereal and came back to the living room to sit with his Mom and watch the news. It was generally pretty bad. What was really sad was that many people had to go to shelters to stay warm because of the power outages. I started thinking about those people up where Gary lived that were homeless, especially Sergeant Hughes. I mean, he only had a tent and a campfire. Was he going to be ok?

I decided to ask Dad to maybe go up there after he got home to see if he was ok or if any other homeless people needed help. I mentioned this all to Gary and he thought it was a good idea too.

"You know," he said, "maybe we should call the City of Mercy shelter. They usually go around and check on the homeless and poor people near where I lived. They've checked on my Mom and me before. You want to call them Davey and check to see if they gone over to where the Sergeant was camping?"

"Sure. That makes more sense than having Dad go up there first."

I got the phone number from a business card that Lori had put in the packet of information we got when we did the charity stuff. When I dialed first, the line was busy, probably because there was a lot going on because of all the snow. It took 4 more tries before I got through. The lady I spoke to said that some of the workers were out checking on the homeless and poor people around the forest area and she offered to call back to let us know the Sergeant's status. We just had to wait now.

— ••• —

In the afternoon the snow stopped falling and the sun started to come out. Gary and I had to finish shoveling and since the puppy had gotten up and tried to pee on the floor, he came out with us. One of us watched him as the other shoveled. Rascal happily played in the snow. By the time we were finished he had done all his business, chased a couple of birds, and barked at everyone that walked by. Those people that did go by all had to stop to ooh and aah at the puppy. Rascal loved the attention and Gary and I liked it too.

When we finally went in, Rascal was very wet and tired. We dried him off and just like usual, he went right to Anna wanting up on her lap. I had to make sure it was ok.

"Anna? Is holding Rascal a problem for you? I mean, we can keep him off your lap if it's a problem."

Anna smiled. "I really like holding the puppy. It makes me feel good. Plus, pretty soon he'll be too big to hold, so I might as well do it now."

She laughed and I knew exactly what she meant and why she was laughing. Rascal was going to get big really fast, so we had to enjoy him as a puppy now.

I lifted the puppy to her lap and he curled up and went right to sleep. He was quiet for the rest of the evening. A little later, about 7:30, Dad got home. He had stopped and picked up some subs, which was great. I asked about Mom and he said she was staying at the hospital until 10 or so and then she would be home. Anna had gotten tired and gone to her room before Dad brought the food, but Gary and I had made her some soup and a peanut butter sandwich earlier, so we weren't worried that she hadn't gotten something to eat. We put the puppy on the couch and he stayed asleep, curled up next to a pillow. He had pooped himself out playing.

As we sat and ate, Dad told us about the accident that Mom had been called to help with. It involved 6 cars and a semi, and a lot of people had been hurt. There had been other injuries around town as well. Most of them were caused by the power outages, but others were from cars sliding on snow-covered roads and people falling on slick sidewalks.

I remembered to ask Dad about Sergeant Hughes.

"Dad, Gary and I were worried about the Sergeant. I mean, he was only living in a tent and it snowed a lot. We called the Shelter and they were supposed to call back to let us know if he was ok, but they never did. We were wondering if you could maybe check on him?"

Of course Dad said he would. Because school was going to be open tomorrow and Gary and I wanted to go along, he agreed to take us along right after school. He always kept his promises.

— ••• —

DAVEY!! Davey, wake up!

Gary was leaning over me holding the puppy under one arm and shaking me with his free hand.

"Wake up! You slept through your alarm. You need to get up now and get ready to go. I'll take care of Rascal."

"What time is it?"

"Almost time to leave. Get dressed. My Mom's watching Rascal until your Mom gets up. I'm taking him out now."

Gary took the puppy and went outside. I didn't have time for a shower, so I cleaned up a little and got dressed.

Gary was at the bus stop waiting when I got there.

"Thanks for waking me up, but why did you wait until the last minute?"

"I didn't know you were still asleep. Rascal was yipping and when I knocked you didn't answer, so I opened the door. You were snoring like crazy."

"I don't snore."

Gary laughed, "Oh yah, you do."

"I even slept through Rascal barking?"

"Well, it was more like a yip."

"Is your Mom going to be ok watching Rascal?"

"I think so. She seems better. She didn't even use the cane when she came out of the bedroom."

"Well, that's good."

It was the first day of November and Halloween had pretty much gotten snowed out. Gary had made lunch for both of us and added some of the candy that would have been given out to the kids. I was not surprised at how Gary did all kinds of stuff to help out. I had almost forgotten about the bus stuff. I mean, there was a reason for what he did and it was a good one.

Anyway, the bus was almost a half hour late. When it did show up and we got on, there were a lot of kids not there, probably because their parents didn't know school was being held or they thought there wasn't going to be bus service.

But there, sitting in her usual seat, was Lori. As soon as she saw us she smiled and waved. Then, she followed us to the back of the bus and sat down next to me. Wow! How lit is that?

"Hi guys! How was your weekend?"

Lori was looking at me waiting for something to come out of my mouth…which didn't happen.

Gary spoke up. "Good. We got a puppy for Davey, a Saint Bernard. We named him Rascal."

Lori got excited. "What? That is so cool. When can I come over and see him?"

Gary spoke up again because I still was not getting any words out.

"I think we'll need to check with Davey's Mom and Dad to see when it would be ok. Is that alright, Lori?"

She smiled. "Sure. Maybe my Mom can come, too. She loves puppies. Just let me know, ok?"

I nodded. I wasn't too happy about Aggie Czech coming over to my house. What if she said something about the demon stuff? I guess there wasn't much I could do about it. I just had to be prepared for anything bad that might happen.

So, I sat there like an idiot not saying anything while Lori and Gary talked about the snow, classes, and dogs. Finally, we reached school and as we got off, I noticed a girl standing near the bike racks. She was watching who got off the bus.

We were the last to get off and when we reached where the girl was standing, I realized it was Debbie Mackenzie. As we walked by, she started walking with us and spoke to Gary.

"Hey Gary. What's going on?"

Gary looked at her and smiled. I think he might have actually liked her. I mean, she was tall, but cute.

"Hi Debbie. Nice to see you recovered from all that dancing with me."

She laughed.

"You know, you really didn't have to ask me. I'm kind of used to not being asked."

"I never do anything I don't want to. Ask Davey."

Debbie looked over at me.

"Well, I can tell you...he really did want to dance with you, Debbie."

She smiled.

"I have to go to history. Maybe I'll see you guys at lunch?"

We all nodded and headed down the other hall to our classes. Gary and Lori had Math and I was going to Miss Montgomery's.

So, this was interesting. Debbie wanted to have lunch with us and I guess that us included Lori. Me and Lori and Gary and Debbie. Wow. It almost sounded like boyfriends and girlfriends. I was thinking so much about this that when Miss Montgomery asked me a question, I didn't realize she had asked. She walked over to my desk, leaned over and said "David? Are you with us?"

I jerked back and everybody in the class laughed. It was embarrassing. I apologized and lied, saying I was just thinking about all the accidents and the people who might have been hurt. Miss Montgomery was a very nice teacher and when I said that she turned to the rest of the class and asked if anyone else was worried about people in town. Most everyone raised their hands.

"So, what can we do to help these people?" she asked.

Everybody just sat there and nobody said anything. So, I guess I had to say something. I raised my hand.

"Yes, David?"

"So, Miss Montgomery, we just finished doing the food drive to help the homeless and anybody else who needed a little extra help. Maybe we can see if anybody that was in an accident or lost power or got hurt might need a hand. Like maybe someone who has a pet and can't take care of them because they're hurt or can't get home? Or maybe they can't get to the store or they need help shoveling their walks? I mean, there's a lot we can actually do to help."

"Those are good ideas, David. Let me talk to some of the other staff and see if we can organize some help quickly. Class, please continue reading Chapter 7 while I run to the principal's office."

Of course, as soon as she left, everybody started talking. My friend, Eddie, who was in my class came over to my desk.

"Davey, you know my Dad's got the limo service. Maybe I can get him to help. What do you think?"

"I think it's a great idea, but I also think we should wait and see what the school says, ok?"

"Sure. Say, you and Gary want to come over this weekend and catch a movie? Dad's going to rent the newest *Men in Black*."

"Sounds good, but I have to check and see if Mom and Dad will watch my puppy."

"You got a puppy? You didn't say anything."

"It was just over the weekend. Gary and I went to the shelter and they had some Saint Bernard puppies. Well I ended up getting one. We named him Rascal."

"Wow! I wonder if Dad would let us get one."

"There were a bunch, Eddie, but you have to remember that they get really, really big. I mean, my Mom had a Saint when she was younger, so she understands the size thing. You would have to make sure your parents understood that, too."

"Well, the size thing might be a problem. Maybe they'd let me get something smaller."

"They had some really neat iguanas there, too. One was 3 feet long."

Eddie scrunched his nose up.

"Yah, I'm not sure Mom would let a lizard in the house. Maybe a smaller dog. Do you and Gary wanna go to the shelter with me on Saturday or Sunday? I mean, just to look. Want to?"

"Sure. We could do it in the afternoon before coming to your house for the movie. I still have to check and make sure they'll watch Rascal."

"Great!"

Just then, Miss Montgomery came back in the room.

"Class, I've spoken with Principal Wilcox. According to him, there's already some people organizing a help initiative. A little later there will be an announcement about volunteering to help and there will also be a sign-up sheet if you want to offer a little of your time. Now, let's get back to work. I just know you were able to finish up Chapter 7 while I was out of the room. So, close your books for a short impromptu quiz on that information."

Everybody moaned and she smiled because she knew no one had done anything while she was gone. Strangely, and mostly because of

Gary, I had already read the materials. Gary always got A's and maybe it was me being a little jealous of how good he was with all the school stuff. Instead of mucking around and playing games and not studying, I actually had read the chapter in advance.

"David, can you please explain the difference between morphology and phonology?"

I think that Miss Montgomery was shocked, because after stuttering like an idiot, I actually did.

"Ahhh...one is kind of how we understand how words are formed and umm...the other is kind of how words sound."

She laughed. "Well, that's kind of right David. Very good."

And with that, she went around the rest of the class asking questions from the Chapter we should have all finished...the one that I HAD finished. I felt really good.

— ••• —

The announcement was made at lunch.

I had found Debbie and Lori sitting together near the windows and sat down next to Debbie (so I could look directly at Lori). A few minutes later, Gary came in. He was walking across the room with the Principal, who was carrying a clipboard. They were talking and laughing. I wondered what the conversation was all about.

When Gary got to our table he was still smiling. I decided to ask.

"So, Gary, what were you talking to Principal Wilcox about? I saw you laughing."

Gary laughed again. "Well, I guess I have the highest grade point at the school and Principal Wilcox wanted me to try out for the Teen Jeopardy tryouts that are being held in Denver in a couple of months. He told me he thought it would be good publicity for the school. Since there is supposed to be an online test in a few weeks, he was hoping I would take it."

I actually wasn't surprised.

"Wow, Gary. That's awesome. You are going to do it, aren't you? I mean, you could actually win a lot of money."

"Only if I actually got picked and then won, Davey. If I didn't, I think I would feel really bad and because it might disappoint my Mom. She's been through enough."

Lori broke in.

"Yes, but if you won…Davey is right—you could win a lot of money. Wouldn't that help you and your Mom?"

She continued…

"And…even if you didn't win, you still get at least $1000 if you get on, don't you?"

Gary nodded. "I think so, but it's ONLY if you get on. Actually, I never thought much about it before."

I knew what he had to do.

"Gary, look, if I were as smart as you and the Principal asked me to do something like that…well, I'd do it in a flash. You're going to do it!"

"I'll have to ask my Mom."

"Your Mom is going to say GO FOR IT!!"

Debbie had been quiet until I said that.

"Look, Gary, don't get too excited. Remember, you have to score well on the online test and then, you have to go and do another test and then, well, I don't know what else you have to do to get on. A lot of kids try out, but only a handful get on the show."

Gary laughed again. "I know, but, I could get on and if I did and I lost, I would get a little money anyway. I guess I should try…if it's ok with my Mom, I mean."

I started wondering how Debbie would know stuff about the Jeopardy process. Maybe she had tried out and not gotten picked. I wasn't going to ask her because I didn't want her to be upset.

Just then, Principal Wilcox started to speak.

"Ladies and Gentlemen…yes, I mean you guys. (We all laughed.) We have an opportunity to help our neighbors by donating a little time from our busy schedules. You might be asked to shovel a walk, babysit,

November - 69

deliver groceries, or do whatever is necessary to help some of the people who have had problems caused by the storm.

I have a sign-up sheet here. If you do want to help, there is also a form your parents will need to sign, giving you permission. Those forms and the sign-up will be near the school entrance.

This is all voluntary. You are not required to help, but your support could make a difference for an individual or a family in our community. Feel free to see me in my office if you want more information.

Thank you and enjoy your lunch."

It was Gary who spoke first.

"I can shovel some walks for people. You too, Davey?"

"Sure. I wonder who organized this. Did the Principal mention it to you?"

"No, he just wanted to talk about Jeopardy."

Lori was listening.

"I can babysit if someone needs it. You know, this sounds like something my Mom would be doing. Or, maybe your Mom, Davey?"

"You're right. It does sound like my Mom. I'll ask when we get home."

I couldn't call because my parents still hadn't let me have a phone and the school didn't allow students to use the pay phone during class hours. Actually, they didn't allow phone calls from personal phones either.

No cell phone was kind of a bummer because a lot of other kids already had one. But my parents...I don't know. I guess they didn't think I was ready for one or maybe that I just didn't need one. Of course, I needed one. Doesn't every kid?

Maybe the demon that Aggie Czech advertised would help with stuff like this. I laughed to myself at the thought. I knew perfectly well that there was no demon. But, wouldn't it be cool if there was something that granted wishes for people? I mean, even a demon?

There was that coat thing for Gary... that was pretty weird. He needed a coat. He got a coat and not just any coat, the coat he actually wanted. Aggie Czech must have something like esp to have known that. Looking over at Lori, I wondered whether she knew her Mom had powers. Wow, maybe Lori had powers, too.

I was sitting there smiling about all the demon stuff when the bell rang for us to go back to class. As we all got up to leave the cafeteria, Gary leaned over and whispered something just to Debbie. She smiled. Whatever he had said made her seem very happy. I would have to ask him what he whispered later tonight after we got home.

— ••• —

The rest of the afternoon went fast. My last period on Monday was always study hall or a club meeting. Since I didn't belong to any clubs, I just used the time to read or try and get my homework done.

When school was out, I met Gary near the door. He had already signed both of us up and picked up the forms we needed for parent approval. As we were getting on the bus I saw Lori walking with that older kid she danced with on Friday. And bummer, he was holding her hand.

I should probably not have been upset, but we had lunch together and I was thinking she liked me. Well, I know she does, but not like I wanted her to like me. Gary noticed how moody I seemed and of course, he had to say something.

"Davey, what's the matter? You look down."

Before I could answer, Lori came back and sat down next to me.

"Hey guys. You signed up, right?"

Gary said we had and I just sat there moping.

Lori kept talking.

"So, I was thinking that me and my Mom could come over on Friday after school?"

"No. Gary and I have other plans."

Gary was surprised.

"We do?"

"Yah. I forgot to mention it to you, the plans I mean.

Maybe you guys can come over in a few weeks. Gary and I will probably be busy that long."

Lori looked a little disappointed but said sure that would be fine. Gary didn't say anything, but I knew he was wondering what was going on.

As soon as we got off the bus, he asked.

"Davey, why the heck are you acting so crappy? You like Lori, don't you?"

"She was holding that kid's hand."

"What kid?"

"The one she danced with."

"Oh."

Gary laughed.

"You know, Davey, it's your own fault."

"What do you mean by that?"

"I mean, you're scared to show you like her. You had a chance to ask her to dance, but did you?"

"Almost."

"OMG, Davey. Almost?"

"I don't want to talk about it, Gary. Let's get Rascal and go for a walk."

Gary didn't say any more and I knew he was right. It was my own fault that Lori had a boyfriend and it wasn't me.

When Rascal heard the door open, he started yipping happily and the puppy ran to meet us. Gary picked him up and he wiggled like crazy and kept trying to lick his face. Even though we had only had him a few days he already looked bigger or kind of fluffier maybe. Just then, Mom came out of the kitchen.

"Guys, what's going on? How was school?"

"OK, Mom. Gary and I signed up to do some more charity work. We need you and Anna to sign permission slips."

Gary handed both the slips to my Mom, who barely looked at them before laying them down on the bookcase that was in our hallway.

I wasn't sure why she didn't seem more interested, but then it hit me that she probably had already seen them and did have something to do with the stuff we were volunteering for.

"Mom? You already know about this, don't you? And, before I forget, Rascal looks bigger. Is that possible?"

"Yes on both counts, David. Yes, some of the nurses thought it would be a good idea to offer some help to people who had problems because of the storm. Of course, they decided I should organize the whole thing. Aggie Czech is friends with your principal, Eric Wilcox. She contacted him to see if any of the kids would like to volunteer. Actually, we had a lot of kids sign up...more than we could use, so you guys aren't going to be needed for this.

She continued.

"However, your Dad is going to be checking on all the homeless and poor people for the next few days and on Saturday. I thought that you and Gary might want to help with that. Yes?"

We both said absolutely.

"Oh yes...about Rascal...well, Anna and I took him out in the back yard, and it was a bit muddy from the melting snow. Rascal got really dirty so, we gave him a bath. He fluffed up a lot and looks really terrific— much cleaner and much bigger."

Gary sounded concerned.

"Mom went outside? Was she ok? Did she stay warm enough?"

"I thought a little fresh air would be good for her. Oh, and don't worry, Gary. I gave your Mom a really warm parka to wear. We sat outside for a while watching the puppy and when she did get tired, we came in and had a little lunch. She's resting now. Really, she's doing great and you know what? It's great having her around. I really like her."

Gary looked relieved. "Great. I'm going to peek in and she how she's doing."

Gary handed me Rascal and went down the hall to check on his Mom. She must have been sleeping because he came right back.

"Mom's resting. You're sure everything's good?"

Mom nodded that it was.

"Just to let you know…this coming Friday, we're going back to the clinic and the doctor is going to check to make sure she's recovering like she should. It's going to take a while, Gary. But really, she is doing great."

There's something about Mom. She just knows stuff about people. She could see Gary was worried, so she reached over and put her arm around his shoulder.

"Gary, you and your Mom…well, we like you here. We want you to stay with us as long as your need to..or want to."

"Thanks Mrs. Allen."

"Call me Kim. Now you guys get started on your homework. We're going to have dinner a little early because I have to go over and meet with some of the teachers and Aggie about what we're going to need to do."

I wasn't crazy about Mom hanging with Aggie, but I couldn't do anything about it. So, I decided, what the heck. If something bad was going to happen, it was going to happen. I wasn't going to worry about it anymore. Plus, they would probably be so busy that they wouldn't have time to talk about me. So, no more worrying…at least for now."

— ••• —

I had been grouchy since I saw Lori and that 9th grader holding hands. After dinner, Gary said he would take Rascal so I could mope without worrying about the puppy. I was feeling a little better in the morning and when Lori got on the bus, she waved, but sat with a couple of her friends toward the front. That was good. What was better was that Eddie Anderson took the bus. He usually gets dropped off by his Dad, but when his Dad's busy, Eddie rides with us.

"Hey guys. So, are you coming over this weekend?"

Gary answered. "We can, Eddie, but we have some stuff to do earlier. Is that going to be ok?"

"Sure. How come you'll be so late? You said you go with me to the animal shelter."

"We're helping Davey's Dad after school for the rest of the week. We're going to be checking on the people up near the woods. We doing that in the morning so we should still be able to meet you."

"Great. Hey Davey, what's going on with you? You haven't said anything at all."

Well, I just wasn't going to tell Eddie that I was upset about a girl. If I did he would tell his sister who would tell the universe. NO WAY!!

"I'm just a little tired, Eddie. Rascal has kept me awake almost every night…except last night when Gary watched him."

Gary laughed and I knew what he was thinking, but fortunately, all he did was laugh.

"Yah, the puppy likes to yip in the middle of the night," Gary added. "We have to keep him in a box because we can't put him in bed with us because he'll pee. He still isn't trained."

"Gee, maybe I can come over and see him?"

"It'll have to be next week, Eddie. Gary and I are helping Dad for the rest of the week. Remember?"

"Oh, yah. Next week is cool."

We had just pulled up to the school and as we got off, I watched out the window to see if that kid was waiting for Lori, but it didn't look like he was. I thought maybe Debbie would be out there too, but she wasn't either. Lori walked ahead of us with her friends.

Later, at lunch, she sat with a bunch of girls on the other side of the cafeteria. I knew she had other friends, so I wasn't really upset about it, although it would have been nice if she'd wanted to sit with us.

— •••—

School went really fast. Dad was waiting for Gary and me when we got home. We didn't have to worry about Rascal because Mom and Anna were watching him. We had bought a dog crate (cage) for when Rascal needed to be left alone, but we hadn't needed to use it yet. I was glad because the cage was really big and Rascal was still pretty tiny.

We were taking one of Dad's work trucks, just in case something electric needed fixing. Gary sat in the front. No, I wasn't just being nice letting him sit there. We tossed a coin to see who would first. Tomorrow, I would.

Anyway, after checking in with Mom and Anna, we headed out. Out first stop was going to be Mrs. Skriver's house. You remember, it was that older lady we took food to? Dad took the same route we had when we did the deliveries. When we got to the turn off where Mrs. Skriver lived, we found that the road was completely covered with snow and there were no tracks at all. That meant that nobody had checked on whether she was doing ok.

The snow was too deep for us to drive through, so we parked at the start of the driveway and walked up to the house. There weren't any lights on and we didn't see any smoke coming from the little chimney. Dad knocked and called her name.

"Mrs. Skriver? Mary? It's Keith Allen. Mary?"

Dad knocked again, this time louder.

We heard a noise inside and the door being unlocked. Mary Skriver peeked out at us and smiled. When she opened the door we saw that she was wearing a heavy coat and had a blanked wrapped around her on top of it.

"Mr. Allen. How nice of you to stop by. My power went out during the snowstorm. I don't have a phone so I couldn't call anyone to help fix it. Maybe you could take a look?"

Of course Dad could. While he was checking out the electrical, Gary and I went and got some firewood from the pile at the side of the house. Mary had a little wood burning stove. She had run out of wood, but didn't want to go out and get more for fear she would fall and not be able to get back in the house. So when the fire burned out, she put on her coat and wrapped herself up in a blanket to stay warm.

A lot of the wood was wet, but there was kind of an overhang that kept some of it dry. We got a bunch of those logs and got a fire started in the stove. We also got more logs and piled them up on the side of the porch, enough, we thought, for at least a couple of days of heat. That would make it easy for her to get pieces of wood for the stove and she wouldn't have to go out in the snow.

Dad had gone around to check the electrical connections and found that some of heavy snow had pulled down a big branch from one of the oak trees and it had fallen on the wire going into the house and pulled it loose from whatever connected it to the outer wall.

While Dad was doing whatever it was that he does with electrical stuff, we got the shovels out of the back of the truck and cleared the porch steps, then made a path to the wood just in case Mrs. Skriver needed to get more. We also dug a path out to the road so she could get to her mailbox and for when somebody from the shelter would come and pick her up to take her to the store, which they did once a week.

As Gary and I shoveled I started thinking about what we could do to help her a little more.

"Gary, I don't know how she can be living out here without a phone. What if she fell down and couldn't get up? I mean she could be laying there for years without anybody knowing. She needs a phone."

"Phones are expensive, Davey."

"Yah, I know, but what if we could got her a burner?"

"You mean a prepaid?"

"Yah. One where we could put in a few dollars so she could call if she needed to. I mean, how much would it cost to get her one of these?"

"I don't know. Maybe $50 would get her a cheap phone and enough minutes for a month or two, wouldn't it?"

"Maybe. I don't know. I'll ask Mom about it."

"Where are we getting the money for something like this?" Gary seemed concerned.

"I've got enough money saved. It wouldn't kill me to use some of it for a phone. I mean, I could ask my parents, but they paid the adoption fees for Rascal, so I figure I can fork over a little money for something like this."

"You know, I've got a few bucks saved from the money your Mom and Dad have given me because I've been helping with the chores. It's not much, but you can have it, Davey if it would help."

"No, you keep that for now. I can pay for this one. I wonder if this is something that would help other people up here. What do you think?"

"I think it's a great idea, but I also think that you can't pay for all the phones we might need to help all the people that need help."

Gary was right. I needed to talk to Mom this week to see what we could do to get enough phones so that everybody that needed one would have one.

Just then, the lights came on in the house. When we went back inside the stove has warmed the room enough so that Mrs. Skriver could take her coat off.

When the power had gone out, she was afraid that the few things she had in her old fridge would rot, so she put everything in a box and set it out on her porch. Because it was cold, it kept the food from spoiling. Now that the power was on, she could put everything back, so Dad had me get the box and bring it in. I felt really bad seeing how little there was. She did have the groceries we had brought her, but those wouldn't last that long. Even the gift card would be gone in a few weeks.

You know, most of us don't realize how hard it is for a lot of people. For a country that is so rich, how can it be possible to have people barely surviving? I mean, if we have this many people just in our town, how many are there living in poverty in the whole U.S.?

We had been at Mrs. Skriver's for almost 3 hours and didn't really have time to go anywhere else because it was already almost 7 and that's when we told Mom we would be home. Dad let Mrs. Skriver know that he would send a crew up tomorrow morning to permanently repair the wiring for the house and get rid of the branch that had fallen. She thanked us a zillion times and asked us another zillion if we could come up and visit again. Dad told her Mom would be coming up to make sure she was ok and to see what else we could do to help.

After we left, when we were driving home, I asked about the Sergeant.

"Dad, I was hoping we could check on Sergeant Hughes tonight. Do you think maybe we could swing by where he was camping and see if he's ok?"

Dad agreed and called home to let them know we'd be a little late. When we got to the place in the forest where the Sergeant had been camping, we didn't see him or his dogs. His tent was still there, but he was gone. I wondered where he was. Dad said he would try and find out a little more about what was going on with him.

— ••• —

It was almost 8:30 when we got home. There were sandwiches for us in the kitchen. Mom and Anna had already eaten and so had Rascal. He was now curled up sleeping on the couch next to Mom. I wanted to talk to Mom about the phone idea, but figured I would wait until tomorrow.

Gary and I were both tired, but we did grab sandwiches and headed off to our rooms to relax. Gary didn't have a tv or a computer, but I let him use my laptop and kind of borrowed Dad's for myself. I mean, he wasn't much of a computer person and hadn't even really missed it. I did leave a note telling him where it was, just in case he did need it... which he hadn't yet.

I had forgotten completely about the puppy, but a few minutes later, there was a knock on my door and it was Mom holding Rascal under one arm and the stuffed puppy toy in the other hand.

"David, did you forget something? Let me give you a hint...something that yips and wiggles a lot?"

"Sorry, Mom. Gary and I spent most of the time shoveling and I was tired."

"Remember what we told you David. You are responsible for Rascal, even when you're tired. What would happen if you were tired and didn't feed him, or too tired to take him out to do his business?"

"I know. I'm sorry. I won't forget again."

Mom laughed. "You probably will. Now, you need to get him out before you go to bed."

She handed me Rascal and left. I went upstairs to see if Gary wanted to go out with me, but when I peeked in it looked like he was already asleep. I wasn't going to wake him up just to get the puppy out.

I took the puppy out in the front and let him run around and play in the snow. It was pretty cold, so after about a half an hour of puppy romping, I gathered him up and went back in.

I was pretty tired, but the puppy was bouncing around and wanting to play. I put him in the box we had and stuck the stuffed animal in with him. There was a lot of whining and yipping, but finally, Rascal calmed down and went to sleep. I was very tired. I still hadn't finished my math homework and had to force myself to stay up and do it. It was almost 11:30 by the time I actually got to close my eyes.

"DAVEY!!"

I had just gotten to sleep or so I thought when I heard Gary yelling my name.

"DAVEY!! You need to wake up. You've overslept again. DAVEY!"

"What time is it?"

"6:40. The bus should be here in 10 minutes."

"Dang. Can you take Rascal out while I get dressed?"

"Sure, but do it fast or we'll miss the bus."

Gary took Rascal outside while I dragged myself out of bed. I didn't have any clean clothes and had to throw on some dirty stuff. Now, that's not my Mom's fault. I'm supposed to do my own laundry and well, I guess I just hadn't gotten around to it lately. I made a note to do a load after I got home tonight. When I came downstairs Mom and Anna were sitting at the kitchen table talking. I noticed that the dog cage had been set up in the corner of the kitchen.

Just then, Gary brought Rascal back in and Mom took him and stuck him in the cage. There was plenty of room for the puppy, plus enough space for water and food bowls.

I made it to the bus stop just as the bus was coming around the corner. I hadn't had time to ask why they were putting the puppy in the cage, but I figured Gary would know. As soon as we got settled in the back, I asked.

"Gary, I'm sorry about this morning...again. I had to stay up and do my math. I mean, I'm not as smart as you are, so it takes me a little longer to finish my homework.

"Not a problem, Davey. I figured you were just getting back at me for all the bus stuff."

I laughed. "Not intentionally, but I really appreciate it. By the way, do you know why my Mom was putting Rascal in the dog cage?"

"It called a crate."

"It's a cage, Gary."

"OK, cage. Your Mom is taking my Mom with her when she goes up to see Mrs. Skriver. I guess Mom wanted to swing by the trailer to make sure we got everything we should have when we went up there before. They have to put Rascal in the "cage" while they're gone."

"Is your Mom going to be ok? "

"I think so. She's been feeling a lot better."

"Great. Oh yah, remind me to stick a load of laundry in when we get home."

"I will, but don't forget we're going up right after school to check on the Sergeant."

"I know. I didn't forget, exactly. I just need to get my laundry done since I forgot to do it over the weekend. Maybe if I start a load before we leave, Mom will put it in the dryer. I'll ask her when we get home."

The rest of our bus ride was quiet and the day went pretty fast, even though I was still tired from not getting enough sleep. In the morning I had noticed that Lori was not on the bus, but I had decided I was done with thinking about her. I mean, she seemed to have an older boyfriend already, so she was definitely not interested in me.

When we got home, Dad was waiting for us and he had Rascal tucked neatly under his arm.

He saw us and came forward.

"Hi guys. I thought I'd get Rascal out while I waited for you kids to get back from school. We need to get moving. I promised the ladies we'd definitely be home by 7."

"Dad, do I have time to start a load of laundry?"

"Go ahead, but hurry."

I hurried in and got a load started, then stopped by the kitchen where Mom and Anna were making cookies and asked if she would stick them in the dryer for me. Of course, she said she would, but reminded me that laundry gets done on weekends on a regular basis. I looked at Anna and noticed she had started getting color back in her face. She still looked awfully skinny, but generally, much, much better. Mom reminded me that we needed to be home by 7 and I let her know that Dad had already mentioned it.

Gary and Dad were already in the truck waiting for me. Right when we started driving through the forest, it started to snow again and we started worrying about the Sergeant and the other homeless and poor people that lived in the area. Dad drove directly up to where Sergeant Hughes was camping, but he still wasn't there, so he decided to go directly up to City of Mercy and try to find out if they had helped him and his dogs.

— ••• —

City of Mercy was farther up at the Northern most part of the forest. They had picked that location, not because of where it was but because of what was there—an abandoned factory in a completely fenced area. The building was big enough for a lot of people to be housed, plus they had offices for the support staff. There was a decent kitchen and a gym where both kids and adults could play games like basketball and volleyball.

This was one of the shelters where we had dropped off food. There was a locked gate, so Dad had to let them know who we were before they buzzed us in. Driving up to the front we saw a bunch of little kids playing outside in the snow. There were 2 men watching to keep them safe.

As we got out of the truck, one of the men approached Dad, greeting him by name.

"Keith Allen, what are you doing up here on the wrong side of town?"

Dad laughed and shook the man's hand.

"Jack, it's been too long. Kids, meet Lieutenant Jack Davis, one of the Army's best members of the special forces. This is my son David and the other lad here is his friend, Gary Morgan."

"Ex-special forces Keith."

Jack Davis stuck his hand out and shook both of ours. He was very tall with a bald head and a neatly trimmed beard. He also only had one hand, the one he shook with. The other was a hook. He saw me staring at it.

"Nice to meet you guys. The kids call me Captain Hook. I just never understood why they would call me Captain when that's not my rank. Kids...what can I say. He laughed and so did we.

"Jack, the boys and I stopped by to see whether a Jimmy Hughes was at the shelter. You might know him? He lives in a tent down a few miles in the forest and he would be with 2 dogs? We stopped down there yesterday and today, but he wasn't there.

"Sure, I know the Sergeant. Kind of a loner and doesn't seem to think he ever needs any help. I guess it was snowing so bad he couldn't keep a fire going and even though he could care less if he was cold, he was concerned about his dogs. One of the guys stopped by and picked them up. He was here last night, but then, he and the puppies ended up going to stay with someone in town."

"Who was that, Jack?"

The Lieutenant pulled a phone from his jacket and used the hook to hold it in place while he looked up information.

"Boy, I sure am glad I have this hook. It makes it so easy to hold my phone, don't you think so guys?"

Jack Davis laughed. Scrolling through a list he had on his phone, he finally found what we were looking for—where the Sergeant ended up.

"Keith, it looks like he and the two doggies are staying with a Ken Grossman."

It was Gary who spoke up.

Mr. Davis, Lieutenant? Is that the Grossman who drives a bus?"

"Gary, right? Just call me Jack or, if you want, you may address me like the kids do—Hook. I don't know what he does. He volunteers here a few days a month. When he heard about the Sergeant and his dogs coming in, he said he had plenty of room at his house and offered to let them stay with him. I don't know what he said to the Sergeant, who tends to be a bit pig-headed about taking charity, but he must have said something that made some sense, because the Sergeant agreed to take the help. I honestly think it was because he was worried his dogs would end up being sent to an animal shelter and he just didn't want any of that.

It sure sounded like the Mr. Grossman who drove our bus. Dad talked a few more minutes with the Lieutenant before we got back in the truck and drove away with the Lieutenant waving goodbye with that hook. We still had a couple of stops to make before we headed home. There was that old couple on social security and the young mother.

We got to the old couple's house first and Dad got out and knocked. A younger woman opened the door and spoke briefly with him before going back inside. When Dad got back, he let us know that the lady was their daughter and she was staying with them for a while to make sure they would be ok. That was great. It was good to see family helping out.

When we drove up to the trailer where the young mother stayed, we found a note on her door saying she had moved back home. I guess trying to work and take care of a little baby was just too much for her to do all by herself.

It was around 6:30 when we headed home.

— ••• —

It bothers me a lot to see all those people having a hard time. I guess that's because I've never been hungry or cold or poor or anything. Gary has. Gary knows what it's actually like. Maybe that's why everything he does is to help people. As soon as we got home, he checked on his Mom and scooped up Rascal to take him outside. Then, he went into the kitchen to see if Mom needed any help.

Me? Well, I really like helping too...but I don't always look for things to help with, like Gary does. When we got home, I went in the living room and talked to Anna while Gary set the table. I did keep an eye on Rascal until dinner was ready and afterward, as usual, I did load the dishwasher, with Gary's help.

I still had that idea about getting burner phones for the homeless people. Yes, yes, I know—they're disposable phones. I guess I just watch too many detective shows on tv. Anyway, I wanted to talk to Mom about it after dinner, but she was busy making phone calls about something. I wasn't sure what was going on, but I had to finish my homework and make sure the puppy was taken care of. I knew Gary would find out from his Mom and then, he would tell me.

Obviously, we hadn't had Rascal very long, but he seemed to be learning that peeing in the house was a no no. He would start yipping like crazy and wiggling around when he had to go out. I know St. Bernard's are smart dogs, but Rascal seemed extra smart.

It was almost 10 when Gary came up to get me and Rascal to go outside. We decided to go out in the back yard because there was a bench where we could sit while Rascal ran around and did his thing.

Gary was pretty quiet. I wondered why.

"Hey Gary, what's going on. You seem kind of quiet."

"I'm a little worried about my Mom. I guess she started having trouble seeing yesterday evening."

"Was that what my Mom was on the phone about?"

"I think so. I think your Mom was looking for specialists. Not sure though. I think I heard her say something about a side effect to her condition that might cause some sort of sight problem."

"You mean the pneumonia?"

"The malnutrition."

"Dang Gary. You mean she's losing her sight because she didn't get enough to eat?"

Gary sighed. "Pretty much, I guess."

He looked really down. I know he worried a lot about his Mom.

"Listen, Gary. I know your Mom will be ok. Have faith."

Gary smiled, but he didn't say anything at all. Just then Rascal started yipping and we heard a little cry coming from the edge of the yard. We both got up and walked to where we heard the noise. Rascal was crouched down right at the line of bushes where our yard stops and the neighbor's starts. Gary grabbed the puppy and I peeked down to see what was there. There was movement, but I couldn't tell what it was.

"Gary, listen, take Rascal in and grab that flashlight that's in the first cabinet in the kitchen. I'll wait here."

Gary nodded and took Rascal in, then came out a few minutes later with the flashlight.

We pointed it under the bushes and were surprised by two furry little creatures—two cute little kitties. They couldn't have been very old at all because they were so tiny. It looked like they were abandoned. They were crying. Gary reached down and picked them both up.

"Davey, look at these little kittens. Wow, do you think your parent would let us keep them?"

"Sure Gary. My Mom's a pushover when it comes to baby anythings."

"So, let's see what everybody says."

Mom and Dad were in the living room. Rascal was now curled up on Dad's lap because Anna had already headed to bed. Mom was sitting on the couch and when she heard us come in, she glanced in our direction and of course saw the bundle of fur that Gary was carrying. She looked surprised.

"What's that Gary? David? Oh my gosh, kittens. Where did you find those tiny little things?"

Mom reached out and took the kittens from Gary. She was smiling like crazy and cupped them in both of her hands.

"We think they got abandoned, Mom. Can we keep them?"

Mom got serious. "You know, guys, kittens that are abandoned when they're this small usually don't make it."

Seeing how Gary and I both reacted to that statement, she continued.

"Look, tomorrow, I'll take them over to the vet and see what we need to do to keep them alive. Are you guys planning to take care of them AND Rascal?"

Of course, we nodded that we were, but we could see how Mom looked at them and knew she would be happy to watch them too. You're probably wondering what my Dad was doing all this time. Well, nothing really. He just sat there holding Rascal and just kind of shaking his head in that knowing what was going to happen way, but not having any control of the situation. Dad loved animals, too, but was more of a dog person. Still, I know he didn't mind that we now had two new additions to the family.

The kittens were crying and Mom took them into the kitchen and held each of them over a newspaper while she rubbed their tummys. The kittens peed and pooped. Mom told us that was how mother cats made their babies go potty—but by licking them. She then took some cream and put it on the tip of her finger and gave each of them a little, then got a towel and Rascal's stuffed toy and put the kittens in a box, with the towel snuggled up around them.

"First thing tomorrow, I'll take them to the vet. But guys, remember what I said. Kittens that are this young when they're separated from their mothers don't usually make it."

With that Mom picked up the box and took it with her into the bedroom. When we went into the living room to get Rascal for the evening, he was pulling on the bottom of Dad's jeans. Dad was laughing like crazy as the puppy growled and wiggled as he pulled.

Seeing us, Dad tried to get the puppy to let go of his pant leg, but Rascal didn't want to. He did when he spotted Gary and me. We were all laughing like crazy as the puppy happily played. Finally, he started calming down and since it was Gary's turn to watch him, he scooped him up, said goodnight and went up to his room.

As I started to leave, Dad touched my arm and gestured that I should sit. I did, but of course, wondered why.

"David, so how's everything going with you and Gary?"

"Good, Dad. Why are you asking me?"

"Well, Gary and his Mom might be staying with us for quite a while. Does that bother you at all?"

"No. I really like them here. The longer they stay, the better."

"Gary's Mom might be having some more health issues. I just wanted to make sure you had no problem with sharing our home."

"Dad, if it were up to me they could stay with us forever."

"Well, forever is a long time, David, but good to hear. And now, I see, you and Gary brought a couple of kitties home?"

"No. they were in the back yard. They were just left there, under the bushes."

Dad laughed. "You realize your mother loves cats. She had a couple growing up and well, David, if you think those babies are going to be yours and Gary's, think again."

I knew what Dad meant. They were now Mom's.

I said good night and went up to my room. I had done all my homework at school, so I only had to worry about my laundry. But there, on my bed, neatly folded, was all my clothes. I put everything away and made a mental note to thank Mom for doing this. I would get another lecture, of course. That was ok though, because there was no excuse for me not washing clothes for myself.

Before I went to bed, I took a few minutes to look up costs for phones. The phones weren't too expensive, and they did come with a few hours of minutes, but you always had to buy more when those minutes ran out. When I was less tired, I would figure out what to do to make the phone thing happen. I wasn't sure how to get the money together. Mom would know how. Mom knows how to do everything.

Gosh, maybe the demon could help. I chuckled to myself. Whatever went on with that sort of stuff really only happened because of Aggie Czech. All I would have to do …at least I thought all I would have to do…was let her know there was something that needed to be fixed or changed or helped with…and Aggie or the demon or whatever or whoever might make it happen. I needed a plan. Maybe tomorrow when I was less tired….

—•••—

Friday! I managed to wake up on time. I got a shower and was just finishing getting dressed when Gary knocked on my door. Rascal was tucked under his arm and wiggling like crazy. Gary was smiling.

"Davey, you got up on time."

"I even had time to take a shower, so I don't smell and now, on top of that, I even have clean clothes to wear so I don't look like a bum."

We both laughed.

"Let's get Rascal out and maybe we'll have time to check on the kittens. I wonder if we should name them."

"I think we should wait on that. Remember what my Mom said about what happens with kittens this young when they're abandoned?"

november - 89

Gary agreed. "You're right. We should wait."

I didn't want to think about the kitties dying and I know Gary didn't either.

When we left for school, we didn't see my Mom. Anna was up sitting at the kitchen table and Gary asked where she was. Anna said that she had left for the vet a little before 7:00 because she wanted to make sure the kitties were going to be ok.

— ••• —

We had to wait until we got home to find out about our new friends. Mom was in the kitchen with Anna and each of them were holding one of the kitties and feeding them with tiny bottles that looked like doll bottles…you know, the kind little girls play with? And yes, Mom told us, that's what they were—doll bottles.

When we went to get Rascal and let him out, Mom let us know that until the kitties were a little bigger, Rascal might have to stay in his crate while the babies were being taken care of. He had been put in the cage while the kitties were being fed but didn't seem to mind too much. He was playing with some new toy that squeaked every time he bit it, which seemed to be all the time.

Gary and I understood. Rascal was huge compared to the kittens even though for a Saint Bernard he was still awfully tiny.

Mom and Anna finished feeding the kitties, did the pee and poop thing and then took them to Mom and Dad's room where there was a big box set up to keep them in. Once they got them safely tucked away, Gary and I got Rascal out. He was absolutely happy to see us and immediately peed on the floor before we could even get to the door. Gary got him outside while I cleaned up the spot. It wasn't on carpet or anything so I didn't have to do much except wipe it up with a paper towel, spray the spot with Lysol and take the towels to the trash.

When I went out it was snowing again. Rascal was having fun playing. Gary had taken a broom and started sweeping the walk. I noticed he was looking a lot better. He had gained a little weight, which was good, but my old clothes were still loose on him.

As we watched the puppy play, Gary brought up the Sergeant. We hadn't been able to ask Mr. Grossman about him because he wasn't on the bus this morning.

"So, Davey, do you think that the Sergeant is staying with our bus driver?"

"Well, I can't say for sure, but based on what we know about the kind of person Mr. Grossman is, it probably is him."

"Does your Dad know him?"

"Don't know, but we should ask when he gets home."

Mr. Grossman was one of those people that would do everything necessary to help you if you needed it. I thought it was kind of odd that he hadn't helped Gary, but, thinking about how well Gary had made everybody think he was just a bully, well I guess even Mr. Grossman was fooled.

As we sat watching Rascal playing in the snow, Dad turned into the driveway. He waved us over to the Jeep. Gary scooped up the puppy and we walked over to talk to Dad. Rolling down the window, he smiled.

"Hello, boys. So, I need to go and check on Mrs. Skriver's electrical. Want to ride along?"

Of course we did. Gary took Rascal back in and let Mom and Anna know what we were doing and that we would be back within the hour, before dinner.

Driving up to Mrs. Skriver's home gave me and Gary the opportunity to ask about Mr. Grossman.

"Dad? Gary and I were wondering if you knew Mr. Grossman? Ken Grossman, our bus driver?"

"Ken Grossman? Sure, I know him. Everybody knows Ken."

"Why is that, Dad?"

"Well, you kids only know Ken because he drives your bus. But before he did that, before he retired, he was a police detective, and before that he was a beat cop. It seemed like everybody knew Ken. I can't tell you how many times he was there when someone needed help. But the reason everybody really knows him is because he put his life on the line to rescue a family whose car had crashed through a barrier going up in the mountains. I don't know the whole story here, but somehow, all by himself, he got that family out of the car before it broke loose from where it was hanging and crashed down the side of the mountain and then, burst into flames. He got a commendation from the city and not too long after that he was promoted to detective.

Wow. That's all Gary and I could say. It's amazing what you learn about people you think you know.

"Mr. Allen, do you think Mr. Grossman was who took the Sergeant and his dogs?"

"Probably. I don't think there are too many Ken Grossmans around here. We'll find out soon enough. Right now, let's make sure Mrs. Skriver has power and isn't having any problems."

Dad was right. Some kind person was taking care of the Sergeant and we were here to help Mrs. Skriver.

Turning down her road, we found that the snow had partially covered it again. There were no tracks in the new snow, so that meant no one had been down here since the crew came and permanently repaired the wiring to the house. There was smoke coming out of the chimney and the lights were on, so we knew she was there.

Dad went up and knocked while Gary and I got shovels and cleared as much of the road as we could while he was checking on Mrs. Skriver. It wasn't too long before he came back down, carrying a paper plate that was covered in tinfoil.

Mrs. Skriver peeked out and waved at us.

"Come back soon," she called out.

Dad said we would try and come up in a few days. He thanked her for the cookies and we all got back in the Jeep and drove off.

It was Gary who spoke up.

"Wow, Mrs. Skriver made cookies? She has so little. Should we have taken them?"

Dad shook his head yes.

"You know, Gary, when someone who has as little as Mrs. Skriver wants to give you something like cookies because they are grateful for your help...well, you take the gift and thank them for their kindness."

Gary and I understood. It also made me think I should work harder on the phone plan I had. I would have to talk to Mom soon.

— ••• —

It seemed like time was passing really fast. It was already almost Thanksgiving and things were going super well, especially with Gary and his Mom staying with us. Grandma Sis wasn't coming to our house this year because she was going to visit Mom's brother in Iowa. I never told you we live in Colorado, did I? Well, we do, near the foothills of the Rocky Mountains.

Anyway, Grandma Sis always rotates visits between Mom and Mom's two brothers. This was an Iowa year for her because she had been at our house last year. Next year she would go to Texas for Thanksgiving.

Because Gramma Sis wasn't coming this year, Mom got it into her head that she would invite some people over for dinner. She asked Gary and me who we would like to come and we agreed it would be nice if we invited Mrs. Skriver, Mr. Grossman and the Sergeant. Mom said that was good and told me she was inviting Lori and her Mom as well. I guess that was ok. Since nothing bad had happened so far about the demon for rent stuff, I had kind of stopped worrying about it. Lori had been busy with her friends recently, so we hadn't really hung out or anything. It would be kind of great to see her. I mean, I'm really no longer interested in a girlfriend arrangement, but she is my friend. You understand, right?

Anyway, Mom kept wanting to invite more and more people and it got to the point where our house wouldn't be big enough for everybody. So, she called Aggie Czech and the two of them came up with a plan

November - 93

to have a Thanksgiving feast at some central location where anybody who wanted or needed a meal and company during the holiday would be welcome. They had thought about doing it at the City of Mercy but agreed that somewhere more centrally located would be better. Aggie called the principal of our school, Mr. Wilcox, but he said he thought there was a better location for a drop-in dinner like they wanted than the school's gym.

There was a brand-new event center that was scheduled to open in a month. It was big enough to seat as many as 1000 people. Principal Wilcox knew the owners...well, actually, they were his sister and brother-in-law. He told Aggie and Mom that they would be happy to have a lunch and dinner there, because it would be a great way to promote the site. The kitchen was fully functional and there were plenty of tables, chairs, and couches for seating, plus all the stuff for serving. They did say that they could supply 2 great cooks (he called them chefs) and a few staff for helping with the meals and for clean-up afterward. Mom and Aggie would have to figure out how to get all the food and the word out. They would also have to come up with transportation for those people that needed it.

Now, with so little time to plan something like this, you might think that it couldn't be done. Well, not so, at least not for Mom and Aggie. They split up the stuff that needed to get taken care of and got busy.

Aggie was going to do the food and the set-up. Mom would make sure that everybody knew what was going on and that for those that needed it, there would be transportation to and from the location. She would also organize the helpers. Of course, Gary and I were going to help. Even Gary's Mom wanted to do some stuff. She agreed to make calls to all the churches and shelters in the area to let them know what was getting planned.

I started wondering why nobody had done anything like this before, but Mom said they had. I guess I just never paid much attention to it until now. You know, this year has been a really big change for me. I mean with all the stuff with Gary and his Mom and all the other charity stuff. I don't know what started it, but I think it was that sign in Aggie Czech's window. The more I think about it, the more I think there's something to hocus pocus or whatever you call it. Or, maybe I just think that Lori's Mom does have some superpowers and does make stuff happen.

So, do you think there are both good and bad demons? Right now, it seems like there are only good ones.

Anyway, Aggie had Lori make a flyer to let businesses around town know what we were doing and what they could do to help. Gary and I got to pass them out. We also got to organize all the donations and food offers that started coming in from all over. In less than a week over $10,000 in donations had come in, plus grocers and food distributors around the area had offered all sorts of stuff. Father James Donovan, who's the head priest at St. Mary's Catholic Church came up with a plan to have people in his parish make side dishes and desserts. He reached out to other churches throughout town to donate as well. They were all different faiths and included 2 synagogues and a local mosque. Everybody seemed to want in on the big party. With all that food and all that money Gary and I figured we could feed billions. Well, maybe not that many, but a lot.

The big day snuck up on us really fast. I think Gary and his Mom were more excited than anybody. It had been tough for them for the last couple of years and I don't think they had celebrated much at all. Anyway, everything was done on time and ready. Anna was feeling pretty good and went ahead with Mom to the location to help supervise the setup. Gary and I went along, too. Oh, don't worry about Rascal and the kitties. They were fed and cared for, then tucked away in the box and dog cage, or crate if you like that better. The plan was to go home in a few hours and let Rascal out and check on the babies. Dad would take me and Gary to take care of our friends and then, we would go back to the dinner.

Mom had arranged for transportation for those people that needed it. Many of the parishioners at our church volunteered to pick up and drop off, plus the City of Mercy and the other shelters had busses that could bring a lot of people.

When we got to the location, Aggie and Lori were there and so were other helpers, including Lori's boyfriend. His name is Charlie Cornish and dang, he turned out to be a pretty nice guy. Lori introduced me and Gary and told us that he had volunteered to play the piano. Wow, good enough to play for a bunch of people? That was something. I was still kind of bummed out about the boyfriend thing, but he seemed pretty nice, so I guess it was ok. Lori deserved someone like that. I wonder if she knows I'm a nice guy, too.

The Wilkinson Center for Events was ready for everybody. Tables had already been set up with tablecloths, glasses, cups, and silverware. Plates were in the serving area that was near the kitchen. As people wanted to get their lunch and dinners, they could simply pick up a plate and get served whatever they wanted to eat. The piano was situated on the side farthest away from the kitchen. That's where most of the couches were. There was also an area where people could dance or where you could set up chairs for a meeting before or after dinner. There was even a big room off the main area that was for kids to stay while adults had meetings. There were toys and games and a big screen tv to watch movies. Two of the teachers at our school volunteered to be monitors. One of them was Miss Montgomery. The other was Mrs. Bissell, the 7th and 8th grade science teacher. Both said they loved little kids which is why they volunteered to do it.

It was about 11:30 when the first groups started to arrive. City of Mercy had brought two busses with families that were staying in the shelters. There were some Dads, but mostly Moms and kids. Some of Lori's other friends were set to greet people and get them situated at tables. Once those first people got here loads of other people started coming in. Dad had gone and picked up Mrs. Skriver. She saw us when they arrived and waved. Dad was carrying what looked like a pie that she had made for the event. There was a table with desserts set up and he put it down with the zillions of other pies and cakes people had made.

The plan was to serve all afternoon, so people could come early or late, whichever worked for them and no matter what time, there would be a good meal for them. The time thing worked really well because of how many people were showing up. Even though many people stayed all day, some just came for lunch and left after eating.

In the middle of the afternoon, Mr. Grossman, our bus driver came in. He was with a very nice-looking guy who walked with a cane. I realized it was the Sergeant. His hair had been cut and although he still had a beard, it was trimmed pretty close to his face. He was wearing jeans and a t-shirt and a nice red plaid jacket. He looked great, nothing like when we saw him back in the woods. Dad spotted them come in and he walked over to shake their hands and get them situated at a nice table kind of toward the piano area. He motioned to me and Gary to come over and say hello. Of course, when we did, we asked how his friends Hank and Wiggles were doing.

The Sergeant laughed.

"Better than they've been in the last couple of years, thanks to Ken here. They have a nice warm place to stay, plenty of food, and a big fenced back yard to play in. You know, guys, I hate taking help from other people, but Hank and Wiggles mean everything to me. When Ken here said he had a big house and wouldn't mind the company, well, I had to accept, for the sake of my dogs, of course.

Mr. Grossman smiled and we understood exactly what that smile meant. We knew that the Sergeant was grateful for himself as well.

Just then Aggie came over and reminded us of what we were supposed to be doing, so we got back to work. I started worrying about Rascal and the kitties, but Dad knew me and Gary were busy so he went home himself to take care of our friends. My Dad…the greatest Dad in the entire world.

— • • • —

It was about 10:30 in the evening when the last group of people started to leave. Mom had kept a count and told us later that we had fed nearly 700 people. We hadn't seen Jack Davis (you remember…Captain

Hook?). A couple of the staff from City of Mercy said that a few had to stay behind to keep the shelter safe. I guess Hook was one of them. When Mom heard, she made sure to pack up dinners for the people that couldn't make it down to the event center.

After everything was cleaned up, we headed back home. It was really late, but Gary and I still had to get Rascal out and Mom needed to check on the kitties and do the pee and poop thing. Dad had taken Anna home about 8 because she had gotten really tired. When we got home we found her asleep in Dad's recliner with Rascal curled up on her lap.

Mom carefully lifted the puppy up and handed him to Gary. She gently touched Anna to wake her up so she could go to bed and then headed to her room to check on the kitties. Gary and I took Rascal out and right after he did his thing we brought him back in because we were really tired. We had started keeping him in the cage at bedtime because he seemed to like it and we wouldn't get woke up with the puppy trying to get out of his box in the middle of the night.

Gary and I were really tired, so we both went to bed right away. I don't even remember putting my pajamas on. I was asleep immediately and stayed asleep until 9 in the morning. Can you believe that? 9 is later than I've slept in years.

When I finally got hooked together, I went to the kitchen and found Gary, Mom and Anna sitting at the kitchen table.

Mom smiled.

"Good morning sleepyhead. It's about time you got up. I was just telling Gary and Anna that we did so well with food and everything, we had money left over. Gary mentioned you might have an idea for how to use it. We've got about $2,500."

Wow. How amazing is that? I needed to find a way to get money for the phone idea and here it was. Wow. It made me wonder even more about Aggie Czech and whether she had anything to do with that. I mean, how would she have known about my phone idea? The only person that knew was Gary. More mystery that I had to figure out.

Gary spoke first.

"So, Davey does have a great ideal to help some of the people who are living in poverty and the homeless. Davey? You want to tell them?"

"Sure. So, I was thinking that we should do something for the people that don't have phones. People like Mrs. Skriver. She doesn't have a phone and lives all by herself. What if something happened? She would have no way to contact anybody. I thought maybe we could give people like her a burner…or, in Gary's words, a disposable phone. The phones don't cost too much and we could make sure they were loaded with enough minutes to get them started. What do you think?"

Mom sat there for a minute before she answered.

Well, it's an interesting idea, David. Let me talk this over with Aggie Czech and we'll see whether we can make your idea work. We do have enough for phones, but it's the cost of minutes that might make the idea not too workable. Let's see what Aggie has to say."

Mom saw that I looked a little disappointed.

"David, it's actually a great idea, so don't start looking down right yet. You know that Aggie is great at figuring things out. Give us a few days before jumping to a negative conclusion."

I said fine and got back to what was the most important right now today—breakfast!

Just then, the doorbell rang. Gary went to open the door and there was Eddie Anderson. I had forgotten that we had told him to come over in the morning to see the puppy. But, it was more of a surprise than we expected, because Eddie was carrying a little dog. It wasn't a puppy. It was a smallish scruffy looking white dog. Eddie looked really happy.

Gary spoke up first.

"Eddie, you got a doggie. What kind and how old?"

Eddie looked really happy.

"Mr. Stevenson said she was a pure-bred Mutt. Her name is LuLu May. He wasn't sure how old she was, but maybe around two or so."

Gary laughed.

"Did you think up that name yourself?"

"Nope. That was her name when she came into the shelter. I took my Mom and Dad down there and when Mom saw her, she fell in love. She said LuLu May looked kind of like the doggie she had when she was a kid. I kind of wanted one of the Saint puppies, but LuLu May is great too!"

Just then Rascal came running around the corner. Mom had let him out of the cage. He was yipping like crazy and ran right up to Eddie. Looking up, he saw LuLu May and the yipping stopped. Eddie smiled and put Lulu May down next to Rascal.

Even though he was just a puppy, Rascal was still a lot bigger than Lulu May. She kind of looked like a Chihuahua, but had short white fur with a few black splotches and black that also circled one of her eyes. Do Chihuahuas have fur like that?

Anyway, Lulu May wagged her tail and took her time checking Rascal out. Rascal just sat there like all was totally cool. Right then Mom reminded us that he needed to do his duty, so all three of us took both doggies out to the back yard so they could run around and maybe play a little.

Eddie really liked Rascal, but Gary and me could tell he was really happy with what his parents had let him get.

The three of us sat on the bench in the back and watched the doggies. Lulu May wandered around sniffing everything and Rascal followed her doing the same. They were getting along great.

"So, Eddie, did you know that Gary and me have two little kitties?"

"What? You've guys got kitties, too? Where did they come from?"

"We found them in the bushes back here in the yard. They're really tiny. We were worried because we didn't know if they would be able to live without their Mom, but my Mom is taking really good care of them, so I think they are going to be fine. We haven't named them yet."

Eddie Laughed. "So, let's name those babies!"

Gary spoke up. "I think we should check with Davey's Mom first... just to make sure she thinks they're going to be ok."

We all agreed that should be the plan. We would ask my Mom whether it would be ok to name them later today.

It had started to snow again. We stayed out a little longer and then carried our friends back into the kitchen to wipe their paws so they wouldn't track all over. Mom and Anna were in the kitchen taking care of the kitties and Eddie just squealed when he saw them, the two furry little balls being fed with doll bottles that were almost bigger than they were.

Mom saw Eddie staring happily at the kitties. "So, Eddie, would you like to finish feeding one of the babies?"

Eddie lit up. "Can I?"

He handed Lulu May to me because Gary was holding Rascal.

Eddie cupped his hands and Mom put the tiny kitty she was holding in the center of his palms.

"Now, Eddie, keep the kitty in one hand and take the bottle in the other, then gently rub the kitty's mouth until she accepts the nipple and starts eating."

Eddie did exactly what Mom told him to do and he was able to feed the rest of the milk to the little girl. Yup, she's a girl. Actually, both kitties are. When Eddie was done feeding, Mom took her back and did the pee poop thing.

I guess it was up to me now to ask if we could name them.

"Mom, do you think we can name the kitties now? I mean, I know it hasn't been that long, but they seem to be doing pretty well."

Mom smiled. "Actually David, Anna and I already named them. Sorry about that."

I laughed. "So, what did you guys name them?"

Anna spoke up. "I hope you two are ok with that."

We both said Of Course!

Gary laughed. "Mom, we're waiting. Will you guys please tell us what their names are?

"Harley and Quinn."

"You mean like Batman's Harley Quinn?"

"Pretty much."

"Pretty much? What does that mean?"

"It means we thought the names were cute and just fit perfectly for our new family members. We just thought the names fit out new furry friends perfectly."

Both Moms laughed. It was kind of surprising because I never realized that my Mom knew anything at all about superhero movies. I guess I was wrong...again.

— ••• —

We spent the rest of the afternoon with Eddie and his new doggie puppy. Rascal and LuLu May were good together. They spent most of the time sleeping in the living room with the moms while we played video games in my room and talked about stuff, including girls. Sure, we talked about other stuff too, but girls...well, you know.

I guess Eddie has a girl he likes. She's new to our school. Janie Miksa is from Illinois. I guess she wasn't too happy moving to Colorado, because Eddie says she seems kind of stuck up...kind of angry, too. He likes her anyway, I guess. That's Eddie for you. Gary asked him if he was going to ask her out. Eddie just laughed.

"You guys..liking someone and asking them out are two entirely different things. I'm not sure my parents would be happy about me dating. What about you guys?"

I spoke up first. "I don't think I'm dating for a long time...forever maybe."

Of course, Gary opened up a can of worms.

"Tell Eddie why, Davie."

Eddie got very interested. "OK, Davie, tell me why."

"The talk, Eddie. Mom told me that my Dad would want to have it with me before I ever even thought about dating, even casual dating. So, why bother with girls at all? JUST NOT WORTH IT!"

Eddie started to laugh so hard he rolled around on the floor. He looked so funny that Gary and I both couldn't help laughing too. I mean, I guess it was pretty funny, but what he said after he stopped laughing so hard was really creepy.

"You guys. I heard my Mom talking to someone on the phone about sex for us."

"WHAT??? What do you mean, Eddie?"

"Sorry, that's not what I meant. I meant that the school is considering a sex education course for all the kids."

Well, that bothered me a lot. "They wouldn't have something like that with us guys and with girls too, would they?"

Eddie just shrugged his shoulders. "Don't know, Davey. They wouldn't be so stupid to do something like that, would they?"

"I don't know. Teachers and parents come up with some weird stuff, so you never know what they're planning. What do you think Gary?"

Gary grimaced. "It was hard enough thinking about my Mom talking to me all alone, so something like that seems pretty nasty. When's this supposed to happen, Eddie?"

"Don't know and I sure as heck am NOT asking my Mom. Davey, why don't you ask your Mom? She seems to always know what's going on. Won't she know?"

"Oh NOOOOOO. There is no way I'm going to ask. Way too embarrassing."

We all laughed and agreed not to worry about it until we heard more. I mean, maybe Eddie's Mom was just chatting about nothing special. That was probably what it was. We all decided not to worry.

— • • • —

We were wrong.

December 4

The weekend went by really fast. Eddie stayed for dinner and then his Dad came and picked him and Lulu May up. On Sunday, Gary and I did some shoveling and took care of Rascal, but that was about it. As Mom put it, we simply vegged for the rest of the day.

I guess it felt good doing nothing for a change. I mean, this year it seems like we were constantly doing something. I'm not saying it's a bad thing because everything that's happened so far has been really, really cool. It was nice just having a break.

Of course, it was just a tiny break and Gary reminded me that we had to start planning for Christmas.

"So, Davey, Christmas is coming up really fast. Have you thought about what we should do for the family and how we can maybe help some of the people we've met in the last month?"

"I hadn't really thought about it, Gary. I usually try and do a few chores around the neighborhood to make a little money. The school has jobs posted too. We should check this week. I agree we should try to do something for some of those hard-up people, especially the Sergeant and Mrs. Skriver. I still want to do the phone thing, but maybe there's something else we can do to help them as well."

"What did you have in mind?"

"I don't know. What do you think? You're the smart one. Come up with a plan, Gary."

Gary laughed. "I think our best bet here is to talk to our Moms and Lori's Mom."

Gary was absolutely right. The Moms would know the best thing to do to help people for Christmas.

I had saved quite a bit of money and told Gary I would share so he could get his Mom something nice for Christmas. He was grateful and told me he would pay every cent back. I knew he would.

— ••• —

On Wednesday of the week after Thanksgiving, when we got home from school, Anna and Mom had news.

Mom was very excited. "Guys, guess what? Anna has something really terrific to tell you. Come talk to us."

When we went into the living room we saw Anna sitting in Dad's lounge chair and of course, Rascal was curled up on her lap. It kind of looked like the puppy had grown a touch because he was filling up Anna's lap more than I remembered from even a week ago. Rascal saw us and wagged his tail, but he didn't move or try to jump down or anything.

Anna knew the puppy wanted down and she gently nudged him off her lap to the floor. When she did, Rascal yipped like crazy and ran up to us wiggling and jumping because he was happy to see us. Once we got him calmed down we waited anxiously to hear what was going on.

Anna smiled. "So…I got a job."

"What?!!!" Gary sounded concerned. "Do you think that's wise? Are you even strong enough to work? Mom? What kind of job did you get?"

"I'm going to do some online tutoring…Math and English. I won't leave the house and since it's only part time I'm not going to get completely pooped out doing it."

"Wow! That's great, Anna. Congratulations!"

Gary was silent. He looked concerned and his Mom could see that.

Anna laughed. "Gary, come on. Don't look so glum. I'm feeling much, much better. I want to do something other than just sit around the house. I want to contribute. Plus, I'm getting paid $35 an hour."

"What??? OMG, Mom, $35 an hour is huge!"

"Don't get too excited, Gary. It's only 2 hours a day, but that could be $350 for a week's easy work. I might not get that many hours, but at least I'll be able to contribute a little and maybe there'll be a little for Christmas, too."

Gary sighed. "Ok Mom. Just take it easy, please?"

"I promise."

With that Gary walked over to his Mom and gave her a hug, whispering something that I couldn't hear. Later, when I asked him, he told me he had said how proud of her he was. Definitely, that's something Gary would say to his Mom. I'm really proud of my Mom too, but I don't have to tell her. At least I don't think I have to. Maybe I should. I will.

— ••• —

It was almost December and we had to start planning for Christmas. Gary and I decided to pool the money we had in order to buy presents for everybody. We had about $430 and figured we needed more to get decent stuff and not crap. We were going to sign up for one of the jobs that the school posted for kids to earn a little cash for the holidays, but we didn't have to. Dad mentioned that Frank, his friend at the hardware store needed a couple of kids to help with the store inventory that he did every year in December. Frank wanted to know if we would be interested. When Dad asked us, of course, we said that we were.

We started this weekend. Dad dropped us off and Frank put us to work right away. It was fun, especially because he was paying us $15 an hour. Can you believe that? I figured he was giving us extra just because he and Dad were friends. Frank wanted us for 4 hours Saturday and Sunday and then the same for the next 2 weekends. That would mean that me and Gary would each make $120 a weekend and he was going to pay us in cash. Wow! $360 added to the $430 we already had would give us $1150 to spend on Christmas. Could it get better than that? Well it did. Frank was so pleased with how hard we had worked that he gave us each an extra $100.

We thought getting the money together would be the hard part, but it turned out to be pretty easy. The really hard part was figuring out what to get everybody for Christmas and who we were going to buy for other than our parents.

Gary went first.

"We should probably get something for Eddie and then, I might want to buy a little something for Debbie…nothing special…just something."

I laughed. "I knew you liked her, but you never said anything to me. Why not?"

"Don't know. I just figured you knew, I guess, plus you've been so upset about Lori, I didn't want to bring it up."

"I'm over Lori."

Gary rolled his eyes looking at the ceiling and shaking his head. "Davey, there is no way you're over her. Don't lie about it, especially to yourself."

Gary was right. I still liked her and even though I thought her 9th grader boyfriend was pretty nice, I still kept hoping they would break up.

"Can we please not get into that right now? We have more important things to think about, like how are we gonna split up the cash for presents and who are we gonna buy for?"

Laughing, Gary agreed and we came up with our list. First, there was our parents, then Eddie and Debbie. Then we decided it would be nice to buy Mr. Grossman a little something since he was always so nice to us and he was taking care of the Sergeant. Then, there was the Sergeant because we didn't want him to think we had forgotten him by buying for Mr. Grossman…and then, there was Mrs. Skriver. I know she would really appreciate a gift, no matter what it was.

Gary wrote everybody down. "So, my Mom, your Mom and Dad,

Eddie, Debbie, Mr. Grossman, the Sergeant and Mrs. Skriver. Anybody else?"

"I think we should get Aggie Czech a little something, don't you think? I mean, she gave you that jacket and did a lot to help with the charity stuff."

"You're right. But Davey, don't you think Lori will feel bad if we don't get her something too?"

Gary was right. I wasn't particularly crazy about doing that, but she probably would be hurt if she didn't get her something too. So, I said ok.

"I think maybe we should get Frank something to thank him for all the work he gave us."

Gary agreed and we had our list. We decided that $25 for each non parent would be enough. That only totaled $200 (plus tax maybe). I didn't think the $25 limit would do it for Mrs. Skriver because I wanted to get her that phone with minutes, so, we upped the non-parent total to $250. That still left us $1,100. If we spent $250 on each of the parents, we would still have $350 left over. I decided we should split it. Gary wanted me to take it, but I said no. We would just split anything after the presents.

After we got all that money stuff settled, we still had the hardest part of the whole Christmas thing to do—figure out what to get everybody.

— ••• —

School was out until after the New Year, so we had plenty of time to shop. Mom dropped us off in the morning at the mall and loaned me her phone so we could let her know when we would be done. We had spent some time last night trying to figure out what we wanted to get for everybody. Gary's Mom was pretty easy because she didn't have much. A lot of her stuff got lost when they didn't have a real home anymore. We figured we could get her a sweater and jeans and then, maybe, a book because she liked to read. My mom was a little harder. I knew she wanted one of those fancy stand mixers, but when we looked up the cost online, they were kind of expensive. I was thinking maybe a cheaper mixer would do, but I wasn't sure. Gary didn't think that would be what she wanted, so we thought maybe a leather jacket for spring. Dad was the easiest. He likes just about everything. Gary had noticed that he was always having to make a new pot of coffee in the morning, so we thought maybe one of those coffee machines that used coffee pods and made a cup at a time. We saw one that made a pot of coffee and let you also make single cup using a pod. It was a little more than what we wanted to spend, but we decided that was ok since we still had extra money that was free.

When we got to the mall we came in through Kohls. It's a department store that Mom likes a lot, mostly because they have Kohl's Cash that lets you buy more stuff after you've bought what you went there to buy in the first place. We went into the kitchen area and found Dad's coffee maker gift. They had a wrapping program where you paid for them to wrap your gifts for you. This was perfect, even though it cost money. So, the $225 coffee maker, plus the 8% tax, plus the $10 for wrapping ended up costing us $253. We were still good, plus we got $40 in Kohl's Cash for some more shopping…maybe for the coffee pods that you needed for the coffee maker.

One down and a zillion to go…or at least that's how it seemed.

The package would be wrapped and we could pick it up after 2, which was great. We wouldn't have to carry stuff all over the mall. We could get everything when we left. They did have carts we could use and we decided to rent one when we were done, just to get everything into the car.

We decided to walk around the mall and see if we could find presents for the Moms. As we came out of Kohls we ran into Aggie Czech coming in. She saw us right away.

"Hi guys! Shopping?"

Gary spoke up. "Yup, but so far, we've only managed to buy one thing and we've got a lot more to get. We're trying to buy for our Moms and that's not easy."

Aggie smiled. "So, what are you trying to buy? Maybe I can let you know where the best place to shop would be."

"Davey's Mom wants one of those stand mixers, but they're pretty expensive, so we were thinking of a leather jacket. My Mom...well, she will probably be happy with just about anything we get her. We were thinking a nice jacket, jeans and a sweater and then, maybe a book, because she likes to read."

Aggie sat her bags down on the floor and reached into her purse. She pulled out a bunch of coupons and started browsing through them, pulling one, then another, out of the stack.

"So, I think I may be able to help. Here, take these. Go down to Best Buy right now, before they run out of stock. And Gary, if your Mom likes to read, she may like an iPad. I think they're on sale."

Aggie handed us 2 coupons, one for 20% off at Best Buy and one for an unknown discount at a store down at the end of the mall. It was one of these coupons that they scan at the register and take that discount off your total. We thanked her and went directly to Best Buy.

It was really crowded because they were having a lot of big sales. We decided to split up. I went to where the mixers were and Gary headed over to the Apple section to see whether we could actually afford an iPad. When I got to the mixers, there was only one left and it was marked down to $243. With that discount coupon, it would take the cost down to just about $200 and that was great. It was a perfect color, too—teal, one of my Mom's favorite colors. I picked it up and found it was pretty heavy, so I got it into a cart and went over to the other side of the store looking for Gary. He was heading toward me with a piece of paper.

"Davey, Aggie was right. They were on sale for $243, so I got one. We have to give them this order card and they'll get it for us when we check out."

"Wow, I got the mixer and they were on sale for the same price. Aggie Czech comes through again for us! We better find something halfway decent to get her."

We had done good, thanks to Aggie. Best Buy wasn't doing wrapping so we took it to the mall wrapping store where we could pick up when we went back to pick up the coffee maker.

With the 3 main people bought for, we decided to get some lunch and figure out how much we had left and what to do for everybody else. We still had to buy for Eddie, Debbie, Lori, Aggie, Mrs. Skriver, the Sergeant, Mr. Grossman, and Frank. Except for Mrs. Skriver (you know, the phone thing), if we kept everybody at $25 we would still have about $395…minus lunch of course.

I suppose you're wondering if I had planned to get something for Gary. Why would you even think I wouldn't? I stashed away an extra $100 just to make sure I could get him something neat. I'm still not sure what it's going to be yet because Gary never talks about wanting anything special. I don't have much time left to figure this out. Maybe the demon will give me some suggestions. Hah!

— •••—

After lunch we started walking through the mall looking in the stores, trying to find neat stuff under $25 that we could get for everybody. Gary had finally figured out what to get Debbie. She had a charm bracelet and he thought it would be cool if he gave her another charm for it. He didn't want it to be anything romantic…just something neat. As we were looking around we saw a shop called Silver Satisfactions. They had tons of stuff and even though a lot of it was expensive, there were things we could afford.

A lady named Maggie was at the counter when we came in. She was very nice and asked us what we were looking for. Gary said a charm for a friend. Hmm..a friend? Ok, we'll go with that…for now. Anyway, they had tons of charms. Maggie asked what it was he was looking for and he asked if they had any dancers. Of course, she pulled out little ballet dancer charms, but that wasn't what he wanted. There were more expensive charms and Maggie pulled one of the trays out. There, in the middle was the perfect charm—a boy and girl dancing. It was perfect, except it was $34.

December - 111

Gary looked over at me and I nodded to go for it. That would mean, with tax, that we spent "almost" $37 on his "almost" girlfriend. Just as we were about to check out, Maggie pointed to a sign over near the store's front display. 'Buy One Item, Get a Second for 50% Off'.

"Would you gentlemen like to pick out a second item? It's a great deal."

Hah! I knew we were gentlemen. We both laughed. Gary looked over at me. "Davey, you want to get Lori something?"

Well, I did want to get Lori something…but jewelry? Not so much.

"I don't know, Gary. What could I get her that says "friend" and nothing extra?"

Before Gary could answer, Maggie spoke up. "We have some really nice purse bling…perfect pieces for girls who are just friends."

Going to one of the corner displays, she pulled out a tray of items that girls hook on to their purses or backpacks. They were silver, with 2 or 3 chains at different lengths with animals or stars or some other shape on the ends. They were actually pretty cool.

I was a little worried about the cost. "Maggie, these look a little expensive. How much are they?"

"$29 each. With the 50% off, you would get it for $14.50."

Great! I started looking at what was available and there it was—a 3-chain bling, with stars on 2 of the chains and on the third, a dragon with a red garnet eye whose tail curled up the chain. It was perfect and the closest to a demon I could come to without being obvious.

"I think that'll work. Gary?"

"It's good."

The saleslady added up everything and the total was $52.38, which was right in line with the amount we were trying to spend on everybody. Maggie had boxes and little gift bags that she gave us for free, so we didn't have to worry about wrapping them.

As we left, Gary had a question. "So, Davey, why the dragon? Any reason?"

"Gary, don't overthink this. I just thought it was cool."

Gary laughed, but didn't say any more. There was no special reason I picked that one. But...it is really cool. I think she'll like it.

Out next purchase was for Mrs. Skriver. We found a store with a sale and there was a perfect phone for older people. It had big numbers and would really be easy to use. Plus, it came with 1200 minutes and for an extra $25, we could get another 500 minutes. We did it, even though it cost us almost $150. I could see why Mom wanted to discuss my phone idea with Aggie and why she was thinking that we needed a lot more money than we had left over from the Thanksgiving meal. After what it cost us (on sale by the way) for Mrs. Skriver, I could understand why Mom was worried about the money for my idea.

We were still doing ok moneywise, although we had spent more than what we had planned to. There was still 4 people we had to buy for and the only one that was going to be easy was Eddie. He has a Playstation and always likes new games. We found one on sale for $29. We made sure to get a gift receipt just so Eddie could return it if he didn't like it.

So, we were down to four—Aggie Czech, Mr. Grossman and the Sergeant and then, of course, Frank, our money savior. We finally settled on a book for Mr. Grossman. He always had a book with him on the bus and they were pretty much all mysteries. We found a brand new James Patterson called *Texas Outlaw*. We figured that would be good just in case Mr. Grossman liked western stories and mysteries. Of course, we had no idea what it was about. Still, it sounded good, so we got it.

Down to three.

We passed a sporting goods store and they had these really neat winter hats, the kind that have flaps you can hook up to the sides or pull down to cover your ears. We figured that would help keep the Sergeant warm, especially if he ended up camping out again. So, we got it. We found out later that he would move in permanently with Mr. Grossman, but at the time, we didn't know that.

Down to two.

When we had been in Aggie Czech's shop the last time, she had been working on her laptop. Gary noticed that her laptop bag looked pretty worn, so we decided to get a new one as her gift. We had seen a display at Best Buy, so we decided to go back pick one up there. As we walked back, we passed a western shop and Gary stopped and looked in the window at some cowboy boots.

"Those are pretty cool. Whadaya think, Davey?"

"I think they're cowboy boots. You like them?"

"Yup. Always have, but I never got them because they were way too expensive, at least the ones that I liked were."

Gary was right. They were $225. I didn't have enough to get them for him. I would have to find a cheaper gift.

Anyway, we went back to Best Buy and picked up a really nice laptop bag that was made of denim with silver studs on the flap and along the edges of the strap. It was a little pricier that what we were hoping, but we got it anyway. After all, Aggie had given that jacket to Gary and we wanted to do something nice for her.

With Aggie's gift purchase, we were almost done. We had seen some gloves back at Kohl's and thought Frank might like them, because his seemed to be a little worn. So we decided to get them.

We called Mom to come and get us, then got a cart and went around to pick up the gifts that were getting wrapped, picking up the gloves when we went back to pick up Dad's gift. As we waited for our ride, we tallied up our spending spree. We had about $145 that was left over. That meant I had an extra $70 dollars to get Gary something cool. Still, the money I had wasn't enough to get those boots he liked.

— ••• —

When we got home the tree was up and it looked terrific. It was a fake because my Mom hated killing trees just to decorate one for a couple of weeks and then throw it out. Still it was really nice. Dad had set it up and the Moms had gotten busy and decorated.

Gary and I got the rest of the presents wrapped and we labeled everything with leftover pieces of the paper because we had forgotten to buy gift tags. It was good, because nobody would care. We thought we would be the first with presents, but when we brought ours down, there was already a lot of stuff under the tree.

Rascal was laying on the floor near the fireplace and when he saw us he wagged his tail, but didn't move.

I wondered why he hadn't, but looking closer, I saw the two tiny little kitties curled up next to him. I told you he was really smart.

As we were finishing getting all the presents organized, both of the kitties woke up and started meowing. Harley stayed curled up next to Rascal, but Quinn got up and came over to Gary, who immediately scooped up the baby and started petting. Quinn purred happily.

When Mom came into the room, she saw Gary holding one of the babies and the other still laying near Rascal.

"Guys, you know, the kitties are starting to use a litter box. We set one up in the powder room and we've been taking them in there to train them. Cats have a natural instinct to go to the bathroom in litter or fine gravel and it didn't take too long for us to get Harley and Quinn doing that. We're still carrying them to the box, but I suspect it won't be too long before they will go in there by themselves. Guys, remember they are still pretty tiny, so you have to be careful not to step on them. We're trying to keep them in the box but they have started wanting out to run around.

Just then Rascal got up and walked over to Gary. Looking up at the kitty, it was almost as if he was checking to make sure everything was ok. Harley followed right behind him and kept meowing.

Gary laughed. "The kitties think Rascal is a big kitty. Look at how Harley is following him."

Gary was right. The babies seemed to have connected with Rascal. When Gary put Quinn down, she went right over to the puppy, meowing and purring, then rubbing up against his side. He sat quietly and allowed it, as if he knew how careful he had to be with the two tiny creatures. Like I said before…a very smart doggie, our Rascal.

—•••—

It was almost Christmas and I still hadn't gotten anything for Gary. Mom agreed to take me to the mall because she had to get a couple other things for people. Dad was taking Gary and Anna for the same reason.

When we got to the mall, Mom headed right to Kohls and I walked down to Gutherie's Western Wear. I saw a sale sign in the window, which was great. When I looked closer at the sign I was bummed out to see that boots and shoes were not included in the sale. I went in anyway, just in case. Browsing around didn't do much good. As I was about to leave and start looking somewhere else, the man behind the counter spoke to me.

"Looking for something in particular, son?"

"Well, I came in to see if those boots in your window were on sale, but they're not. I wanted to get them for a really good friend."

"So, I assume you didn't pick up one of our surprise coupons at the beginning of the month? They were scratch-off cards giving you from 5% up to 50% off a single item."

When he said coupon, I remembered that Aggie Czech had given us a couple when we had seen her in the mall before. I still had it and dug it out of my pocket.

"Is this what you're talking about?"

"Yes sir. Now give me that coupon and let's see what kind of discount you'll be getting. You haven't scratched it off yet, so let's do that now."

With that, the man pulled a coin from his pocket and scratched off the silvery ink, revealing a 40% discount. 40% off! Wow!

"So, how much are those boots you have in the window?"

"$225, but if you use the coupon, your cost is $135."

Dang, I had just enough money to buy the boots. Fred, who was the salesperson helping me asked me what size I needed.

"I'm not sure. I think it's a size 8 or 9 because my friend has worn my shoes and they've fit him pretty much."

"Well, I only have an 8 ½ or a 9. Want to try the 8 ½? We do take returns so if they don't fit, he can come in and exchange them for something else."

I said ok, so Fred totaled up the purchase, which came to almost $146. After I paid, he asked if I wanted them wrapped, which I did. He did it no charge which was great. He had put a gift receipt in with the boots so if they didn't fit Gary or he didn't want them anymore, he could bring them back.

Thanking him and wishing him happy holidays (because you never know if someone celebrates xmas or not), I left and headed to meet Mom. I was totally glad that my shopping was done and to make it even better, I had managed to end up with a little cash left over. This was definitely a first. Most years I've had to borrow a little from Mom and Dad just to be able to buy something decent for everybody.

Anyway, Mom was waiting for me at the entrance to the food court. She had bunches of stuff she had bought in that really short period of time, probably at her favorite store, Kohls. She always told me that when a store, that most of the time gives you money back when you buy stuff, is a great store, with a great marketing plan. I believed her. Anyway, she asked if I wanted to get lunch, but with all the bags she was carrying, I thought it would be better if we just went home.

When we got there, the house was dark. Rascal was in his cage and Mom went right to her room to check on the kitties, who were fine, sleeping in the box.

I stuck the present for Gary under the tree and headed to the kitchen to make a sandwich. Peanut butter was always good and since Mom liked them too, I made her one. When she came back out of her room, the sandwich and a glass of milk were waiting for her on the counter.

Seeing her smile when she saw it made me feel pretty good. She came into the living room with the food and plopped down on the couch next to where I was sitting, leaned over and kissed me on the cheek.

"So, are we done with shopping now?" she asked between bites of sandwich.

"I guess. Listen, Gary and I bought stuff for some people other than family. Do you think you or Dad can drive us around tomorrow so we can deliver the stuff?"

"Sure. Where do we need to go?"

"Well, we bought a phone for Mrs. Skriver with a bunch of extra minutes. That's the first place we need to go. Then, we got something for Frank at the hardware store and some presents for Aggie and Lori."

Mom laughed. "So, you got something for Lori, huh? What did you get her?"

I felt my face go red. "Gary bought a charm for that girl he likes and there was a 50% off a second item. I got Lori this thing that hooks on her backpack or purse. It's has a couple of stars on chains and a dragon with red eyes. I only got it because it didn't cost too much."

Mom laughed again. "It sounds nice David. I'm sure she'll like it. You got Aggie something as well?

"Yup. She gave Gary that jacket. We wanted to do something to thank her, so we got her a new laptop bag."

"That is nice. I'm sure she'll like it."

Just then there was a whine and several mournful yips. No, I hadn't forgotten Rascal. I just wanted to eat all my sandwich without the puppy begging for part of it.

Of course, I let him out and he was so happy to see me he peed immediately. Mom came over telling me to take him outside so there wouldn't be any more accidents and she would clean up the mess.

As we left the house Dad, Anna, and Gary pulled into the driveway. When Gary got out of the Jeep, he saw me and waved.

"Hey Davie, let me get this stuff in the house and I'll be out in a sec."

I nodded and saw them all going into the house with a bunch of bags. More stuff for under the tree. I started thinking about how lucky we were compared to people like Mrs. Skriver. There had to be more we could do for them. I was hoping Mom and Aggie could come up with a plan for the phones.

It was just a few minutes before Gary came out. Of course, Rascal was happy to see him and wiggled and yipped as Gary petted.

"You get everything done?"

"Yes, we did. My Mom had a great time shopping. It's been a while since she was able to shop because of what had happened with us. You know what I mean, right?"

I nodded that I did. "You know, Gary, I wish there was more stuff we could do for all those people that need help. I almost feel guilty about all the presents under our tree when I think about the people that don't have as much."

"Well, come up with a plan, Davey. You're smart."

"Not as smart as you. So, I'll talk to Mom. Hey, now that you're home, maybe we can get some of the presents delivered today instead of waiting until tomorrow."

Gary agreed and I went in to ask if someone could take us to a few places today. Dad said he would in a few minutes.

We got Rascal back in the house and gathered up the gifts. Dad was sitting in the Jeep when we got back out.

"So, where are we going guys?"

Gary spoke up first. "We got a present for Mrs. Skriver, so can we go there first?"

"Sure. What did you guys get her?"

"A cell phone with big buttons to make it easy for her to see and dial. PLUS, we got her a bunch of extra minutes. Unless she decides to talk to someone for hours, the minutes should last her for a really long time."

Dad smiled. "I'm impressed. A very thoughtful, yet practical gift. How did you come up with that?"

We laid it all out for Dad and told him how we thought maybe we could help some of the homeless or poorer people with phone gifts and that Mom and Aggie were going to try and figure out how we could do it. I really did think that Dad was impressed.

— ••• —

Anyway, we got to Mrs. Skriver's house a little after 4. We could tell that no one had been there because there were no tracks in the snow leading up to her porch. Smoke was coming from her chimney so we knew she was home.

Dad went up first and knocked on the door. Mrs. Skriver peeked out the window and seeing it was Dad, immediately answered the door. He spoke to her for a minute then motioned for Gary and me to come up.

We had wrapped the present in pretty snowflake paper that said Merry Christmas and when we handed it to her, she started to cry.

"I wasn't expecting any presents and I have nothing for you."

Gary spoke up. "We didn't expect anything from you, Mrs. Skriver. We wanted to give you something just because we like you...plus you make great cookies and pies!"

Mrs. Skriver smiled and wiped the tears from her eyes. "Can I open the present now or do you want me to wait for Christmas?"

"No, if you want, go ahead and open it now." I told her.

She laid the box on the table, took a scissors and carefully cut along the edge of the paper where the tape was so it wouldn't damage the wrapping. When she opened it and saw the phone, she stopped and put both hands over her mouth, as if she was amazed at what it was. Picking it up, she sat silently staring at it, then turned to Gary and me.

"It's a wonderful gift, but so expensive. I really don't know what to say."

Dad spoke up. "No need to say anything Mrs. Skriver. The boys just hope you like it."

"Oh, I love it. I haven't had a phone for so long, I'm not even sure I remember how to us one."

We all laughed, but then Dad had another thought.

"Mrs. Skriver, would you like to join us for Christmas Dinner? We can come get you that morning and you can stay all day. We can bring you back home after dinner. Would you be interested?"

"Oh, I don't want to put anyone out."

"You're not going to put anyone out. We'd love to have you. Will you join us?"

Tears welled up again in Mrs. Skriver's eyes and she nodded that she would come to our house for dinner.

"Can I bring anything?"

"Well you don't need to," Dad answered, "but we sure enjoyed those cookies you made."

Mrs Skriver smiled. "Then it's settled. I'll bring cookies."

I was happy that Dad had invited her. We spent a little more time showing her the phone features and letting her know about the minutes and, of course, giving her Mom and Dad's number so she could call if she needed something. After an hour, Dad said we had to get back, so we said goodbye and reminded her that we would come and get her Christmas morning.

It had gotten too late to deliver any more of the gifts, but Dad said he would take us around tomorrow. That was good because I was a little tired and, as usual, hungry.

When we got home, dinner was almost ready. I knew what it was immediately—some sort of pasta. I could smell garlic bread toasting in the oven. My favorite dinner!

Anna had set the table and made the salad. Mom had done the rest.

"Guys, go get washed up. It's almost dinnertime." Anna was smiling and she was looking really good. Her face had color and she had gained a little weight. I was also surprised to see that she was wearing glasses. I had to ask.

"Anna, you have glasses? I don't think I've ever seen you wearing them. Now, don't get me wrong or anything—they look good, really good."

Anna smiled. "They're new. Your Mom helped me get them. The glasses are just one of the thousands of reasons I am grateful to her and your Dad and, of course, to you.

"I'm really glad you guys are here. So far, this has been the best year ever."

Just then Mom came out of the kitchen with a big bowl of spaghetti and Gary was right behind carrying the garlic bread. We all sat down and Dad said a little prayer thanking God for the food and for all the other good things that have come our way this year.

After he was done, we all dug in. As we ate there was a lot of talk about Christmas. Dad let Mom and Anna know that we had invited Mrs. Skriver for Christmas dinner. Of course, Mom said it was perfectly fine. She continued.

"That reminds me, David, Aggie and I did talk about your idea and we think we might be able to make it work. Now, don't get too excited yet. We're not going to do anything until after New Year's, when things calm down a bit. Then, you and Gary will need to put in a little time helping get this initiative off the ground. You guys are up for it, right?

We both said yes. Mom stopped us when we started asking questions and said we would all work on it after January 1st and we would get the answers then.

That was that. We finished up dinner, did the dishes, and took Rascal out. We hadn't been out for more than 10 minutes when Mom came to the door to tell us that Eddie was on the phone. I went in to answer while Gary finished up with Rascal.

When I picked up the phone, I could hear yipping in the background.

"Hey Eddie. So, what's going on with Lulu May?"

"Oh nothing. Dad was trying to teach her to sit up by giving her treats, but she wouldn't. She started barking when he wouldn't fork over any more snacks."

"Ok, so what's going on? You called."

Eddie was really excited. "My parents are going to have a big New Year's Party and they said I could invite a bunch of kids over. You and Gary are gonna come, right? You guys can spend the night."

"Yah, it sounds like fun, but I have to make sure it's ok with my parents first. Can I let you know tomorrow?"

"Sure."

"So, Gary and I are stopping by tomorrow to drop off your xmas present. Are you going to be home?"

"Sure. Wow, you guys got me something? I didn't get you anything."

"We didn't expect anything. We kind of had extra money this year and you're a friend, right? We wanted to share."

"How'd you guys get extra money?"

"We worked at the hardware store helping Frank the owner do his inventory. He paid us a lot."

"Cool. Sometimes I help my Dad, but he just gives me a little extra allowance."

"Frank and my Dad are friends. That's how come we got the work. I mean, we worked really hard for the money and he was very happy with what we did. When he paid us, he gave us extra…so we got you something."

"Thanks! So, listen, let me know tomorrow if you guys can come over and then spend the night."

"We will. Ok, I've gotta go. We'll talk to you tomorrow."

When I got off the phone I went back outside.

Gary was curious. "What did Eddie want?"

"He wants us to come over for New Years because his parents are having a big party. He wants us to spend the night."

Gary looked a little disturbed. "You know, it sounds like fun, but I don't want to leave my Mom all alone. I mean, I know your parents are there, but she's had a really hard time. I don't want to go off and have fun and just leave her."

"I totally understand. I'll tell Eddie no."

"Davey, you can go. I can stay home with Mom."

"Nope. I'll stay home, too. Not a big deal, Gary. Eddie won't care. He'll understand."

"You want to spend a boring New Year's Mom-sitting with me?"

"Who knows. Maybe something cool will come up…like maybe Aggie will come over."

"And bring Lori?"

"Oh no, I wasn't thinking that."

"Oh yes, you were."

"God, Gary, I am over her."

"You're lying to yourself if you believe that."

"Dang, Gary, don't be a smartass."

"Don't swear Davey."

"Dang."

Gary was right. I was still interested in her. I kept hoping that Lori and the 9th grader would break up. I actually hadn't seen them together for a while, so, maybe they had. I mean, even if they had broken up, there was no guarantee she would be interested in me. Still…maybe the demon could help…I wonder…would the demon help?

"Come on, Davey, let's get Rascal in."

Gary's voice brought me back down to Earth.

Rascal and Gary were already heading back to the house and I trailed behind. When we came in, we saw one of the kitties laying on the couch with Mom. The other was curled up sleeping on Anna's lap. After we cleaned off Rascal's paws so he wouldn't track, he went right into the living room and up to where Harley was, next to Mom. He put his head down next to the kitty, happily wagging his tail.

Harley seemed to like the attention. He purred contentedly, then stuck his tiny paw out and touched Rasal's snout. Mom was smiling like crazy.

"Guys, look at this. Have you ever seen anything so cute? The kitties love Rascal!"

Gary spoke up. "They think Rascal is a cat."

Anna laughed. "So, is there really anything wrong with that?"

Gary smiled and shook his head no.

It was cool that our ever-growing-bigger puppy loved the kitties as much as everybody else did.

I started to head to my room, but Mom called me back.

'Guys, we don't know if you have any plans for New Years, but Anna, Keith, and I have been invited to a party. We'd love to go, but we wouldn't want to leave you both celebrating alone."

Whose party, Mom?

Your friend Eddie's parents invited us. You guys wouldn't mind, would you?"

It was Gary who answered.

"We got invited too, by Eddie. He invited us to spend the night, but we didn't want to leave you guys alone. If you're all going, do you think it would be ok if Davey and I stayed over at their house? Eddie wanted us to."

Anna spoke up. Well, I have no problem with it, do you Kim?"

"Nope. It's ok by me. I'll make sure Rascal goes out in the morning. It sounds like fun."

I was curious. "So, who else is going to the party?"

Mom shook her head. I don't know who their friends are. I thought we got invited because of you guys. Why do you ask?"

"Oh, I was just wondering what other kids would be there.

Gary snickered. "Who were you thinking of Davey?"

"Oh, nobody in particular."

"And??"

"Oh, nobody in particular." I repeated the statement just so Gary thought I meant it. I did...kind of.

Gary started to laugh. Mom and Anna looked at us and I'm sure they were wondering what Gary thought was so funny. Fortunately for me, the Moms didn't ask. Very, very fortunately.

"Listen, I'm going up to my room now. Mom, can you put Rascal in the cage when you go to bed?"

Mom nodded that she would.

"Gary, you want to come up and play some games?"

"I will in a minute. I've got something to show you. I have to get it."

"Ok."

I had barely gotten to my room when Gary came in. He was carrying a magazine and he handed it to me."

"Take a look at this Davey."

It was actually a catalog called Friends Furrever and had bunches of things for dogs and cats.

"Wow, where'd you get this?"

"I saw it on a table in the mall with a bunch of other advertising stuff. I said to myself, self, Davey and I need to get something for our friends and this is a perfect place to look."

As I paged through the catalog, I saw a whole bunch of neat collars and loads of other stuff for both cats and dogs. There was even a bunch of pages with clothes for them. I mean, clothes?? Who would put their friends in clothes? There were even boots and that was interesting. How cool would it be to NOT have to clean Rascal's feet every time he came in from outside? There were also tons of toys.

"This is pretty neat, Gary. Did you see anything in particular?"

"Oh yah. Look on page 10, I think. There are some really nice collars for big dogs."

I opened the catalog to that place and there they were. Heavy black collars with silver studs all around. There were even some with spikes, but I wasn't sure Mom would approve of spikes. I mean, Rascal, the Goth Saint Bernard? No, I don't think so. Not that there's anything wrong with Goths I think they dress really cool. But the spike thing… not so much.

"Gary, I think these collars are great, but a little too expensive for me right now. I've managed to spend most of the cash I had. Plus, I think we should probably wait to get an expensive collar like this for Rascal until he's full grown or at least, almost full grown. These collars are $79.00 each."

"Ok, that sounds right. I don't have much cash left either. I think we should pool a little of the allowances we get and get this in a few months, and…take a look at page 34."

I opened to page 34 and there were all these cute glittery collars for kitties. Perfecto!! The kitty collars cost $28 each.

"So, we'll probably need to save at least $175 to get this stuff. It has to be at least that considering the cost, plus tax, plus shipping."

Gary agreed. "If we plan on getting the collars sometime in May… well, that would mean we would each have to each save about $22 every month until then. That's just $5.25 per week. You think we can?"

"Sure, I think we can swing it."

"So, are you excited about New Years?

"Excited about what?"

"The party."

"I don't know. It sounds like it should be fun, but the parents are going to be there."

Gary laughed. "Do you get wild and crazy at parties, Davey?"

"Oh God, no. I guess it doesn't matter if they come. Other than relatives, I really haven't been to any parties with my parents."

"Then you shouldn't worry about it. Maybe Lori will be there."

"You think so?"

"I don't know. Maybe. You never know. Maybe we should ask Eddie."

"NO!!! Then Eddie will start wondering why we're asking. I don't want to have to explain."

By now Gary was bent over laughing, so I slugged him in the shoulder, which made him laugh even more.

"Dang it Gary. How come it's easy for you to have a girlfriend and for me, it's so tough?"

"Because I admit I have a girlfriend…kind of. All you ever do is deny wanting one."

"Ok, ok, ok. Can we talk about something else, like maybe what we'll wear to the party? I want to look cool, just in case."

"Just in case, huh?"

I laughed. "Yah, just in case. Maybe we'll get something for Christmas that we can wear…something neat."

"There's a lot of stuff under the tree."

Gary was quiet for a moment before he spoke. "You know the old saying "feast before famine"? Well for me and my Mom, we went through a lot of famine. Now with you and your parents, it's like having a huge feast.

"You think it's a good feast, Gary?"

Gary shook his head yes. "The best feast ever, Davey. The best feast ever."

— ••• —

I suppose you're wondering what day it is. I had actually started losing track of time until Gary reminded me that it was almost Christmas.

"Davey, you know it's Wednesday. Christmas Eve is tomorrow and we've got to get the presents delivered. Want to get up?"

Gary and Rascal were standing quietly at the foot of my bed.

"What time is it?"

"A little after 9. Your Dad is waiting to take us around with the gifts. Want to get dressed?"

"Yes. Give me a minute. Has Rascal gone out?"

"Oh yes…twice. So, get dressed and let's get moving.

Gary headed out with Rascal and I brushed my teeth really fast and got dressed just as fast. When I went out of my room and into the kitchen Dad was standing there drinking a cup of coffee.

"Hey sport. About time you got up. Ready to go?"

I shook my head yes.

"Good. Gary has already put the packages in the car, so let's get moving."

With that he went out to the Jeep and got in. Gary came out of the living room and as soon as we got in Dad backed out and headed down our street.

"So, where are we going first?"

"Well, we thought we could drive down to the hardware store first and then see if Aggie was at her office and drop off their presents.

We're not sure where Mrs. Grossman's house is. You do know, don't you Dad?"

"Sure, I do. We can go there last."

It didn't take us too long to get to Frank's store. We all went in to see him and after we gave him his present (yes, he was surprised), Dad started chatting away. That was ok. Gary and I told them we would just walk over to Aggie's office and drop the gifts off while they talked. Dad liked that so we left and headed to Aggie's.

It was great walking through town. All the stores were decorated for the holidays and to top it off, it was lightly snowing. The town even had a sleigh ride that you could pay for to take you up and down the main street.

"Davey, I think my Mom would like that and I bet your Mom would too. You want to see if we can get some tickets?"

"Sure, but how much does it cost? I've got a little left, but not much. Plus, I'm not sure how long the town is going to be doing these rides. Maybe Aggie will know."

Gary agreed and we headed down the street looking in all the windows, listening to holiday music, and enjoying the snow, which had started coming down a little heavier. As we came up to Aggie's office, we saw that the light was on and Aggie was working on her computer at the counter. When we opened the door, she saw us and waved.

"Hi guys. Nice to see you. How's everything going?"

Gary spoke up. "Good. We just wanted to stop by and drop off a couple of presents for you and Lori."

I had been carrying the gifts and laid them on the counter.

"Wow. This is unexpected. Thanks so much!"

Reaching under the counter, Aggie pulled out a bag. She smiled. "We didn't forget you either. Lori wants you both to know that your help during the food drive was truly appreciated."

She handed the bag to Gary. "David, tell your mom we'll be over at about 11:30 on Christmas."

"You're coming over?"

"Yes, we are."

"Lori's coming?"

"Yes, she is."

I felt my face go red.

"Listen, Aggie, Davey and I have to get back to the hardware store. We've got some other things to do today. See you on Christmas."

We said goodbye, left, and headed back to Frank's.

Gary wasn't talking, so of course I had to say something.

"Well, what do you think?"

"About what?"

"About them coming over for Christmas."

Gary laughed. "You're worried about nothing, Davey. I'm fine with them coming over…or really, I should say…I'm fine with Aggie AND Lori coming over. You should be too. Outside of you wanting her as a girlfriend, she is our friend. Right?"

"Right. Maybe everything will be ok. I mean, we can play games and walk Rascal and…and…"

"Don't overthink this, Davey. Everything will be cool."

"You think?"

"I know."

"You think she's still seeing that 9th grader?"

"Does it make a difference?"

"No, I was just wondering."

"God, Davey, we've got to find you another girlfriend."

"You're probably right."

"Maybe we can take an ad out in the school paper."

I slugged Gary on his arm and he laughed like crazy. He was right. I needed to get over Lori. A new girlfriend? Hmmm.

Dad was waiting for us when we got back. "Where to next, guys?"

"We need to drop off Eddie's present and then we've got something for Debbie Mackenzie.

"Well, I know where Eddie lives. Do you have Debbie's address?"

We had looked it up before we left and gave it to Dad when he asked.

"Ok, we'll go to Eddie's, then to Debbie's house and then, to Ken Grossman's place. Any other presents we have to deliver or anything else we have to do?"

Gary spoke up. "Davey and I were thinking that my Mom and Kim would maybe like a ride in the sleigh that goes up and down the main drag. We were going to ask Aggie about the cost but forgot. If we have a little time, do you think we could swing back and see about the rides?"

Dad said yes and he turned the car around and went back to the end of the street where the sleigh rides started. There was a makeshift booth set up and a woman bundled in a heavy parka was standing in the front. Gary and I got out and when we did the lady smiled and greeted us by name.

"Hi David and Gary. It's so nice to see you!"

It was Mrs. Montgomery. I wondered what she was doing selling sleigh rides on cold days like this, but then I remembered that one of her kids owned a working cattle ranch not far north of here, kind of near the Wyoming border. Every year for the last 6 years, the city had contracted with him to give sleigh rides to the residents from a week before Christmas all the way to New Years. It wasn't until just now that I realized it was Mrs. Montgomery's son.

Gary spoke first.

"Hi Mrs. Montgomery. Merry Christmas. We didn't know you were doing this ride stuff."

Mrs Montgomery smiled. "My son Charlie is running it. I'm here to help out and of course spend a little time with one of my kids. What can I do for you gentlemen?"

Gary and I both smiled and Gary continued.

So, how much would it cost for two people and when would it be available?"

She beamed. "Are you planning on taking your girlfriends?"

Gary laughed. "No, we wanted to get a ride for our Moms."

"Now, that is really nice boys. Well, the cost is $25 for each person, but we're completely booked up through New Year's Day. However, we always get cancellations, and I can call you when the next time slot opens up. Will that work for you?"

Of course, we said yes and gave her Dad's phone number so she could call when a time freed up.

With that, we headed over to Eddie's, dropped his gift off and then went on to Debbie's. Her house was situated high up in the foothills. We had to go up a long driveway that must get pretty slick when it snows. Later Debbie would tell us that a lot of times during the winter they would have to leave their car at the bottom of the hill and walk to get home. Luckily, we were able to drive all the way up to the house. It wasn't ultra big, but it seemed pretty modern, with windows all along the front. I could see why they wanted to live up here, because you could see for miles.

A white picket fence surrounded the property and the yard had beautiful fir trees plus a large oak tree with a swing hanging from it. I remembered that Debbie did have a younger sister and the swing was probably for her. Just as Gary was about to get out of the car, Dad stopped him and pointed to the far edge of the yard. Standing there were two deer staring down at the car. We had seen deer before, even in our yard at home. Still, this was cool. We sat there and watched them for a while and finally, they wandered off.

When Gary did get out of the car, the front door of the house opened and Debbie came out on the porch. She must have seen us from the window and knew who we were. Gary walked up the steps and they spoke for a minute before he handed her the little bag with her present. I could see Debbie smiling and then...OMG...she leaned over and kissed him right on the mouth! The mouth! Wow! I think he liked it, but he turned red anyway. He said something and then came down the steps and got in the car. He wasn't saying anything. Dad turned the car around and started down the hill to head for Mr. Grossman's house. Nobody said a word for a long time until Dad couldn't hold it in any longer.

"So, how'd it go, Gary?"

I couldn't help it. I started to laugh and so did Dad. Gary was beet red, but he started laughing, too.

"She surprised me. I had no idea she was going to do that."

Of course, Dad asked a stupid question.

"Well, Gary, was that your first kiss?"

"DAD, PLEASE!!!"

Dad started laughing like crazy and so did we, but that's all that was said about it. And yes, Gary told me later that it was his very first kiss.

— • • • —

Mr. Grossman lived in a big house at the edge of the forest. Dad said he had 20 acres and most of it was fenced, making it perfect for the Sergeant's dogs. The house had belonged to his parents and before that, his grandparents. Dad had to get out and open a gate to get into the property. As we drove up, we could see the house. It looked oldish, but still in really good condition with fresh paint and what looked like a new roof. Even though there was snow in the yard, it seemed like it was very well kept.

Dad told us to stay in the car while he went up and rang the doorbell. When he did dogs started to bark and a minute later the Sergeant opened the door. The men shook hands and exchanged a few words, then the Sergeant motioned for us to come on up. Dad had already gone in and the Sergeant told us to follow Dad into the living room. The doggies greeted us and we took the time to pet both of them. When we did go into the living room we were surprised to see Mr. Grossman with a cast on one of his legs. When Dad asked what happened he told us that he slipped on the ice up at the City of Mercy as he was clearing the steps so that no one would fall.

He laughed. "Can you believe it? Down I went on my keister. They had to cart me to the hospital and now, I'm in this cast for at least 4 weeks."

The Sergeant chimed in. "He doesn't have to worry about anything because I'll be taking care of everything while he recovers."

Looking at the Sergeant I could see he meant it. He was a really good person who just needed a little help. That help had come from Mr. Grossman and now he had the opportunity to give back to someone who really deserved it.

Dad let them know we couldn't stay too long and that we had something for them.

"Me and Gary have a couple of presents for you. I see you have a tree. Can we put them under it?"

Ken Grossman smiled. "That's really nice of you. We didn't get you anything."

It was Gary that spoke up. "We didn't expect anything."

I put the presents under the little tree. There were a couple of little things there already, but nothing like we had at home. I started wondering what they were doing for Christmas dinner and Dad must have been thinking the same thing.

"Look guys, why don't you join us for Christmas Dinner. Ken, I know it might be a little difficult with your leg and all, but I can pick you both up Christmas morning and you can stay the day. Oh yah, bring the puppies. Our puppy can have some friends to play with."

"That is a nice invitation. Sarge? What do you think?"

The Sergeant laughed. "Well I was planning on making franks and beans, but I guess we could put off that special dinner to come over. You really don't mind that my doggies come along?"

Of course, we said it was all good.

Dad was smiling. I think he was ultra-happy that he would actually have someone to talk to, other than girls and kids and pets.

Ken spoke up. "You don't have to come and get us, The Sarge can drive us over. We got his driver's license renewed.

Well, that was cool. I had thought that the Sergeant couldn't ever drive because of him only having a partial left leg. I guess I was wrong and glad I was. I need to be better about making judgements about people, like I did with Gary because of the crap on the bus.

Dad looked at his watch and let them know we had to get home. He told them to be over before lunch because there would be two meals served and plenty of stuff to eat between them.

We said goodbye and headed back home. We were feeling good about getting all the presents delivered and I know Gary was feeling way good after that smooch. Someday maybe I'll get kissed. I'm wondering who it will be and no, really, I wasn't thinking Lori. Really.

— ••• —

I've heard that as you get older time speeds up. Well, time is zooming by now, so I can't imagine how fast it would be when I'm old, like maybe 40? Anyway, it was suddenly Christmas Eve day and Gary and me were really excited about all the stuff under the tree. Mom and Dad always let me pick a present to open after dinner and that tradition was going to continue, except it would be me and Gary. Plus, we decided to let Anna open a present, too. That was because she had gone through so much. It was only right that she also got to open something early.

I usually got to pick what we had for Christmas Eve dinner, but I thought Gary should pick. He actually picked something I like—stuffed porkchops. In the afternoon Anna and Mom spent a lot of time in the kitchen getting stuff ready for dinner and some dishes for tomorrow. Dad, me and Gary set up the dining table where the older people would sit. Us kids would be at the kitchen table. That was ok because I hated sitting with the grownups and listening to the talk. At least we would be able to talk about cool stuff. I'm not sure what, but I know that whatever it was would be a lot cooler than whatever they talked about.

Anyway, after we got the house all set up for guests, we took Rascal for a long walk. We had been so busy doing all the X-Mas stuff that we hadn't spent a lot of time with our biggest friend. As we walked him down the block we saw that there was a house that just got sold. Of course, we wondered who bought it.

"Maybe a girlfriend for you will move in, Davey. Wouldn't that be great?"

"No. I don't need a girlfriend."

Gary shook his head. "That's exactly what you need."

"I'm not ready to have Dad do the talk thing. I don't want to hear it. WAY TOO EMBARASSING."

"How do you know what your Dad is going to say?"

"You know Jason Dickerson, right?"

Gary nodded.

"Well, he told a bunch of us about when his Dad had the talk with him. There was a lot about treating girls with respect and never doing mean things to them. But there was also a whole bunch about you know what."

"What?"

"You know—the where babies come from stuff."

"Oh, that stuff."

"Yup.

"Well, at least you have your Dad to talk to you about it. I only have Mom and I think the talk is a lot worse when it doesn't come from a Dad. I mean, would you want your Mom talking to you about that stuff?"

"I don't even want my Dad talking about it, but I do see your point."

It was starting to snow again, which was really cool. I mean, you always want it snowing over Christmas. Rascal really liked it and as we walked, he tried to grab the snowflakes as they fell to the ground. We had gone about 6 blocks, then turned back toward home. As we went past the house that had been sold, we saw a car pull up in front. The people in the car didn't get out. They just sat there and looked at the house. There were two kids in the back seat and I thought I recognized one of them as the new girl that came to our school right before holiday break.

"Gary, is that the new girl at our school?"

"I'm not sure. I only saw her once. I think her name is Jane somebody. You think that's the family that bought the house?"

"I don't know. Maybe."

"Do you know where they came from?"

"I think Eddie said they were moving here from Chicago, but I'm not sure. Maybe Eddie will invite her to the party and you can get to know her better…comprende?"

"God, Gary, get off the girlfriend stuff. I mean, we don't have a clue about this girl. She could be mean."

"Mean Jane? Cool. Davey and Mean Jane…now that sounds just about right."

"Oh pleeeeaze, stop it. I think I remember that Eddie was interested in her. That was Eddie who mentioned her before, wasn't it?"

Gary started to laugh. "You're right, but maybe there will be other girls at the party."

"Maybe, but I'm really not interested. Besides, there's nobody that's going to be interested in me."

"Why do you think that, Davey? Have you looked in the mirror lately? You've grown a bunch and you look good."

I actually had noticed that my jeans seemed shorter, but I didn't really connect it with getting taller. Gary was getting taller, too.

"You think I look better? I figured that girls only like taller blonde kids…like you."

Gary laughed again. "Don't sell yourself short, Davey. Girls love blue eyes."

"My best feature."

"Oh, yes."

"I think I might have grown a little."

"Yes, and what else?"

"What do you mean, "What else"?"

"Dude, something else has changed and I'm surprised you haven't noticed."

I put my hand to my face thinking that he was talking about the tiny bit of fuzz under my nose. "You think I need to start shaving?"

Gary could barely contain himself. "God No!! Davey, haven't you noticed…you've lost weight."

What? OMG! I hadn't noticed, but now that Gary mentioned it, it did seem my jeans were a little looser.

"Wow! I weigh myself every day and my weight hasn't changed."

"Maybe not, but you've grown an inch or so. Your weight spread out more."

"Dang, and I was thinking I would have to start shaving."

Gary smiled, "Well, there is a bit of fuzz."

"You think I should do it?"

"Geez, Davey, a little fuzz does not require a shave."

"So, you think I look good enough to find a girlfriend?"

"You've always looked good enough to find a girlfriend. Again, and emphatically I say, stop selling yourself short."

"Thanks, Gary."

It was a little after 4:30 and as we got back to the house, we could see that my Dad was home already. Usually, he gets home later, but because this was Christmas Eve, he was home now. He had given all the people that work for him the day off, keeping only a couple of volunteers ready for any emergency that might come up. Of course, the volunteers always got time off later and usually, bigger bonuses than the rest of the crew.

We thought that we would clean off the walks when we got home, but it had already been done. I knew it had been Dad helping me and Gary out so we would have more time to relax. There were a lot of great smells coming from the kitchen and I realized how hungry I was. We got Rascal's paws cleaned off and went into the living room where Anna and Dad were sitting and holding the kitties.

When Anna saw us come in, she smiled. "Hi guys. How was your walk?"

"Great, Mom, but now we're really hungry and everything smells great! Do you need us to help with anything?"

"Nope. Everything's ready to go. Listen, we made eggnog. Go grab some. It's non-alcoholic."

Gary went right into the kitchen to get some, but eggnog never did it for me. I mean, raw eggs and cream and sugar? Nope. I'll stick with

Coke. I followed Gary into the kitchen and of course, Rascal trailed behind us. He was already 50 lbs and it looked like he was going to be on the bigger side of the breed when he got to full size.

A lot of food was ready and on the island that sat in the middle of the kitchen. Mom had made a Chocolate Macaroon bundt cake for dessert tomorrow. It was my favorite. Just as we were about to go back in the living room, a noise made us both turn, just in time to see Rascal up on his hind legs at the island and a goodly piece of the cake gone.

We both screamed and Gary got to him first, grabbing him by the collar and pulling him from the counter. Just then, Dad ran into the kitchen. He was about to ask what the scream was when he saw the partially eaten dessert. Dad chuckled, covering his mouth with his hand to stop from outright laughing.

Between chuckles Dad told us to put Rascal in his crate, at least through dinner.

I was a little concerned, because dogs are not supposed to eat chocolate.

"Dad, is Rascall going to be ok? I mean he had a big bite of the cake. Did he eat too much chocolate?"

"Let's ask your Mom." Dad yelled down the hall and Mom stuck her head out of the bedroom. She had just gotten out of the shower and her hair was still wrapped in a towel.

"What's up?"

"There was a teeny accident in the kitchen, Kim. Rascal decided he wanted dessert before dinner and took what amounted to a couple of slices of your wonderful dessert. The boys were concerned about the chocolate and whether our very rambunctious puppy would be affected badly by it."

Mom came out of the bedroom and into the kitchen. The towel was still on her head, but she was fully dressed in jeans and a nice short sleeve shirt. Of course, she saw the cake right away and laughed. Taking a knife, she cut the bitten portion away and dumped it into a wastebasket at the corner of the island.

"I should have done this before," she noted as she put the cover on the cake carrier. Sorry guys. Oh yes, don't worry about the chocolate. The amount he ate, based on his size, is not going to affect him at all. From now on, I'll keep the goodies more toward the center of the table, especially chocolate goodies. Now it's almost time for dinner. Let me get my hair dried and Anna and I will get everything served."

With that she headed back to the bedroom and we all went back to the living room to wait for dinner.

— ••• —

Dinner was fantastic and when it was dessert time, we all had a good laugh about Rascal and the cake. After we finished up, Gary and I did the dishes, then headed back to the living room to do the single gift opening. I told Gary that I always picked something tiny like socks so everything big would be saved for Christmas morning. He agreed that it was a cool plan.

Anna picked first. She thought about it for a few minutes and picked a soft smallish bundle that was from Mom. It turned out to be a really cool winter scarf. Of course, she said she loved it.

Now, Gary and me got to pick. We did the smallish present like we had discussed. Gary picked one that also was from my Mom. He opened his and there were some socks, just like we thought we might get. Gary smiled like crazy and thanked Mom a ton. I picked a smallish square present that was from Dad. It turned out to be a book called Train Your St. Bernard in 10 Easy Steps. As I was saying thanks a lot, I was thinking that it was a hint from my parents about taking good care of the puppy. I always planned to, but I was hoping we could send him out for training. Me getting that book said that was probably not my parent's plan. It was cool. I know Gary would help and we would get Rascal trained in no time.

After that, we watched a little tv and then took Rascal out to do his business before we went to our rooms to try and get some sleep.

It was always hard for me. Christmas morning with all the present opening was totally awesome, especially because there was always a very special present. I mean, it wasn't always something I had asked for. A couple of years ago I got Skis and lessons in Aspen instead of the Playstation I wanted. That was cool and I really enjoyed it. I got the Playstation later, on my birthday in August. I was wondering what this year was going to be, especially with Gary and his Mom living with us. As I started to doze off, my mind was thinking about girls... well, girl. She was coming over for dinner. I was wondering if she ever thought about me.

— ••• —

"Davey!"

Gary's voice and a slobbery lick across my face woke me from a very peaceful sleep. I had asked him to get me up so we could get Rascal out, eat breakfast and take care of any chores we had to before we opened our presents.

"Let me get dressed and I'll be down in a sec."

Gary said fine and took Rascal to the living room to wait for me. It didn't take me long to get myself hooked together. When I came out, Gary was sitting on the couch with Rascal laying quietly at his feet. I saw that Mom had hung stockings for everybody and we always looked at what was in there after opening everything else. I could hear some noise coming from down the hall and that meant everybody was probably getting up.

"Let's get Rascall out, ok?"

Gary nodded and we got our coats on and headed to the door. I could see it was snowing and knew we would have to get the walks and driveway cleaned off, especially so our guests wouldn't have to walk through a couple of inches of snow.

"So, Davey, are you excited? I sure am."

"Yup. Don't be surprised if there's a special gift that you didn't think you would get. My parents like surprises. I'm just wondering what they're going to do this year."

"To be honest, I'd just be happy with some new clothes."

"Oh, you'll get clothes. I hope I get something cool that I can wear."

"You mean, to impress Lori?"

"No, of course not."

"God, Davey. Get with a reality check!"

"Fine. I want to look good for her."

Gary snickered and I punched him in the arm, making him laugh out loud.

We had a longish chain for Rascal so he could stay out while we shoveled the snow and we did it faster than usual, because we wanted to get to the gifts. As soon as we finished, we got Rascal's paws cleaned off and when we came into the kitchen, Mom and Anna were standing in the kitchen drinking coffee and laughing. Seeing us come in, Mom asked if we wanted breakfast before opening the presents.'

"Mom!! Are you kidding?"

Both Moms smiled.

"Well, ok. Let's all go into the living room."

Gary thought it would be a good idea if we put Rascal in his cage… ok, fine, crate. Rascal wasn't happy and whined, but I agreed that at least while we were opening stuff, Rascal had to stay in jail.

Dad was already sitting on the couch when we all went in. After everybody got settled, Dad got up and started passing out the gifts. There were so many. Each of us had a big pile and I knew a lot of them would be clothes. That was ok.

Dad asked, "Should we take turns or all go at it?"

"All at it, Dad. We'd be opening all day if we did it one by one."

"Well, then, let's go!"

I always go for the little stuff first and work up to the bigger things. So, there were socks and t-shirts and jeans and a really cool sweater that I decided to wear today. There was this one big box and it was from Gary. When I opened it, I was surprised to find a bomber jacket just like his, with a note that said "Now we are twins." I immediately put it on and it fit great.

"I love it! Thanks, Gary. I love it!"

Gary hadn't opened the boots yet. One of the bigger boxes he opened was a laptop. When he opened it I think he was really surprised. I mean, the gift was super and I could get my laptop back. But, surprise, surprise. I also got a laptop to replace my old one. What great presents!!

Anna, Mom and Dad were opening theirs as well. Mom squealed when she saw the mixer and when Anna saw the iPad, she cried. But she cried even more when she opened a tiny box from Mom and Dad. Inside was a set of keys to a car, with a note…It's not new, but it'll get you around. The car had been sitting in front of our house. I had asked Mom about it, but she said not to worry about it, that it was supposed to be parked there.

Gary whispered, "Did you know about this?"

I just shook my head. "I had no idea."

"Was this the big surprise stuff you were talking about before?"

"Well, it was a big surprise, wasn't it?"

"Yes."

"OK. Open that present from me, Gary."

"Oh, right."

With that, Gary opened the box and when he saw the boots, he just stared at them for a minute, before turning to me.

"You got me the boots I wanted. They were really expensive. How did you do it?"

I laughed whispering, "The demon…well, actually Aggie Czech. She gave me a coupon for that store."

Gary looked surprised. "No way! She gave me a coupon for Macy's, or I wouldn't have been able to afford that jacket. Davey, she probably is the demon."

"Shhhh…let's keep that between us and see how she acts when she comes over."

"Agreed."

Mom interrupted out discussion, "Guys, Santa left presents too. Go get Santa's gifts, guys."

She took two stockings off the mantle and handed them to Anna and Dad. Gary and I grabbed ours. Of course, there was a lot of stuff like candy and socks, but buried way down at the bottom was a little box wrapped in Santa paper.

"OMG!! A cell phone. Wow! Thanks guys!"

Mom's sock had a little box too, but hers turned out to be a FitBit and a gym membership. Anna got a phone and a gym membership, too. Wow! Great surprises, but then I thought of Dad. Had Santa given him something special?

"Hey Dad. Did Santa give you something cool?"

Dad was smiling. "Well, it's really hard to beat a coffee setup like I got from you guys, but Santa managed to give me something neat—fly fishing gear and the lessons that go along with it! Gosh, thanks, Santa!!"

Everybody was happy. Everybody loved everything, especially the phones. Well, at least Gary and I really loved the phones. This was the big surprise I had told Gary about, although a car for Anna was huge.

Mom reminded us that it was about time we got everything ready for our guests. Dad was heading out to go pick up Mrs. Skriver and everybody else was told to be here before noon. Gary and I cleaned up all the wrapping stuff in the living room while the Moms finished up the food we would have for lunch.

We let Rascal out of his cage and he went right to the couch where both kitties were curled up. He sniffed a couple of times, then plopped down on the floor as close to the babies as he could. It was like he wanted to protect them.

He was already close to 50 pounds. We didn't know exactly when he had been born, but the shelter people had put August 15th down as his birthday. That made him around 4 months old. Dad said he thought Rascal was going to be bigger than most Saint Bernards because of how fast he was growing. I wasn't too crazy about leaving him in that cage all day, but thankfully, Mom said we could leave him out so long as he didn't do anything weird...like eat sombody's food without permission.

After we finished cleaning up the living room and getting the chairs organized like Mom wanted, we both went back to our rooms to get cleaned up and ready for our guests. I had gotten a really neat gray sweater from Anna and I wanted to look good. No, please don't jump to THAT conclusion. I wasn't thinking about Lori. Really...I wasn't.

Anyway, just then, my new, fabulous, better than almost anything, phone rang. It was Gary. I mean, who else would it be?

"Hey Davey."

"Wow! My first call. I still haven't got your number put in yet. "

"I wanted to get my Mom's number in, so of course I put yours in, too."

"Of course. I haven't done it yet. I had to change. That sweater your Mom gave me is really cool."

"I bet you look good."

"You think?"

"So, you want me to say she's gonna like how you look? Ok, I'll say it. Davey, she's gonna like how you look. Better go talk to your Dad."

"Why?"

Gary laughed. "The talk, Davey. It's time."

"Dang, Gary. I'm not THAT interested in her. No, no talk for me."

"I figure the talk is more about how you treat girls. The sex part is only a little bit of it."

"How do you know? I mean, you haven't had the talk either."

"Come on, Davey. Don't you think your Dad figures you already know where babies come from? Do you really think that's what the talk is about?"

I shrugged my shoulders. "Honestly, it was just the thought of talking about anything related to that stuff."

"Well, don't sweat it. I figure it's really about respect, about how you treat people...all people really, but the talk probably is mostly about how you treat girls."

"Well, I guess that doesn't sound too bad, but why is it even necessary? I already know how to treat girls."

"Because it makes parents feel like they've done a really important thing for their kids. That's teaching them to be good people. Oh yah, I put on the boots. They fit great!! Thanks!!"

"So, come down to my room."

"On my way."

It was just a second, then a knock, and Gary came in. He was wearing the boots I had gotten him and they did look great. He had on a new shirt that was Western too. I mean, it wasn't one of those weird shirts with fringe and pictures of horses and stuff. It was plain white, but all the buttons were pearl snap types. He also had on a leather vest that was pretty cool.

"You look like a cowboy, Gary."

"This is Colorado. Why can't I look like a cowboy?"

"It's cool. I like the shirt."

"Yah, me too."

Just then the doorbell rang and we could hear voices. It was Mr. Grossman and the Sarge.

Mom yelled for us to come out and say hello to our first guests, so carrying our phones, we went out to the living room. Mr. Grossman was still in a cast and Mom got him settled in Dad's recliner. Sarge had his dogs on leash and both were behaving really well. Rascal came up and sniffed both of them, then wagged his tail, which said that he was happy for friends.

The Sarge looked great. He still had a nicely manicured beard that had flecks of silver, making him very distinguished. I could tell the jeans he wore were new and to top everything off, he was wearing the cap we had given him. How lit is that?

Anna had taken Mr. Grossman's coat to hang in the closet and she asked Gary to take the Sergeant's. He was still standing by the door holding his doggies' leashes. Mom came over and told him that his puppies didn't need to be held, so he took the leashes off. When he did, nothing happened. Hank and Wiggles just stood there next to the Sergeant. He was still walking with a cane, but he wasn't wobbly or anything. Actually, he was walking really well. When he went into the living room, his dogs followed him and when he sat down on the couch, both of them laid down next to him.

The doorbell rang again and it was Aggie and Lori and Lori's little brother, Kenny. I had forgotten she had a brother, probably because he was still in grade school and I never saw him much. He didn't seem too interested in anybody and was actively playing a game on a hand-held he probably got for Christmas.

Aggie was carrying a pan of something and Lori had a bowl of something else. I had figured the Moms had made everything, but when they put the stuff in the kitchen and uncovered it, I saw snacks. They had brought a lot of goodies for before and after our meals.

The front door opened again and it was Dad and Mrs. Skriver. She was carrying a pie and I could see that Dad had the plate of cookies she promised she would bring. Gary took her coat and Mom came up and gave her a hug before taking her into the living room.

Lori had gone into the kitchen with her Mom and her brother was just kind of standing next to the door. I thought I better make myself useful.

"Hey Kenny, remember me?

Kenny glanced up from his game, shook his head no and went back to playing.

"So, come down to the basement with me. There's a couch where you can sit and play your game, plus there's a tv down there if you want to watch something.

"Ok."

As we started down to the basement, Mom stopped me and suggested we take Rascal down there with us. Rascal liked it downstairs because the floor was tile and cool for him to lay on.

I haven't really told you much about our basement. Sure, you know the laundry is down there, but did I tell you we have a pool table and a foosball game? There's also a big screen tv and a nice sectional couch, plus an old fridge that works fine for keeping pop and snacks. It was Dad who got the pool table a few years ago. He doesn't play much anymore. I guess he's just too busy. Gary and I play sometimes, but we're not good like Dad was…or still is, I guess.

"Gee, this place is neat!" Kenny had finally glanced up from his game. He walked over to the pool table and ran his hand over the felt.

"Any chance we can play?"

"Sure, but later. Gary and Lori will be down in a few. We can play then or after lunch. Can you do me a favor and keep an eye on my dog while I run upstairs for a minute?"

Kenny hadn't really noticed Rascal until I said that, but when I asked him, he looked over and saw the puppy and immediately squealed.

"Wow! That is a big puppy. What kind is he?"

"He's a Saint Bernard, Kenny. He's going to get really, really big… much bigger than he is now.,

"Cool!"

"Then you will watch him for a few minutes?"

"Sure!"

Kenny had already laid his game down on the couch and was over sitting on the floor next to Rascal petting him like crazy. Rascal loved it and flipped over on his back so he could get his belly rubbed.

I went back upstairs to see what Gary and Lori were doing and found them in the living room talking to our other guests. Mrs. Skriver saw me and waved for me to come over. When I did, I saw she handed me little package.

"I hope you like it," she said.

I opened the package and found a knit ski cap. Gary already had his on and Dad did too. They were kind of the same, mostly red, white and black with a tassel on each.

"Gee, Mrs. Skriver, thanks. I like it a lot."

I stuck it on my head and it fit perfectly.

Mom was smiling. "You know, Mary, you didn't have to do that, but I must say they are very, very nice. You can really knit."

Mrs. Skriver seemed genuinely grateful. "Well, thank you Kim. I've been knitting since I was just a child."

Aggie Czech had listened quietly, but then, just like usual, she came up with a wonderful idea.

"You know, Mary, you could sell some of those hats. Do you make anything else?"

"Oh yes, gloves, mittens, scarves, and knit throws. I can do sweaters, but they take so long, I don't do them too often. Do you really think I could make a little by knitting?"

Aggie laughed. "I know you can make a little and maybe more than that. Why don't we plan on talking after the first of the year?"

It looked like Mrs. Skriver was going to cry. She had pulled a Kleenex out of her little purse and held it ready for tears that might come soon.

"You know, Aggie, I certainly could use the money. Even a little would help. When you mentioned that I started thinking about some of the people who live near me. Do you know Linda Williams?"

When Mom and Aggie shook their heads no, she continued.

"Linda's a nice young lady who's had a turn of bad luck. She takes care of her mother who has Alzheimer's. Do you remember that big farm store that went out of business—Evans Company Farm & Feed? Well, she worked as kind of a woman of all trades, doing books, marketing, acting as a secretary…well, just about any office work a company might need. I know she worked hard for them, but when Nate Evans closed the store, for no good reason, I might add, he did so without thinking of any of the employees. There was no severance, no nothing. Linda did collect unemployment, but it just wasn't enough to keep her apartment and take care of her Mom. She found a little house back where I live and got a job down at the Local Grocery Store. Tom Ford, the owner… he's a really nice man. He lets Linda bring her Mom with her to work. He has a little tv in his office and she sits there and watches all the time while Linda works.

We were all really quiet, waiting to hear what Mrs. Skriver was going to say, but she stopped talking for a few minutes, so Mom had to break the silence.

"Mary? Were you going to tell us something else about Linda?"

Mrs. Skriver sounded startled when she answered.

"Oh, oh yes. I'm sorry. I sometimes forget what I was saying, now that I'm so old.'"

She laughed and continued.

"Linda makes stained glass planters and things. They're lovely. She has a few at Tom's store, but they are mostly too expensive for the people that shop there. Here, I have a picture."

Mrs. Skriver dug down into her purse and pulled out a wallet that turned out to hold photos. She opened it and slowly turned from picture to picture, looking for a few seconds at each before going to the next. From what I could see, most of the pictures looked like family members and maybe I shouldn't have, but I asked.

"Mrs. Skriver? Are those pictures of your family?"

"Oh yes."

She held up the wallet so everyone could see the picture she was on.

"This is my husband, Harry. He passed almost 40 years ago."

She turned the page and held up a picture of her and her husband and 2 kids.

"This is my family—my husband, Nora, my oldest, and Jeremy, my little boy. Well, I suppose I shouldn't say little. He's 43 now."

I started to ask where her kids were, but my Mom frowned and silently shook her head no, so I stayed quiet. I guess she was right. I mean, why would her kids let her live like she did, all by herself and with very little money and almost no help? I would have to ask Mom later. Maybe she already knew what was going on.

Anyway, Mrs. Skriver flipped through the pictures until she found the one she wanted to show us. Holding it up, I saw there was a kind looking lady holding a planter that I guess she had made. Actually, it looked pretty nice and I could see that it would be something that people like Mom would really like. You know, people who like to plant things? Well, that's definitely Mom. Of course, it was Mom that spoke up first.

"Mary, that planter is lovely. How much is she selling them for?"

Mrs. Skriver sighed.

"$100. There's no one up where we live that can afford to buy a planter for that much money. I told her, but she said it cost her quite a bit to make and took her a really long time to do it. She figured she wouldn't make any money unless she charged that much.

Mom was smiling. "Well, I think it's worth every cent and I'll bet she could sell them easily here in town. I have a gallery friend who I'm sure would put a couple in her shop and probably at a much higher price than $100.

Dad, who hadn't said a word until now, also had a great idea.

"Well, you know, I have this friend, Frank. He owns a hardware store that has a big garden section. I'm sure he would put a couple in that area.

Of course, Mrs. Skriver started to cry. I guess it's just something she does when she's happy and I figure she does it when she's sad, too.

"I just can't tell you how much I appreciate your help and I'm sure Linda will be very happy" she said, wiping her eyes with the Kleenex she had been holding ready to use.

— •••—

Anna had been working in the kitchen and when Mom went to help, she let me know that all the kids should get ready to eat. I went and got everybody together. Mom and Anna had decided that because there were so many of us they would make it a buffet where we could go and take whatever and then sit wherever. The table in the kitchen was just a little too small for us all to sit, so we decided to get food and go back downstairs.

I had planned on putting Rascal in his crate, but he was behaving so well, I decided to leave him out. You know, I've made a few mistakes in my life...nothing too bad, but leaving Rascal loose during a lunch buffet, especially after he ate that cake, was not necessarily the smartest thing I've ever done. As the bunch of us kids got our food and went downstairs, I wasn't really watching my big puppy.

We had just started to eat when a loud yell came from upstairs.

"David! Get up here now.

It was Dad and he wasn't sounding too happy. When I got upstairs, I found him in the dining room. He was holding Rascal by the collar in front of all the food. At the edge of the table there was a plate of sandwiches...or rather, there was a plate that was half full.

"Dad! There was egg salad there and it has onions. Rascal could get sick. Why didn't you stop him?"

Well, that did it. Dad was pissed.

"OK, young man. This dog is YOUR RESPONSIBILITY. YOURS, NOT MINE I shouldn't be the one to stop him from eating a bunch of our lunch sandwiches at a time when he should have been crated so he wouldn't try. It happened with the cake yesterday and now, sandwiches. I don't expect this to happen again. Do you understand me, David?"

I nodded.

"Now, go call the emergency vet clinic to see if we have a problem. The number is in your mother's address book in the top drawer by the phone.

As I started toward the phone, Dad stopped me.

"One last thing, David. There will be some extra chores for you in the next few days. Understood?"

I nodded again. I had a feeling that was going to happen...no, I knew it was going to happen, but I didn't know when or what I would end up doing. I would just have to wait and see how many chores I would have to do to make up for not watching Rascal well enough to keep him out of trouble.

— ••• —

When I called the vet she told me that because of Rascal's size and the fact that there probably wasn't enough onions in the sandwiches to make him sick, I really shouldn't worry. That made me feel better.

The rest of the day went pretty smooth. Rascal stayed in the crate except for when we took him outside and after everybody had eaten and the leftover stuff had been put away or up so high he couldn't reach. The Sergeant's dogs were really well behaved. They didn't have to be on a leash or in a crate or anything. Just remember, they are older and I figure when Rascal isn't a puppy any more, he'll behave as well. At least, I hope he will.

It was fun having Lori over. We all ended up playing Monopoly. Her little brother even played. I kind of forgot about the boyfriend/girlfriend thing, because it was just a bunch of friends hanging out. Well, that didn't last because Lori asked about the party that Eddie's parents were holding.

"Are you guys going to Eddie's party?"

Gary answered.

"Of course. It sounds like fun. Davey and I are spending the night. "

Lori smiled. "That's cool. Who's watching the puppy?"

"My Dad, kind of. He'll just swing home to check on him."

As soon as I said that the thought came into my head that Dad might not let me go because of the Rascal stuff. I had never seen him so angry about anything and when he did mention extra chores, I hadn't thought that he might include the party on the list of potential punishments. I mean, the party wasn't a chore, but staying home watching Rascal would be.

I wasn't going to let that happen. I would need to apologize like crazy and tell him I was up for any extra chores that might be necessary to make up for the problem that Rascal had caused. Hopefully the party wasn't on his list.

"Davey?" Lori reached out and put her hand on my arm. (OMG!!)

"Davey, Gary said you guys got phones for Christmas. Give me yours and I'll put in my number so you can talk to me whenever. OK?"

Wow. Lori wanted to talk to me whenever. Handing her my phone, I felt really great, but then, she asked Gary for his phone, too. Why, I ask you, why would Lori ever want to talk to Gary?

—•••—

Christmas dinner came and went. Mrs. Skriver used up all her Kleenex when Mom and Aggie said they would help all the ladies sell their crafty stuff. The Sergeant spent a lot of time talking to Anna. I'm pretty sure he liked her and I'm thinking she liked him, too. I decided not to mention it to Gary right yet, because according to him, his Mom was still married to his Dad who took off. I didn't want to get him more upset because it had already been pretty bad for him for a long time.

After we took Mrs. Skriver home, Gary helped Mom and Anna clean upstairs and Dad and I started on the basement. That's because he needed privacy to lecture me on responsibility. He had calmed down a lot, so the chores he assigned me weren't as bad as I thought they would be (clean the garage when it got warm enough). Unfortunately, the punishment was way worse. I spose you're wondering what I mean. Well, Dad started his lecture about responsibility with Rascal, but then, he hit me with a real zinger.

"David, now that you understand what I expect from you as a responsible member of this family, I think it's time we talked about another important issue—girls and sex."

My face felt like it was burning off and I sat paralyzed waiting for Dad to lecture me on something I didn't want to hear. It started with Dad asking me questions.

"David, do you know where babies come from?"

OMG, this was horrible and I made it worse when I tried to lighten the conversation.

"The stork brings them?"

"DAVID!! RESPONSIBILITY!! Now, answer honestly. Do you know where babies come from?"

Embarassed to the nth, I nodded that I did. I mean, how many kids my age don't know that already? Do parents really believe they don't?

"Good, then we don't have to talk about the details. You'll get more in your sex education class that I believe will start in March some time."

"Dad, what about that?"

"We had to sign a release for you to take the class."

"What? Why would you do that?"

"Because it's important and learning it in school will be a lot easier than talking to me about it. And, since you already know that babies are not delivered by storks, we still have to talk about how you treat girls."

"I know how to treat girls."

Dad laughed. "You might know how to treat girls now, but when you start actual dating, a lot of things change."

"Like what?"

"Well, most kids go through many relationships as they grow up… before they find someone to settle down with…like me and your Mom. We saw different people before we got together and I have to tell you, David, not all those relationships ended on a positive note."

"So, you broke up with some girl. That doesn't mean you can't still be friends, does it? I don't see how you would treat them any different than before."

Dad shook his head. "Everything changes, David. There's a lot of hurt sometimes, because a breakup is usually instigated by only one of the people. It's not always mutual and most of the time, unfortunately, that's how it usually is. There's a lot of hurt involved sometimes and sometimes a lot of anger."

"C'mon Dad, I know how to treat people and I don't think a break-up would make me treat someone differently."

And then Dad hit me below the belt.

"David, you're interested in Lori, aren't you?"

I felt my face go entirely red and as I shook my head no, Dad just sat there staring at me.

"Look, sport, don't you think I noticed when you wanted to go over to Aggie's office more than once? I mean, what other reason would you go over there, except to try and see Lori?"

Dang, if I said no, he would start asking me why I went over there and I didn't want to tell him it was to hire a demon to do stuff. I had to think fast.

"It was just for the charity stuff."

"You gave her a Christmas present, didn't you? That kind of sounds like you like her."

Dang, Dang! Couldn't Dad just drop this?

"Well, that was only because I didn't want her to feel bad when we gave Aggie, you know, her mom, that computer bag. Dad, wouldn't you feel bad if someone left you out and didn't get you something but got mom something? Wouldn't you?"

Dad chuckled. "Ok, ok let's just leave it at that, sport, but just remember what I've told you. Relationships can be difficult. No matter what, you should always treat others with respect, especially the girls you date, even if they break up with you or, if it happens, that you break up with them. No matter what, you understand?"

"Yes."

"Great. Now, let's head upstairs and get a late-night snack. There's lots of leftovers from dinner."

"I'm not hungry, Dad."

"What? Not hungry? Not possible or...was it just too much uncomfortable talk that made you lose your appetite? Dad chuckled.

"Please, Dad, no more tonight? Please?"

Dad slapped me on the back and headed upstairs and into the kitchen with me following. We found Gary still there finishing up wiping down the counters. Mom and Aggie had already gone into their rooms for the night.

After making himself a turkey sandwich, Dad headed into the living room to watch a bit of tv. As soon as he left the kitchen, Gary whispered a question.

"So, how'd it go?"

"Not well."

"How come?"

"Well, it started as my responsibility lecture and ended up as a talk about girls and dating."

"You mean the sex talk?"

"Yah, but he didn't talk about sex. He just asked me if I knew where babies came from."

Gary burst into laughter and I punched him in the arm, making him laugh even harder.

"Don't laugh too hard stupid. You're not going to like what I found out."

"What?" he asked, continuing to snicker.

"We have to take sex education in March"

"What? How do you know?"

"Dad said he had to sign a paper for me to attend. If he did that, I'm pretty sure your Mom did it too."

"Dang."

"So, what did you tell him when he asked you where babies come from?"

"The stork."

Gary broke into more laughter and I had to laugh, too.

"It was totally embarrassing, Gary. I'm almost relieved that the sex stuff is going to be a class."

"No kidding. That's bad enough, but worse when it comes from a parent."

"There was more...Dad knows I like Lori."

"How?"

"He figured I did when I kept wanting to go over to Aggie's office. I sure as heck wasn't going to tell him it was to rent a demon. That would have been bad. I could have been grounded until I was 50."

"Well, I won't say anything about the demon and you do like Lori."

"Ok, yah, I do like Lori, but you know, she's seeing that kid."

"Davey, things change. Be patient or find a different girlfriend."

"My Dad kind of said the same thing, that we would go through a lot of different girlfriends. So, maybe you're right."

"So, is there anybody you might be interested in?...other than Lori, I mean."

"No. Do we know who's coming to Eddie's party?"

"No, but I'll bet there'll be kids from other schools. Eddie's Dad knows a lot of people."

"Even Eddie found a kind of girlfriend. I mean, I have to say kind of because I don't think she knows he likes her."

Gary and I both laughed.

"Listen, Davey, you're looking pretty good. You've grown quite a bit and got skinnier. I think you need to get your hair cut. You'd probably look pretty cool if you did something with your hair."

"Like what?"

"Well, I don't know for sure, but I'm getting my hair cut before the party and you should, too."

"What if they mess it up?"

"Davey, when was the last time you got a new hair style?"

"Never. Mom just had the cut people trim a bit so it didn't go in my face and get so long I looked like a girl."

"Well, I'm going to get something new, too. Mom scheduled an appointment at a salon."

"Like a girl salon?"

"No, dummy. It's for both guys and girls. It's called Moxie Magic."

"Moxie Magic?"

"Oh ya, because when you got moxie you gotta look the part. That's the magic part and what their sign says."

"How much does it cost? I mean, I've got a little left over, but not much."

"I'll bet if you asked your Mom for a haircut, she'd spring for it. My Mom said she would, now that she's making money. Don't worry about it though, because I still have a little cash if she doesn't."

— ••• —

But she did. She chuckled when I told her it was Moxie Magic and when I asked why, she said that I would have to wait and see. I would find out soon enough and it wasn't a bad thing…once I got used to what they would do. Wow, now I'm wondering what Gary got me in to.

— ••• —

The Moxie Magic Salon sat high in the foothills overlooking the town below. The road to get there first curved around and then straight up about 2 miles. Mom hated driving roads like that, so Dad offered to take us and wait until we were done. Gary's appointment was at 9:30 and mine was 9:45. As we pulled up into the parking lot behind the house (and yes, it is a house), we saw Eddie and his Mom just leaving. His red hair that used to look kind of like a bowl cut that hung down over his ears was gone and Eddie didn't look like Eddie anymore. Nerdy Eddie with the bowl cut was now super-slick, cool-looking Eddie. His hair was short on the sides with the top longer and brushed toward the front in a ragged sort of way. He was wearing a black leather jacket that he must have gotten for Christmas and the whole thing made him look like a flashy boy band person.

Eddie waved as we drove by.

"Dang, Eddie looks good." Gary commented, staring out the window and waving back at Eddie.

"Wonder if we'll look as good."

Dad laughed. Listen carefully. Now when the stylist asks you what you want, tell that person something fantastic, because the less you try to tell them, the better you'll look,"

"Dad, how do you know?"

"Ask your mother when we get home."

Dad was chuckling as he pulled into a parking spot at the edge of a wooded area farthest from the house. As we started to get out of the

Jeep, a man standing near the front of the salon yelled at us to get back in the car.

"Bear!!"

"Boys, get in the car now!!"

We all got back in and locked the doors. Don't know why we did that because I'm not sure a bear would know how to open a car door.

About 10 feet from the car, a black bear lumbered out and toward the car. It came right up to the window and stared in. Gary was the closest and wasn't just staring back; he was using his phone to take pictures.

Just then, a shot rang out and the bear made a kind of roaring sound and crumpled to the ground. We were all horrified, until the man carrying what looked like a gun walked up to the bear and pulled a tranquilizer dart out from his shoulder. What a relief. None of us wanted any harm to come to the bear, just because he got near our car.

Another man came up carrying a stretcher and the two men loaded the bear onto it and stuck it in the back of a van. We later found out that they took him up a few miles higher in the mountain and dropped him off. I guess this has happened before and the guards here always tranquilize the bear and cart him away. Once they got the bear into the van, the man with the tranquilizer gun turned to us and gave us a thumbs up.

Cool, we got out of the Jeep and headed into the salon.

— ••• —

I don't know what I was expecting. I thought salons were for girls really, but when we walked through the front door, there were a bunch of guys waiting to get their hair cut. Some of them we recognized from school, but others were older.

There was an oldish lady sitting at the reception desk. She looked like she was as old as Mrs. Skriver, but I wasn't sure. She had bluish hair. I'd seen other older ladies with hair like that. I never figured out why they wanted blue, but a lot of them seemed to like it.

"Hello gentlemen, Keith. Do you have appointments?" The lady at the desk addressed Dad by name and I wondered how she knew him.

Dad spoke up. "Good morning, Martha. The boys have appointments at 9:30 and 9:45. They need the works."

Martha, the blue-haired lady, smiled. "The works? Well, Keith, that will require two of our best stylists. Let's see. I'll assign Marco and Nora. How's Kim doing?"

"Great. Thanks for asking."

"Keith, you know where the waiting room is. There's coffee and soda and some cookies while you wait. It may take a little longer to get you in, but, as you know, the wait is worth it."

Dad thanked her and headed down the hall, with me and Gary following and then, he turned into a room facing the front of the house. I had thought the waiting room was in the front, but I guess that was just for people trying to get an appointment if there was an opening. The real waiting room was where we ended up and boy, it was something.

Floor to ceiling windows spread across the full width of the side facing a spectacular view of the mountains , plus there was a nice patio with tables that we couldn't go out to because of all the snow. There were a couple of people waiting there for appointments, but I didn't know either of them.

One of them was a super cute blonde girl. I thought maybe I had seen her before, but she was definitely not in our grade or I would have remembered. I had been staring at her when she looked up from the book she was reading and smiled. Of course, I looked away instantly, but I could feel my face doing the beet red thing.

Gary was standing by the window staring out at the mountains. He turned just in time to see me turn red again because of some girl. He started to chuckle and just when I was about to punch him, a really tall man walked into the room and said his name.

"Gary?"

"I'm Gary."

"Nice to meet you. I'm Marco. You ready?"

Gary nodded.

"So, follow me and let's get started."

Marco turned and walked down a side hall. I gave Gary a thumbs up and as he left the room, I wondered what he would look like when his haircut was done.

I walked over to the window to keep myself from looking at the blonde girl. Snow was lightly falling, but not so heavy that you couldn't see the town below. It seemed really peaceful. As I stood there staring out at the mountains, I heard my name.

"David?"

Turning, I saw a woman standing in the doorway. She had pink and purple hair that seemed like it was all over the place and her clothes looked very old and ragged…OMG, she kind of looked like a homeless person. If this was the style lady that was going to do wonderful stuff to my hair…well, I was a little worried. No, I was real worried.

"David?"

"I'm David."

"I'm Norah. Nice to meet you. Follow me, sir. It looks like we've got a lot of work to do."

She turned and headed down the hall and I followed even though I wasn't sure I should.

Her area was next to the place Gary went with Marco. There were no windows, but she had strung sparkling Christmas type lights all over the walls and across the ceiling. There was a counter with scissors and other hair stuff plus a mirror mounted over the counter. At first I thought I would be able to watch what she was doing but when I got into her styling chair, she turned it away from the mirror. Dang!

"So, David, what did you have in mind?"

"I, I'm really not sure. My Dad said you would just do it."

Norah laughed. "Keith would say that. You know, he used to be my best customer."

I was surprised. "You did my Dad's hair?"

"Oh yes! Your Dad used to come up regularly. That was when he was dating your Mom, Kim."

"Wow. That was a long time ago. How long have you been doing this stuff? I mean, doing hair."

"I started right after high school. Your Dad...he was one of my first regulars."

"Wow!"

"So, let's get busy David. Do you trust me?"

"I don't know. I guess so."

"Good enough."

She put one of those bib thingys around me, sprayed my head with water, then took a comb and ran it through my hair. That was all ok because I had washed it before coming up here.

Then, she started. I wasn't sure what she was doing, but I could see my hair being snipped off in little chunks. She was working quickly and once she got everything the way she wanted with the scissors, she took a razor and did some shaving on the edges of my head. Then, she took a dryer and blew it dry, using her hands to do whatever to make it look cool. When she was done, she took a tiny little bit of this stuff called hair wax and rubbed it all over my head. She worked on it for a few minutes, then took the scissors and cut a couple places that still didn't seem right to her and when she was satisfied, she stepped back and took a look.

"Well, David, ready to see what I've done?"

I nodded and she swung the chair around so I was facing the mirror. OMG!!! What I saw wasn't me. My hair was cut short on the sides and the top was ragged and kind of stood up all over, plus the front kind of came forward in kind of a windblown way you might see on some movie star or model. Wow. I looked like a movie star!

"David? What do you think?"

"Dang, Norah, I look good. Wow! What do you think?"

"Oh, I like everything I do and so will your girlfriend.

"Actually, I don't have one yet."

Norah laughed. "Well, that won't last long."

"You think?"

"Honey, I am the best at what I do and now, my dear, you are the King. Whoever that girl is you might like…well, I don't think she could resist you now."

"Really?"

"You're just going to have to find out for yourself, David. Now, let me get you out to your Dad."

Norah removed the bib thingy and brushed the hair pieces off around my neck. I put my glasses back on and stared at the mirror. Even with them on, I didn't look bad. Still, I decided to leave them off because I looked really cool glasses free.

As I walked back in the waiting room I saw Gary standing next to Dad. He turned and I could see surprise on his face. He smiled.

"OMG, Davey, you look great!"

"Thanks. Without my glasses on, everything is kind of fuzzy, but I look a lot better without them."

Just then I realized that Gary looked different too. Well, not as different as me. Gary didn't need as much change because he was really cool looking already. His hair didn't stand up like mine. It was short on the sides like mine, but the top kind of laid toward the front. I mean, it wasn't flat. I'd seen a picture of Brad Pitt when he was younger and Gary's hair looked a lot like his. It was similar to Eddie's style, but it definitely looked different enough that they wouldn't look like twins.

"You look good, too. I'm sorry I didn't say anything right away. I guess I was liking how I looked so much I didn't even think about it. But Gary, bro, you always look good."

Dad had been talking to Norah and I heard him laugh and then give the lady a hug. She turned and waved at me, then walked back to her room. Dad turned to us.

"Gentlemen, are you ready to go?"

Gary and I both nodded yes and we all started heading back to the front. Just as we were leaving I felt a tap on my shoulder and when I turned, I was surprised to see it was that cute blonde girl.

"You're a friend of Eddie's, right?"

I nodded and she smiled.

"Well, you're probably going to his party, so I'll see you there, won't I?"

"How do you know Eddie?"

"My Dad uses Eddie's Dad's limo service quite a bit. I've been to Eddie's house a few times and once, I saw you and your brother there. That's why I was thinking you might be going to their party. I've been invited, too. Well, my parents got invited and I was included. So, are you going?"

Gary had been listening and he wrapped an arm around my shoulder and smiling answered her.

"Yup, my brother and I are going. Why do you ask?"

She smiled again. "So, I go to a different school and don't know anybody that's going to be there, except Eddie and, well, since I've seen you there and now here, I kind of know you, too. I figured I could hang out with you guys at the party if that's ok?"

I could just feel what Gary was thinking and before I could say anything, he answered for us.

"Sure you can. Me and my girlfriend and Davey would just love to have you hang with us."

I could feel my face going red again because he had made it seem like it was going to be him and his girl and me and whoever she was… like a couple. I mean, I was hoping that Lori would be there without that kid. Now, she would see me with this girl and assume the worst…well, assume I wasn't interested in her. I mean, not that she ever thought I was interested in her in the first place…I mean…DANG!

"Guys, can we get going?" Dad interrupted my crazy chain of thought. "Nice to meet you, young lady and I'm sorry, I didn't hear your name?"

"It's Ronnie, sir."

"Well, Ronnie, the boys will see you at the party. We have to get going now."

Gary spoke up before I could even say anything.

"Davey and I are looking forward to seeing you at the party tonight. Bye for now."

My red face nodded at her as we walked out.

After we got into the car and started down the mountain, Dad asked what we thought. Of course, we both said great, cool, the best, and a lot of other words.

"That's good. Glad you both liked your stylists."

I decided to mention what Norah said.

"So, my stylist said she used to do your hair, Dad. Is that true?"

Dad chuckled. "You bet. I attribute Norah's fantastic redo as the main reason your mom and I got together in the first place."

"Really?"

Dad laughed. "Well, maybe it wasn't the only reason, but I thought you'd enjoy the story, since now you guys look better than I've ever seen you look. And, if you don't have girlfriends now….well, that won't last long."

"OMG, DAD, don't. You guys…I'm not interested in girls except as friends!"

Gary couldn't hold it in and started roaring with laughter.

Unfortunately, I was in the front seat or he would have gotten punched hard. All I could do was tell him to shut up and of course, that made him laugh harder.

—•••—

It took us a little longer to get home because it had started snowing harder and the roads were a bit slick. As we pulled into the driveway, we saw Mom and Anna out in the front with Boomer, who was happily rolling around in the snow. I still didn't have my glasses on, but I could see well enough, although everything was kind of fuzzy.

As soon as Gary and I started getting out of the car, both Moms started squealing. I really don't understand why girls squeal about stuff, but now I know that Moms do it too. They were smiling like crazy and Mom had her hands crossed across her mouth. Both of them walked up to us and ooed and aah'd, saying how great we looked. Heck, we knew how great we looked. I mean, even Eddie had looked super when we saw him leave the salon.

It was middle of the afternoon and we weren't going to Eddie's until about 7. Dad has asked us to take care of the walks and driveway. I didn't want to put a hat on because I didn't want to mess up my hair, so I let my ears get cold. I mean, I wanted Lori to see me and be awed with how I looked. Well, maybe that's a total exaggeration…yah…over the top. No really, I just wanted her to notice me as more than a friend. I wonder if that would be possible. She likes that kid. I mean, he is nice. Still…

— ••• —

That afternoon Eddie called and asked if we wanted to go to the party in a limo. It was just for us kids he said and when we asked, the parents said sure. I had decided not to wear my glasses, but I took them along just in case we ended up watching a movie or something on their big screen. I could see just fine. It was just a little fuzzy, that's all.

At about 6, the limo rolled up in front of our house. It was one of the really long ones that would hold a bunch of us kids. We were waiting inside by the door and watched as Eddie got out and came to get us. He was looking really good, too, with his neat hair cut and nifty leather jacket. Me and Gary were wearing the bombers and dang, we looked great, hot even. I'm glad Mom can't read my thoughts because she would have something to say about me thinking that.

We told the parents we were leaving and headed to the limo. There were some kids in there already. There was JJ and her brother, Scott and Steve, Jane, the new girl, Lori, and, unfortunately, her boyfriend.

I haven't talked about JJ and her brother yet, have I? Well, JJ is Jasmine Jones and her brother is Jake Jones. The parents are John and

Janece. I guess they thought it would be fun if everyone in their family had a J name.

Anyway, JJ and Jake are only two of a handful of black kids who go to our school. Once in our history class the teacher mentioned JJ was African American and he asked her where she came from. JJ said Cleveland and when the teacher said he meant where in Africa her family was from, she said her family was from England and had lived there for over a hundred years and how far back did he want her to go? JJ knew what he meant. Later, she told a bunch of kids that she didn't think it was right that a teacher would ask where she was from and not ask the same thing to everybody else.

JJ is really smart and really cute and up to a few months ago, a lot taller than me and the other kids my age. Her brother Jake is in the 9th grade and is almost 6 feet tall already. The high school is waiting anxiously for Jake to get there because they think he'll be perfect for basketball, but Jake is more interested in computers than sports. His Dad is a computer analyst of some kind and he wants to be like his dad.

When we got in the limo everybody noticed how we looked and there was a bunch of lookin' good and you guys are rock stars kind of comments. Even being with her boyfriend didn't stop Lori from commenting.

"God, you guys look fantastic. Where'd you go? Up the Hill?"

Gary answered that we had and Lori laughed.

"I think those guys up there do actual magic. You guys all rock!"

I guess I hadn't noticed, but when she said that, I looked over and saw that both the brothers must have been there as well because they looked pretty darn good, too. Well, not as good as me and Gary, but pretty darn good anyway.

I hadn't thought about the demon for a while, but when Lori mentioned magic, I was thinking there must be some hocus pocus going on. I mean…her Mom and now the place we got our hair fixed or styled or whatever you call it for boys. And, if you recall, that place is called Moxie Magic. What do you think?

Anyway, Eddie said we weren't going to the party right away, because we were first going to stop for Pizza at The Mad Italian. It was his parent's treat. We love that place because the pizza is really good and they have an arcade right next door, so a lot of the kids from our school and the high school hang out around there.

There were quite a few kids and parents standing around the front of the restaurant when the limo pulled up and we all got out. We knew some of them who were there and at first, I think they thought we were some famous movie stars or musicians because they just stared and smiled at us. That only lasted a few seconds because someone recognized Eddie. Then they saw Gary and me and a couple of the girls giggled and started whispering to each other as they stared at us. Of course, I wondered what they were saying.

One of them, a girl name Marsha somebody, walked right up to Gary and whispered something in his ear. He shook his head no and I heard him say "thanks for asking." Turning to the restaurant door, I saw Eddie open it and motion to all of us to follow him in.

"We've got a reservation," he said.

I was kind of surprised because it was almost impossible to get reservations for this place, but later, Eddie told us his Dad and the owner were really good friends. So, when Eddie had asked about getting pizza somewhere, his Dad called Lou Pavia, to make sure we got tables. Lou was coming to the party as well, so we were able to thank him when we saw him later.

The place was really crowded and I saw a lot of kids from our school. The hostess lady led us to a side room where a big table was set up. Eddie said something to her and she nodded, then walked back toward the kitchen.

"The food is already ordered," he said.

Just then, she brought two more kids into where we were sitting. One of them was Ronnie, the cute blonde girl we met at Moxie. The other was a 9th grader, like Lori's boyfriend.

"Guys, meet Ronnie from Longfellow Middle School and most of you know Deacon already."

I was sitting between Steve and Gary, but when Ronnie went to sit down, Gary moved over one and told her to sit next to me.

"Hi David," she said. "You and your brother look great. That place is the best, don't you think?"

I nodded yes and for whatever reason, could feel my face turning red. What, exactly, is the matter with me? Why do girls make me so nervous?

"Gary isn't my brother. He's my best friend and he and his mom live with us."

"Cool," she said, "so, are you with anybody tonight?"

More face redness…

"No."

"Great! We can hang out then, ok?"

"Sure, I guess." She was really cute, but she wasn't Lori, but Lori was already busy with her 9th grader. I mean, maybe if Lori saw me with another girl…maybe she would dump that guy. Hah! What a plan! I was going to hang with Ronnie and make Lori jealous.

— ••• —

I told you before about Eddie's parents and that his dad had a limo service and his mom was an event planner. What I didn't tell you was that they lived at the edge of our town, near the foothills, on a bunch of land. It's kind of near where our bus driver, Mr. Grossman lives. He has a lot of land, too, but I don't think he has as much as Eddie's parents.

Anyway, his mom pretty much works at home because they have an event building right on their property. It's not huge but Eddie says they had nearly 400 people there before. That's where the New Years bash is going to take place, at least for all the parents. The kids are going to be in Eddie's house in their family room. It's pretty big, too. It's not as big as the event building, but I think Eddie can get at least 50 kids in there with no problem. They have a live-in housekeeper and she volunteered to keep an eye on the kids while all the parents were partying in the event building. Why do they think bad stuff could happen with us kids?

Parents...I don't think they realize we're not bad. I know you're remembering the demon stuff. That...well, I didn't want to hurt anybody. I just wanted the bullying to stop...and dang, it did. Now I'm wondering if the demon had something to do with that as well. Probably not...but you never know.

From what I've been telling you, you also probably think that Eddie's family is rich. You know, maybe they are, but you'd never know it from talking to Eddie or his parents. They're some of the nicest people I've ever met. They treat everybody with respect, no matter how much money they have. I just don't understand why money makes such a big difference in how people treat each other. That will never happen with me. I won't let it.

— ••• —

There were kids that had already gotten to the party before the bunch of us in the limo got there. I didn't know a lot of them, because they went to other schools. Most were my age or older. More food. Loads of little sandwiches, chips and dip, cookies and cake and, of course, soda. I mean, the pizza was great, but snacks like this...well, you just gotta eat it!

Mary Ellen, the housekeeper took all our coats so they weren't just laying around anywhere. I was glad, because I didn't want that cool bomber jacket ruined by some kid spilling on it.

A tap on my shoulder got my attention away from the goodies. It was Eddie.

"Davey, we're. gonna do some dancing, so you'll ask someone, right?"

"C'mon, Eddie, who wants to dance with me?"

Eddie laughed. "Have you looked in the mirror lately? You are totally cool! Every girl in here is gonna want to dance with you."

"Every girl?"

"Yah, pal. Wow, you are interested in somebody aren't you? Who is it? You can tell me and you know, I won't say a word to anybody. Does Gary know?"

I had to lie because Eddie couldn't keep a secret. He always ended up telling his sister and she was a blabbermouth. No way I was telling him anything!

"Nobody, Eddie. Why would you think that?"

"C'mon, Davey, like I said before, you need to look in the mirror. You've grown a foot and lost a ton of weight and God, that hair thing Moxie did…well, pretty much all the girls will think you are totally hot!"

"No hotter than you, Eddie."

Eddie laughed. "Ok, maybe, but I'm still short. You're a lot taller than me now. Girls like tall guys better."

"I hadn't thought about that. You sure?" I was actually interested because Lori's 9th grader had been a lot taller than me. Wow, maybe Lori would be more interested because I was just about his height now.

"Of course, I'm sure. My cousin has a degree and she told me."

"A degree in what?"

"Restaurant Management."

"Geez, Eddie, Restaurant Management? How would she know anything about tall kids and what girls like?"

"Davey, you gotta understand people to get a degree in Restaurant Management. She knows."

Eddie is one of my best friends, but some of the stuff he says… GEEEEZ. Still, it sounded right. Actually, I wanted him to be right. Gary was taller and girls liked him better than me. Well, now that I was about as tall as Gary, maybe that would change.

— •••—

By 9:30, the party was starting to get fun. More kids had arrived, including a few high school kids. When they saw that we were mostly 7th thru 9th, they took off, either going to the parent's party or leaving entirely. The music had been turned up and it was great—a super cool mix of slow and fast stuff. A DJ friend of Eddie's mom had recorded over 4 hours of it for us kids to listen to and of course, for dancing.

Eddie was over talking to Jane, the mean girl. She didn't seem too interested, but Eddie is one of those kids who never gives up and finally, she got up and walked to the dance floor with him. Gary was already dancing with Debbie, so I started back toward the food. There was a tug on my arm and I figured Ronnie had finally come over, but when I turned, I was surprised to see it was JJ.

"Hey Davey, wanna dance?"

"Gee, JJ, I'm not too good."

"Oh, for heavens sakes, just look over there. All you have to do is wiggle and bounce back and forth. I mean, I can show you, so come on!"

"Ok, if you really don't think I'll be bad."

"No worse than any of the other kids." She laughed. "Come on." She grabbed my hand and led me into the middle of the group.

She was right, especially because all I had to do was wiggle a little and sway back and forth. So, pretty cool. I was enjoying myself and then, the song changed to a slow one. I mean, I'm pretty bad at the wiggling and weaving, but I'm even worse at the slow stuff. We had dancing in one of our gym classes and the girl I had to dance with complained to the teacher that I was constantly stepping on her feet every time I moved mine. I ended up having to sit and watch everybody else. Pretty embarrassing.

"Thanks, JJ. I had fun." I turned to walk away and she grabbed my arm.

"No way, Davey, we're not done dancing. Here, put your arms around me." As she said that, she reached up and put her arms around my neck.

"JJ. I'm horrible at dancing. I'll just step on your feet and I could hurt you."

"Oh, come on. You just have to move your feet a little and weave like before, but slower."

JJ is smart, one of the smartest kids at our school and she's really popular, and, I was pretty sure that she had a boyfriend and that he was here at the party. So, why was she wanting to dance with me? We were friends so I decided to ask.

"JJ, what's going on? Don't you want to dance with Andy. He is your boyfriend, right?"

"Nope, I want to dance with you."

"C'mon, JJ, you and me are friends. What's going on?"

"I broke up with Andy," she whispered.

"Why?"

"He wanted me to bleach my hair blond. My mom would have killed me and more important, why would I want to? I like how I look."

"Dang, JJ, what's with Andy? I mean, why would he want you to do that? You're...well...you're really pretty the way you are."

JJ, who had been frowning as she told me about what Andy wanted, now had a big grin on her face.

"Gee, Davey, you really think so?"

"Sure, plus why would he even want you to be blond? You're... You're..."

OMG...before the sentence came completely out of my mouth, my miniscule brain kicked in and I stopped talking.

JJ stared at me and being the direct kind of girl she was, she finished my sentence.

"Black? You're saying I wouldn't want to be blond because I'm black?"

My face went bright red. "Well, no, that's not what I really meant."

"Well, what did you "really" mean?"

I was burning I was so embarrassed.

"Dang, JJ, you and I have been friends since the 2nd grade. I wasn't trying to say anything about black. You're just pretty, that's all, the way you are now. Why change a good thing?"

JJ burst into uncontrolled laughter. When the laughter turned to a snicker, she leaned over and hugged me.

"Davey, you are a really nice guy. I'm sorry I did that. I knew exactly what you were trying to say."

"Then why would you do it? I was feeling awful."

JJ frowned again. "I get a lot of uninformed "black" comments, like my teacher asking where I was from in Africa and how long does it take to style my "Afro". C'mon, ask me about my hair or where I'm from. Don't make it a black or white thing.

"I wasn't trying to do that, JJ. You know I wasn't, don't you?"

She smiled. "Davey, you are one of the nicest guys I've ever met. I know your family's the same, because you wouldn't be you without them being them. You know, your mom and my mom are friends."

I did know. JJ's mom was big on making things better in the community. She was always doing food drives and helping the homeless. It was obvious that my mom and hers would be friends.

I was just about to comment when Andy interrupted our conversation.

"Davey, sorry about this, but I need to talk to JJ."

"Sure, Andy." I started to walk away, but JJ grabbed my arm. "Davey and I aren't done dancing. Find someone else and try to bleach her hair."

Andy shook his head and frowned. "C'mon, JJ, can't you take a joke? I'm sorry...I am totally sorry. I didn't know you would get that upset."

"Then why did you even suggest it?"

"I don't know. I screwed up. Gonna forgive me or not?"

"No."

"Please?" Andy made a really sad face and JJ laughed.

"Don't ever try and make me a blond again, promise?"

"I promise. Now, can we dance? You don't mind, do you, Davey?"

"Nope, Andy, go for it."

Andy put his hand out and JJ took it and smiled as he led her back to where they were dancing. I started back toward the food and was just about to grab a sandwich when Ronnie came up next to me.

"Hey Davey, glad you guys are here. Are you going to ask me to dance?"

"I'm not a particularly good dancer, Ronnie."

"Well, you looked pretty good dancing with that girl."

"JJ. Her name is JJ."

"Ok, you looked pretty good dancing with JJ. So, c'mon, let's boogie!"

Boogie? That was something mom always said. Before I could say a word, Ronnie was dragging me back to the dance floor. I guess that was ok because she was really cute…well, no comparison to Lori…still really cute. I guess I was having a good time. Yup, I was.

— ••• —

I spose you're wondering what happened the rest of the evening. Well, when Ronnie made me dance, it was already after 11. I spose you're thinking I might have gotten kissed at midnight. Sorry, but it just didn't happen. After dancing for a while, this kid I didn't know cut in and she spent the rest of the night with him. I'm pretty sure he was older, maybe 14…not sure.

Anyway, right before midnight, a bunch of parents came over, probably to make sure there was no hanky panky going on. There wasn't… much. A couple of kids would probably have kissed, but with parents around..well, nobody wanted to get in trouble.

After we all watched the ball drop, Eddie's mom, who was one of the people that came over, told us to all go over to the event building. When we did, we found Eddie's parents had set up a buffet of breakfast stuff. That was cool.

After a lot of the people had eaten, they left, including my mom and dad and Gary's mom. I'm sure they left because they had promised to make sure Rascal and the kitties were ok because Gary and me were staying over. I have to say...we really have great parents.

Anyway, Eddie told us to get food and bring it back to the house because we were going to watch a movie. He didn't say what movie, but I knew it would be good. It was the newest Jurassic movie and we hadn't seen it. It was great.

When the movie was over, it was morning. Eddie said if we wanted to sleep a while before going home we could, but Gary and me said no. So, around 7, after eating more good stuff Eddie and his dad took us home. No, not in a limo; in their car.

We thanked them a lot for the good time and headed into the house, only to be met with a happy bouncing Rascall. Mom was there and told us he needed to go out. It was cool. We were tired but awake enough to take care of the puppy.

Snow was starting to fall again as we headed down toward where we had seen Jane moving in. Gary was pretty quiet as we walked and that seemed to me a little strange. I decided to find out.

"Gary, you're being pretty quiet. How come?"

"Debbie wants to go steady."

"What? You mean steady steady? Like boyfriend and girlfriend steady?"

"Yup."

"What did you tell her?"

"I didn't know what to tell her. I mean, she's kind of the only girl I've ever been interested in."

"Yah, but what did you say? You had to have said something."

"I told her I'd think about it. When I said that, she seemed hurt and got pretty quiet."

"And?"

"And then her parents came over and they all left."

"Geez, Gary, what are you going to do?"

"Don't know."

"If you tell her yes, what does that mean?"

Gary signed. "I guess she would expect that I would have lunch with her and hang out on weekends with her and do our homework together, and…and…I don't know what else. God, Davey, I don't think I'm ready to go steady."

"Then just say no."

"I spose. I guess that's the smartest thing to do, but I like her, Davey. I still want to hang out with her.

"Then figure out something to tell her."

"What?"

"I don't know."

Gary sighed again. "I'm too tired to think about it. Ask me again after I get some sleep."

I knew what he was saying because I was awful tired, too. We finished walking Rascal and because it was snowing pretty hard now, we figured we would be asked to shovel before we relaxed. Well, when we got home, we found the walks had already been cleared. I know Dad did it because he knew me and Gary would be pretty tired. I gotta say… BEST DAD EVER!!

As soon as we got in, we headed to our rooms to get a little sleep.

That was it. I didn't wake up until late afternoon.

— ••• —

January 5

I have to say, New Years was pretty cool, but now it was January and the next big event coming up was Gary's birthday at the end of the month. I had talked to Dad about what we could do to make it special. After all, Gary hadn't had much at all for birthdays for the last couple years.

Dad suggested we go skiing. He loves to ski so the suggestion was kind of for him too. Mom liked to ski, but not as much as Dad. When we talked to her and Anna about maybe taking Gary skiing, they both said great and that they would stay home and plan a little party for the day we got home.

This was all super. Dad would take care of the trip and Mom and Anna would plan everything else. Done! I didn't have to worry about it anymore.

There was a lot of stuff going on in school and the announcement was made in assembly that we would all be taking sex education at the end of February. After the groaning and booing ended, they also announced that we would have a Sadie Hawkins dance for Valentine's Day. Since most of us didn't know what that was, they did explain that the girls would be inviting us guys.

Ok, cool, another thing I didn't have to worry about…you know, having to try and ask a girl to a dance, but I also figured nobody would probably ask me, either. Did I want to go with someone other than Lori? No, I did not. She was going to ask that kid, so did I care if nobody asked me? No. Well, sometimes things don't go the way you think they will.

— • • • —

Everything was set. Dad, me, and Gary would head up to Aspen after school on Friday, spend the night, ski all day Saturday and come home Sunday morning. Then we would have a party for Gary's birthday, which was actually on Sunday. Since Monday was some sort of teacher day at our school, it was closed, making a party for Gary perfect. A few of our friends were coming—Eddie, Lori and her boyfriend, Jane the mean girl, the Cooper boys and of course, Gary's girlfriend, Debbie. Andy, JJ and her brother were invited too, but they weren't coming because their family was going over to Grand Junction to visit a friend of her mom's. Andy could have come by himself, but he didn't want to without JJ.

Dad was going to do a winter barbeque. I always loved those because, for whatever reason, they always smell so good, better than summer cookouts. I knew everybody was going to have a great time.

So anyway, about a week before our ski trip, I was at my locker getting a book for the next class, when "these two girls came up to me.

"Hi David," a kind of tall girl with brown hair and a ponytail greeted me.

"It's just Davey to my friends. I don't know you, do I?"

Both girls laughed.

"Sure, you do. Don't you remember gym class? You and me were dancing?"

OMG…it was the girl whose feet I stepped on.

"Sure, I remember now. You asked the gym teacher to bench me because I was dancing so bad. Yup, I remember you now."

She smiled. "Sorry about that. I just didn't want to get stepped on by some creepy nerd."

"I don't know your name, do I?

"It's Beth."

"Well, Beth, this creepy nerd has to go to class, so ta-ta"

With that, I walked away, leaving them to stare after me, but still I wondered what they must have wanted.

It was the last period and when I met Gary at the door to go home, I told him what had happened and how I had wondered what they wanted.

He laughed. "Have you looked at yourself lately? You look quite a bit different than you did when you had that dance class."

"It hasn't been that long, Gary. Ok, I did grow a bit and lose a little weight and yes, I've got a different hair look and I'm trying not to wear my glasses and…and…oh."

Gary was right. I did look different.

"Girls like you, Davey."

"Not all girls."

"Still hung up on Lori?"

"She's still hanging out with that 9th grader."

Gary snickered. "We all know that, but you still didn't answer my question…you still like Lori, don't you?"

I sighed and nodded that I did.

"Get over it, Davey. Things could change in the future, but right now…nope. Plus, I bet one of those girls that came up to talk to you wanted to ask you to the Valentine's dance."

"You think so?"

"What other reason would they just come up and start talking to you?"

"I don't know."

"So, Debbie has already asked me to the dance."

"Hmm…what about that going steady stuff? Did you take care of that?"

"Yup, used Mom as an excuse. Told her that Mom might get upset if I went steady with somebody and because she'd gone through a lot, I didn't want to take the chance that would happen."

"Well, that's pretty close to true, I guess."

Gary smiled. "It is true. Honestly, Davey, like I told you before, I'm just not ready to go steady. I mean, I'm only 12."

"13 in a few days."

"You're right. Wow, I'm getting old."

We both laughed and headed out to the bus. When we got on, of course I looked for Lori, but she wasn't there. We headed back to where we usually sit, only to find a bunch of girls in our place. They were staring at us and whispering. Gary stopped at the first empty bench.

"Let's sit here," he said sliding over to the window seat.

I sat down next to him and turned back to look at the girls. When they saw me do that they giggled. Of course, my face did the red thing.

Gary looked back.

"Who are they? I don't recognize any of them," he whispered.

"Probably the bus driver knows. We can ask him when we get off the bus. Wish Mr. Grossman would get back. He would definitely know."

Gary nodded. For the rest of the ride, we were quiet and didn't turn to look at them at all. The bus always went thru town on the way to dropping all the kids off near their streets, but today, the driver stopped and let all 4 of the girls off near the rec center at the edge of downtown. As the girls passed us, one of them leaned over and whispered in my ear.

"Dana likes you."

She laughed and they all headed out the door.

I was turning red when Gary asked, "What did she say, Davey?"

"She said Dana likes me. I don't know any Dana, do you?"

"No."

"Ok, tomorrow, let's find out if any of our friends know a Dana.

Well, no one actually seeme to know, so the next day, when we got off the bus at school, we stopped to ask the driver.

Gary was direct, "Mrs. Granger, there were some girls sitting where we usually sit at the back of the bus. We didn't know them. Do you know who they were?"

Mrs. Granger, a nice lady who substituted for drivers who were out, nodded. "There's a little overcrowding at Meyers Middle school, so 100 or so kids in your grade thru 9th are transferring here. I believe the girls you mentioned were here yesterday because they missed the orientation that was being held for those kids. I think they sat in on a couple of classes and got their books."

I was curious. "You mean, those girls are all coming here? Are they always going to ride our bus?"

"No, I don't think so. One of them might. I was just asked to let them off near the rec center so their parents could get them after some gymnastics thing or maybe something else...I just don't remember."

"Oh."

Mrs. Granger smiled. "What about those girls? Why do you want to know?"

I could feel my face turning red. "No big reason. They were just sitting where we usually sit. We had to sit somewhere else."

"Oh, I see. Well, they won't be here tomorrow. One of them might."

"Which one?"

"I don't know. I guess we'll find out when she gets on the bus."

Yes, we were going to find out and then, maybe, I would see who Dana was.

— ••• —

That day, after school, when we got on the bus, there were no new girls at all. All the kids that had been transferred were coming in a few days. I guess that was ok, although I wanted to find out who that girl was, that Dana. Lori wasn't on the bus either.

No biggie, because we had other things to plan and do— tonight, we were telling Gary about the trip to Aspen for his birthday. It was great!

When we got home, we saw an unfamiliar car parked in front of our house. Coming inside, we could hear a man talking and saw Mom and Anna sitting with him. Rascal had been put in his crate cage and I could see that there was another stranger sitting there as well.

Mom saw us come in and got up to talk to us.

"You need to take Rascal out on his walk and try not to disturb us while we have company."

"Who are those people?" Gary asked, staring in at his Mom, who was sitting in the recliner with one of the kitties on her lap.

"I'll explain later. Now, get Rascal…quietly."

We got the puppy and headed out for a walk. When we returned, the car was gone and the Moms were in the kitchen getting coffee and cooking something that smelled pretty good.

Of course, I asked immediately.

"So, who were those guys, Mom?"

"Private detectives."

"Private detectives? What for?"

Mom smiled. "I'll let Anna explain."

Gary and I stared at her, waiting anxiously.

"Well, as you know," she slowly spoke, picking the right words to say, "my husband left us several years ago. It's time I make the separation permanent and get a divorce. The problem is, we have no idea where he is. The men you saw talking to us, they're private detectives. They are going to locate him so I can serve him papers and get the divorce proceeding started. Ok?"

I didn't say anything, but Gary nodded his head. "It's all good Mom. It's about time."

"I'll give you more details when we have them. Also, there's something else, I need to tell you," Anna continued, "I've started seeing someone recently."

Gary looked surprised but managed a "good to hear" acknowledgment. I wasn't sure how he really felt because he didn't even ask who it was or anything. Later, he told me he was concerned because he didn't want his Mom to get hurt again, like his Dad had hurt her. Still, he wasn't going to say anything negative because she had been through so much bad stuff. He was not going to make it worse telling her it wasn't a good idea. Well, when we found out who it was, everything was cool.

With that and without asking any more questions, we let them know we would be in our rooms if they needed us and left the kitchen. I'm sure Gary's Mom wondered why we hadn't asked about who she was seeing.

— ••• —

At dinner, we surprised Gary with the ski trip for his birthday. We were telling him early so he could be ready right after school on Friday. He seemed pretty excited. Dad had scheduled ski lessons for him on Saturday morning. I didn't need them because I had been skiing for a few years already. I wasn't great, but I sure could get down a hill pretty fast.

We didn't tell him about the party we were having for him Sunday night. The whole weekend was going to be super terrific!

On Friday, after school, as we got home, we saw Dad packing up the Jeep with out stuff. He and I both had skis and we had rented Gary all the equipment he would need. Our stuff was tucked away in the back and all the ski gear was on the rack on top of the car.

We thought we were going to be walking Rascal, but it had all been taken care of, so we dropped our school stuff off, said goodbye to the Mom's and headed out to our fun weekend.

— ••• —

And, it was fun. Gary was a natural and after the couple hours of lessons, he was up on the hill going down like a pro. I was on the same slope with Gary, but Dad always did harder runs. Someday, when I get better I will, too.

We skied for hours and then Dad took us to this really cool restaurant that served breakfast all day and night. Well, Dad got steak, like usual, but Gary and me got some breakfast stuff. When we got done, we headed back to the condo that Dad had rented for the night. There was a fireplace and we had cocoa and sat in front of a fire while Dad told us stories about his time in the military.

186 - Demon for Rent

I tell you…it can't get much better than that.

— ••• —

We left early Sunday and got home before noon. The Moms were in the kitchen baking and Rascal was in the kitchen with them, waiting for some sort of treat or anything that might get dropped on the floor that he could eat. The kitties were there, too, probably also waiting for something to eat. One was up on the counter and the other sat right next to our big puppy. I always figured that the kitties thought Rascal was a kitty, too…a big one, but still a kitty.

When the Moms saw us come in, there was a lot of Happy Birthdays and hugs for Gary. He liked it, I could tell. Then Mom said that dinner would be about 5 and there would be some special presents. Everything sounded perfect. No, everything was perfect.

— ••• —

At a little before 4:30 there was a knock on the door. Mom said for us to answer it and when Gary opened the door he was surprised to see Eddie and the Cooper boys, with presents! A few minutes later Lori and her boyfriend got to our house. Then Debbie showed up with Jane and I figured that was it. But there was another knock on the door. When Gary opened it, he saw it was Mr. Grossman and the Sergeant. The Sergeant was carrying a present, too and when we let them in, he handed it to Gary.

"Hope you like it," he said.

Gary thanked him and said he was sure he would. He put it with the other gifts the kids brought and Mon had told him he would have to wait until after dinner to open them.

I wasn't exactly sure why they had been invited to Gary's birthday bash, but then, I figured that Dad had wanted some older guys to talk to. Well, I found out later that wasn't the only reason.

Dad was a great barbeque person. He liked doing it. For the birthday, there was steak and ribs and chicken and burgers. The Moms had set up stuff in our dining room and had done a lot of cooking to go along with what Dad was making. Gary's favorite was macaroni salad and his Mom had made it just the way he liked it, with little pieces of tomato and black olives, along with all the other usual stuff. I could see why it was his favorite. Heck, I really liked it too.

We stuffed ourselves. Eddie really loved the steak. He said his Dad didn't barbeque much and so this was a real treat. After we had finished eating, Gary got to open his presents. He got a t-shirt from Eddie with a St. Bernard on the front, Debbie gave him a book called Winning at Jeopardy, and the Cooper boys gave him a Swiss army knife. I wasn't really sure about the knife, but Gary seemed to like it. Because my parent's present was the ski trip, they didn't give him anything. His Mom gave him a Fitbit, which was neat. The last present was from Mr. Grossman and the Sarge. It was a Chess set, a nice one.

Gary thought it was really neat.

"Glad you like it," Jimmy Hughes said. Your Mom told me you used to have a set, so Ken and I decided this was the right gift."

Gary smiled and thanked everybody for the great stuff. All was good.

The adults went and sat in the living room to talk and us kids went downstairs to play games and watch tv. It was about 10 when Eddie's Dad came with a limo to take everybody home.

We were just about ready to go to our rooms when Anna called Gary to come talk to them. I went to my room, so I didn't hear the conversation until Gary knocked on my door about twenty minutes later.

"Well, guess what?" he said.

"I give up. What?"

"So, my Mom is going on a date with the Sarge."

I was surprised. "Like a date date?"

"Yup."

"Cool…wait…do you think it's cool?"

"I don't know. I like him. I just don't want her getting hurt."

"He doesn't seem like the kind of guy that would hurt somebody, like..like…

"Like my actual Dad?" Gary interjected.

"I guess."

"He wants to come over and play some chess with me."

"He's not going to take your Mom out?"

"No, dummy. He said he wanted to get to know me a little better and figured playing chess would give us a chance to talk. He's taking Mom to dinner next weekend."

"Oh."

"Oh? No other comments?"

"No, I like him, too. Remember, he's a dog person and dog people are usually pretty darn good people. Plus, Dad liked him. That says something, because Dad can judge people pretty well."

Gary signed. "Yah, you're right. He is nice. I guess her going out with him is ok. How about you ask the demon to keep an eye on my Mom and the Sarge when he takes her out?"

"Ask the demon yourself, Gary." I laughed, but Gary just smiled a little.

I could tell that Gary wasn't completely sold on the idea of his Mom dating, especially with the demon comment. Plus, there was also that detective stuff. I didn't know how Gary really felt about that, but I think it bothered him. Gary never talked much about his Dad, so I didn't know if they had been close or what. I wasn't going to ask him, at least not yet.

— ••• —

Just a side note…that weekend, the date went just fine. His Mom came home happy and told Gary all about what they had done and everything.

I think that made Gary feel a lot better. I knew everything was ok. The Sarge is cool, plus he has two great dogs.

I wondered whether he was serious about Gary's Mom. I guess that didn't matter. As long as he treated her right, all was cool.

february 6

February! 7th grade, so far, had been a totally amazing school year. I was flying high. I don't know if the demon had anything to do with it, but thanks demon, if you actually did.

But then...the first nasty thing happened—Mom and Dad and Anna signed the forms for the sex education classes the school would be holding in March. I saw those forms. There was a box you could check to let the student opt out. I don't know why they didn't. Mom said it was because it was important for us to learn everything from someone trained to talk impartially with kids the right way. Dad said, when Mom wasn't listening, that he was glad he didn't have to go into it with me. Well, it was not something Gary and me were looking forward to.

That's how the month started. Even with that setback, school was actually going pretty well. I was getting a book at my locker when a girl I had never seen before came up to me.

"Hi David, remember me?"

I had no idea and shook my head.

She laughed. "Remember when you were looking at puppies at the shelter and there was an attendant there that let you see them? Remember that she held the little puppy you were interested in? Well, that person was me."

I did remember there was some girl that was helping at the shelter, but this girl I wasn't sure looked like her. That girl wore a hat with her hair tucked up under it and she had glasses. This girl had dark hair that went down to her shoulders and she wasn't wearing glasses. I decided to ask.

"I kind of remember someone, but I don't think she looked like you."

"That's true. I keep my hair tucked up in my hat and wear glasses, because dust and stuff gets up in my contacts and hurts my eyes. I'm Dana, by the way."

Dana! So, this was the girl who was supposed to like me. Actually, she was pretty cute, not as cute as Lori, but pretty cute anyway.

"Well, nice to meet you, Dana. Listen, I gotta get to math class."

"Sure, but before you go I wanted to ask you if you would go to the Valentine's Dance with me…I mean, if you haven't been asked yet, have you?"

I was surprised, but she was cute and nobody had asked me. So…

"Sure, I guess. I mean I don't know you very well."

She laughed again. "That's great. I'm new at your school. Maybe we can have lunch together and you can get to know me."

"Sure."

She smiled and said she'd let me know when her and her parents would pick me up. Then, off she went. I was still kind of surprised about the whole thing and layed it on Gary when we went home on the bus.

"I met Dana."

"Yah?"

"Yah. She asked me to the dance."

"Did you say yes?"

"Well, I guess so."

"What does that mean? It's either yes or no."

"I said yes, but that I didn't know her very well."

"And?"

"She didn't seem to care."

"She's cute."

"Yup. You know, she was the girl that showed us Rascal"

"She was?"

"Yup."

Gary looked surprised. "Wow, I would never have known. So, what's her last name?"

"God, Gary, I don't know. I guess I just forgot to ask."

We laughed about it. Here I had a date with someone I barely knew. A date...can you believe that? I'd never even been to a movie with a girl.

We got on the bus and I saw a couple of new people. Lori was there talking to some girls and said Hi as we went to where we usually sat. The ride home was pretty uneventful, and Lori waved at us as she got off at her stop. I wondered how long she planned on having that boyfriend. I mean, next year, he would be at high school and when you're in 10th, do you really want to go with someone in middle school? No, I don't think so. Maybe that would be my chance. Yes, things might just work out with Lori.

—•••—

And then...

The worst thing in the universe happened.

The week before the dance, I was having lunch by myself. Gary had a meeting with the principal (that Jeopardy thing again) and some of the other kids we ate with were helping with decorating the gym and get everything ready for the dance. Just as I was about to get up and go to my locker, I saw Lori heading my way. She waved, so I stayed put, wondering what she wanted.

"Hey Davey," Lori greeted me as she put her backpack down on the chair and sat right across from me.

"Hey Lori, what's going on?"

She smiled. "I meant to talk to you before, but I got caught up in some charity stuff we're going to be doing at the end of the month. Anyway, Steve and his parents are going out of town for a few days and he won't be able to go to the dance. I was wondering if you'd like to go with me?"

OMG!!! Lori wanted me to go with her. I started to speak and suddenly realized I had a problem.

"I...I...I'd really like to, Lori, but I didn't know you were going to ask me, so I told someone else I would go with them. I'll go ahead and tell her I can't go with her, ok?"

Lori frowned. "NO! Not ok. You can't just say yes to someone and then turn around and cancel. It is simply not acceptable. NO, not acceptable at all."

Of course, I was turning red. I really wanted to go with her. I should have known she would say something like that. Lori is one of the nicest people you will ever meet. She would never hurt some other girl just for a date.

"Ok, I'm sorry. What are you going to do? Will you still go?"

"Sure, I figured if you were busy, I'd ask Andy, JJ's boyfriend. She's not going to be here for the dance either. She told me to ask Andy because she knew she could trust me, since we're friends and I wouldn't try to "move in" on him, like some other girl might."

"Oh."

And with that, she got up to leave. "Thanks anyway, Davey. See you on the bus."

She walked away and I felt awful. My first real chance to be with her and I blew it. When Gary and me got on the bus, I told him what happened. He shook his head.

"Davey, girls are NOT going to want to hang out with you if you treat them crappy. It's a good thing Lori said something. Plus, girls can be really mean about stuff like that.

"How would any other girls know?"

Again, Gary shook his head. Girls talk. You know how fast something like that would get around? Every girl in school would know about it in days, if not hours, and, when I say every girl, I mean, EVERY GIRL. You can't keep stuff like that secret. And...every girl in school would always remember what kind of a kid you were...a schmuck.

"Schmuck?"

February - 195

"Yup!"
Dang!

— ••• —

The Valentines dance was being held the Friday before Valentines, which fell on a Tuesday. Gary and I got to go back to Moxie to get a little trim so we looked as cool as we did on New Years. I decided to wear the sweater Anna had given me for Christmas and a pair of Khakis, because Mom said that me wearing jeans was unacceptable and when she saw I was wearing my Jordans, she did a second no and made me change shoes. Gary was wearing slacks, too, with that white shirt with pearl buttons and his leather vest. He looked like a fancy cowboy, except without the boots. His Mom, Anna, told him to wear loafers, so he did.

The dance was starting at about 7 and we were both being picked up by our dates about 6:30. Debbie and her Mom and Dad got to the house first. Her Mom came up to the door with Debbie, introduced herself to Anna and said they would have Gary home by 11:30. She seemed pretty nice, plus she was also one of the dance chaperones. I was really happy that my Mom wasn't chaperoning. I mean, she's cool, but dang, my first dance and all? Nope, Nope, Nope.

It was a little later that Dana and her Dad knocked. You know, until I opened the door, I still had no idea what her last name was. Dana Stevenson! She was Mr. Stevenson's daughter, the person who ran the animal shelter and a friend of my parents.

My Dad came up and shook his hand. "Charlie, nice to see you. Hello Dana, you look very nice."

What? My Dad knew Dana? I guess I am totally out of it. I didn't even know who she was, but my parents did. Geez. Anyway, the Dad's chatted for 10 minutes and finally, Dana said we had to get moving or we'd be late. It was a little after 7 when we got to the dance.

— ••• —

A real band was playing and there was a ton of kids already there. I saw Eddie across the room. He was wearing a suit. He looked ok, but seemed a little overdressed, although I could see some of the other guys had worn suits too. I'll bet it was his Mother's idea. She's more formal than Mom and Anna.

Eddie was with one of the new girls, a Jennifer somebody. He had wanted Mean Jane to ask him, but she asked some 8th grader. He was smiling so I don't think he was too bothered by it.

A couple of the Moms were checking coats and they gave us a little heart ticket with our coat number on it.

Dana had worn a red cloak and when she took it off, I saw how she was dressed for the first time. I had noticed that a lot of girls were wearing red and white...you know, because of Valentine's day. Not Dana. She was wearing a dark blue velvet dress that had a kind of slit on one side where there was a lacy white ruffle showing under the velvet. The sleeves were long and each also had a slit with the white lacy stuff plus it wrapped around her wrists. Actually, she looked pretty neat. I'm not much on girl fashions, so I hope my description was ok. Later, I found out that her Mom is a seamstress and made the dress. Wow, pretty cool!

I looked around but did not see Lori. I saw her Mom talking to a couple parents, so I figured she was somewhere. I could see JJ's boyfriend over by the food talking to some other 9th graders. Next year he goes to high school along with Lori's boyfriend and that could be it for them. I mean...do high school students want to have boyfriends and girlfriends in middle school? Nope, I seriously don't think so.

Gary was out on the dance floor with Debbie. Well, it's really our gym floor, but they made an area for dancing by putting removable red tape in a square. You were supposed to stay inside that area to dance. It was pretty big and could hold a lot of kids.

Some girls spotted Dana and started toward us. When they did, Dana put her arm through mine. It kind of surprised me, but then, I figured it was some sort of girl thing to let them know that I was her date for the evening and not theirs. I don't know if that's what it was or not. You know, you can't really tell sometimes what a girl means by some of the stuff they say or do.

We didn't dance right away, because Dana loved to talk and she seemed to have a lot of friends, so, it wasn't until after 8 and when the band was playing something slow that she decided it was time.

"Davey? Can we dance now?"

"You know, I'm not very good, Dana. Do you want to take a chance that I step on your nice shoes?"

She laughed. "They're just shoes, so no biggie. Come on."

She took my hand and led me on to the dance floor. I was nervous that I would be a complete klutz, but Dana said to relax and not worry about it. When I did, it seemed to go pretty well, although I'm sure I stepped on her feet a few times. She never said a word about that, so everything was cool.

After two or three different dances, a kid in my class came up and asked if he could cut in. Of course, I said sure, although I'm not sure Dana was too happy about it.

As I was starting to walk off the dance floor, there was a tap on my shoulder and when I turned I saw it was Lori.

"Hi Davey! Are you free for a dance?" Lori was smiling and I was starting to melt.

"Sure...I guess"

"Well, come on then."

Lori took my hand and led me back to the dance floor. My heart was beating so fast I thought maybe I'd pass out. The dance had just started and it was slow. She turned to me and put her left hand on my shoulder. I just stood there and she laughed again and took my left hand and put it on her back at the waist. Then, she leaned forward and whispered "Thanks for dancing with me, Davey."

"Why did you say that, Lori? Didn't Andy want to dance?"

"Well, I never got around to asking him to the dance, so I came by myself...well, with my Mom, who is chaperoning."

"Gee, Lori, I'm sorry. If I had known you were going to ask me, I'd…" Lori interrupted me in mid sentence.

"Stop Davey! Dana is really nice. I'm glad she asked you. I'm glad you said yes. Now let's dance."

She leaned her head against my shoulder. I hadn't realized how much taller I was than her. I guess I had grown a lot. It was perfect..until the dance was over and Dana came back and cut in.

Lori turned to her. "Thanks for letting me dance with Davey. With that, she walked away. I must have been staring at her because Dana tugged on my arm.

"So, you like Lori, don't you?"

I could feel my face turning red. "Of course, she's my friend."

"No, that's not what I mean. I mean you LIKE her, don't you?"

"She has a boyfriend, plus, she and I are just friends. Please don't say any of this stuff to Lori. I don't want her thinking something that's not true. We're only friends, OK?"

Dana shook her head ok

"Can we still dance or maybe you want to get something to eat?"

I didn't want to be schmuck so I told her I wanted to dance a little more. I guess that made her feel a little better because I think she was kind of hurt thinking I had a thing for Lori…which I do. I mean, Dana is nice, so dancing with her was ok. I decided to make her feel cool.

"You know, Dana, you look better than any of the other girls in here. That dress is pretty neat. Did your Mom help you pick it out?"

She smiled and then told me about her Mom making it. I guess saying that made her feel really good, so when we finally walked over to the food, she was happy and chatty, introducing me as her date to all her friends.

Andy Chen was over talking to Eddie and his date. He had come with JJs brother who also came by himself. Andy is a real brain. He belongs to Chess club and Debate club. I mean, I bet he's cool at debate. He really knew how to get JJ worked up about something and I think that's what you do in that club. I think Gary might join when she gets into 9th. It's not open to 7th or 8th.

Dana seemed to be pretty popular. Anyway, we got some food after she stopped chatting with everybody and sat down at one of the tables near Andy. He saw Dana and smiled.

"Hey Dana, so you knew JJ wasn't going to be here. How come you didn't ask me to this soiree??

What?? Soiree?? How fancy schmancy can one person get?

Dana laughed. "C'mon Andy, JJ told Lori to ask you. How come you didn't come with her?"

Andy looked surprised. "Lori never asked me and I didn't know that someone was 'designated' already to be my date. That JJ. We will definitely have to have a talk when she gets back."

Dana snickered, "Well, you better include the hair thing, Andy. JJ was not happy about that."

"GOD, don't girls get over stuff like that?" Andy sounded annoyed.

My comment made him laugh. "As far as I can tell, Andy, they NEVER forget. You'll be 75 and JJ will bring it up.

"You're probably right. I should never have asked her to go blonde." He sighed and I knew he regretted ever saying that.

— ••• —

We talked to a few other kids for a while, then went back and danced a little longer. I was having a good time, even though it wasn't Lori. Dana was really nice.

A little before 11:30, the principal announced that the dance was ending and to get in line to get our coats. We did and when we want outside, Dana's father was waiting for us. He was nice, too and asked how it was going with Rascal and was I happy getting a Saint Bernard. Of course, I told him I was.

It took about 25 minutes to get to my house. Dana and I had sat together in the back seat and she got out with me, squeezed by hand, and thanked me for going with her. Then she hopped into the front seat. Mr.

Stevenson waited until I got in the door before he drove off.

Gary was already home and was in the kitchen making a sandwich.

"So, how'd it go, Davey? Did you have fun?"

"Well, it wasn't Lori, but she's really nice...pretty too, and very popular. Everybody was coming up to talk to her."

"So, did you have fun or not?"

"Yah, I guess I did."

"And are you done pining over Lori?"

"I don't pine over anybody."

"Ahhh, yes you do."

"She came by herself to the dance."

"And? So what? A lot of kids came by themselves."

"Lori came by herself. She asked me and I was going to cancel with Dana, but Lori got pissed and told me not to, because that would be really mean."

"She was right. It would have been really mean. You should never do something like that. Girls will never ever forget."

"Yah, I know. That's what I told Andy when the blonde thing came up. I can't say I didn't have fun, because, well...I did. Dana is really nice and very cute."

"See? There are other girls you could be interested in...right?"

"I guess, but..."

Gary interrupted. "No buts, Davey, time to find a new girl interest."

I nodded like I agreed. but knew that the only girl I was interested in, really, was Lori.

Doe the demon know how much I like her?

— ••• —

March 7

The rest of February breezed by and March rolled around, with the dreaded sex ed classes starting the first week. They were being held in two larger classrooms and all the kids who had to go were assigned certain times. Gary was in one of the first groups. It was held in the morning, so at lunch, I asked how it went.

"Not well," he replied. "A couple of the guys were making weird sounds and some of the girls got upset. So, they cancelled it and now, I have to go again tomorrow. Yuk."

"What was it like with girls there?"

Gary shook his head. "I don't know why the school decided to do these classes with both guys and girls. I mean, it started out and immediately got embarrassing and then, some of the guys started making those grunting sounds and the girls flipped out."

"Wow, I am not going to look forward to that."

"I don't think you have to. The lady who was teaching the class… Mrs. Davis, went to the principal and I guess they're changing it to boys only and girls only."

"Well, that's a relief. Will they change the teacher, too? I mean, a guy for guys?"

"I don't know, but it might be easier to listen to if it wasn't a woman."

Well, it wasn't a woman for some, but my class wasn't so lucky. Mrs. Davis taught mine. I don't think I've ever felt so embarrassed about anything. I mean, Mrs. Davis was matter of fact about everything and I guess I did learn a few things. Still, it was not my idea of a good time.

Gary got lucky. A Mr. Donaldson came in to teach some of the classes. I guess he was pretty cool and he tried to make a point about all of it, about the good, the bad, and the awful of sex.

And yes, that's what Gary said that he actually said. And then he said that Mr. Donaldson explained in detail why he said that.

At least we were now done. I hope we don't have to take any more of these classes. Stuff like that should be for older kids, not us.

— ••• —

March was filled with interesting stuff.

One Saturday, Anna had a talk with Gary. I was in my room playing games when he knocked.

"So my Mom filled me in on some stuff," he said.

"What stuff?" Of course, I was curious.

"They found my Dad in New York City. He was working for some book publisher and was sharing an apartment with some floozy."

I laughed. "Floozy? Do you even know what that means?"

"Ya, it means he's just about the worst Dad ever."

"Well, I don't think that's what it really means, but I get it. So, now that they found him, what's going to happen?"

"Well, I guess they're going to give him divorce papers. He doesn't have to come back here or anything. I guess all Mom has to do is show the court that they can't be married anymore."

Gary looked kind of down and I guess, up until now, he was actually hoping his Dad would come home.

"You know, Gary, he's been gone for pretty long. Your Mom shouldn't have to stay married to him."

"I know. You know she's started dating."

"Ya, I know...the Sarge. He's nice."

Gary agreed. "The Sarge is a really nice guy and seems to like

Mom a lot. I guess, when we were on the ski trip, they went on a date—dinner and a movie."

"So, are you cool with this?"

"Don't know yet. I'll have to see how serious it gets. I mean, I guess they really only started dating a little while ago. You know, Mom and my almost ex-Dad started dating in high school and look what happened."

I tried to say something positive. "Gary, you never really know if parents are going to work out. No one knows why stuff like that happens, but it doesn't mean it will always happen. I mean...the Sergeant... he's had it tough, but look at how good he is to his two furry friends. That says something about what he's like. He cares."

Gary sighed. "I guess. I'm glad Mom's getting out. Did you know she had an interview with the school board about a job teaching when the new elementary opens?

"Wow! I didn't know. That's great. When will she know?"

"I'm not sure. I figure in a few weeks. She would have to be available for orientation at the beginning of August, so there's still a lot of time.

"She'll want to move into her own place won't she? That'll be a bummer."

Gary nodded. "She did talk about it and talked about paying your parents for room and board."

"Geez, she doesn't have to do that. My Mom and Dad are pretty well off. They really wouldn't need her to pay them."

Gary smiled. "I know, but she doesn't like to take handouts. She wants to pay our way wherever we are."

I knew what Gary meant, because my parents were like that as well. My biggest worry was them moving. I really liked them staying with us. Best times ever and that goes for Mom and Dad, too.

—•••—

204 - Demon for Rent

By the end of March, Anna had made it to court and the divorce was in the process of being finalized. One of the conditions written into everything was that his Dad had to pay back child support and continue to pay until Gary turned 18. Of course, his Dad got an attorney to contest it, saying that he didn't make enough money to do back child support and pay every month. The court made him supply employment and salary records and worked out a payment plan for the next couple years.

Then, his Dad tried to get custody of Gary, probably so he wouldn't have to pay, but William Donahue, the attorney representing Anna (and a friend of Dad's) demolished that in court. In the end, full custody was given to Anna with visitation privileges for the Dad, although they would be confined to the state of Colorado.

I mean...why would the court do that? Gary's Dad didn't care about him or he wouldn't have split. I don't think Gary wanted to see his Dad, but I didn't know for sure. Gary never talked at all about him...ever. The only thing he said before was that he had trouble holding a steady job and that sometimes, he would work a few months for someone and then...well, he would either be fired or laid off.

I guess they would catch him playing games on the computer instead of working. Well, that's not good. Why he would do that was completely unclear. His Dad seemed to think he had A.D.D, which is Attention Deficit Disorder. I thought that was only a kid's problem, but I don't know. I guess it can happen to older people, too.

— ••• —

Boy, was I glad that March was over. Those nasty classes were, well, nasty. I hated being taught sex by a woman. I mean, how does she really know how guys feel and act? Anyway, we got through it and we also got through most of the divorce proceedings, although it would not be finalized until June.

April 8

April brought more interesting stuff. The weather was changing and we were getting rain, which Rascal seemed to love. Every time it rained, he always wanted to go out. He had gotten really big and getting him in and drying him off after a walk was a real chore. I mean, dog hair can stink and with a dog as big as Rascal…well you get what I mean.

Jeopardy auditions were the second week of the month, down in Denver. Gary had taken the online test and aced it. I took it, too, but I'm not as smart as Gary and obviously, did not make it. I was surprised to find out that picking contestants to go on was not just because they had done well on the test. From people who passed, people that got to go on were picked from a random pool of those who passed the audition. Gary was lucky that he got picked. I mean, he did do great on the test, but I guess he was just one of the lucky ones to get picked for the audition. It was being held on April 14th. I wanted to go along with him to the tryouts, but it was during school and I couldn't, plus I guess a parent was the only one allowed to be there.

When I got home from school, they were already there. I had a lot of questions.

"So, how'd it go?"

"Good, I guess."

"What does that mean? I bet you did great on your test."

"Ya, probably, but again, they only pick actual contestants from the people who pass and that's random, just like the first test."

"Dang, Gary, does that mean that you might not be a contestant?"

"Yup."

"Dang. I didn't know it was that hard."

"Well, it's easy, but you never know if they're going to pick you. It's cool with me. You know, when the principal wanted me to apply, I don't think he knew how random it was. I think he thought if I passed the tests, I would automatically become a contestant and not just go into a contestant pool. I think he thought it would be good for the school. I mean, a kid from the school getting on Jeopardy…that always looks good."

"Well, I know they'll pick you. I have faith and oh yah…maybe the demon will help."

We both laughed. We knew the demon was just imaginary, made up by Lori's Mom. But, sometimes, we still wondered. Sometimes, things we just couldn't explain happened. Sometimes…

— ••• —

The letter came three weeks later indicating that Gary was in the final contestant pool. Dates had not bee set yet, so of course, there was the possibility that we could wait over a year. I had faith that Gary was going and…road trip!!! Mom and Dad said that if and when they called him, we would all go. Yay!!!

— ••• —

May 9

May! It had rained a lot thru April and flooding and landslides had caused a lot of road closures and accidents in the foothills and the mountains. One of the rains was so heavy that basements around town filled with water. Dad had put sump pumps in ours and luckily, the power had remained on and our basement stayed pretty dry.

We were a lot better off than some of our neighbors and the friends we had in the mountains. One family we knew lost their entire home when a mudslide came down the mountain area where they lived and literally filled their house. It was a complete loss. The family and their pets were safe, but pretty much everything they owned was gone.

Mom started worrying about Mrs. Skriver, so Dad and one of his men went up to make sure she was ok. They found that much of her road had been washed away, but her home was intact and so was she. Her power had been knocked out and it looked like it was going to take a few days to restore the lines and the connections, partially because the crews couldn't get to the problems because of the road.

They decided to pack her up and bring her down to town to stay for a few days or at least until the road could be repaired and the power restored. At first, they had planned to put her in a motel, but Aggie, when she found out, said no, that Mrs. Skriver could stay at her house. She had the room.

A lot of people had been forced out of where they were living back in the woods, so the City of Mercy opened their doors to everyone who needed a place to stay and made it clear that they could stay as long as was necessary.

So many people needed help. Our community came together to do what they could for neighbors, friends, and even strangers. The churches all held food, clothes, and household item drives and many of the businesses gave money or goods, depending on what kind of stores they were. Dad volunteered his crew to help restore power where it was possible to do so. Mom's clinic treated anyone that came in for free. The schools had closed for the rest of the week while everybody tried to get back to normal. A lot of kids from our school volunteered to help people clean up where the rain had caused damage.

Gary and I worked around the neighborhood, doing whatever the families needed us to do. Anna helped too. She took care of some of the younger kids or babies whenever a family needed a safe place for them while they tried to recover what they could from their homes.

— ••• —

The schools stayed closed for a whole week after the disaster, so instead of having classes end the first week of June, they continued thru the seconed week. Gary and I had lined up some mowing jobs to make a little money, but that was mostly on weekends, so the end of school date change didn't really make a difference to us.

— ••• —

Gary's Mom's divorce was finalized June 15th. I wanted to ask Gary how he felt about it, but decided to let him bring it up himself, if he ever wanted to. Anna got an offer from the new elementary school to teach 4th grade. She accepted, but still kept tutoring online. I know she was trying to save every penny so they could move into their own place. I didn't want that to happen, but I understood why.

The Sergeant started coming over regularly on weekends to see

Anna. It was cool. Sometimes Mr. Grossman came along. He was walking with a cane, but his leg had pretty much healed.

Gary started playing chess with the Sergeant, but pretty much got beat every time. Jimmy Hughes was really a good chess player and said that the reason he played the way he did was strategy he learned in the Army. Cool.

When he was playing chess with Gary, Mr. Grossman played bridge with Anna and my Mom and Dad. I guess, before all the crap with Gary's Dad, Anna used to play once a week at a club in the area. She said Mom and Dad were kitchen table players...whatever that means, but Mr. Grossman was really, really good and was at some rank in the bridge community. I think she said he was silver, whatever that means.

I pretty much watched Mom and Dad when they played. I like cards, but bridge seems a little hard. There's all kinds of stuff you need to learn. Chess is hard, too. It's all strategy. Once Gary gets the complete hang of it, I know he will probably beat everybody, including the Sergeant..

—•••—

Rascal had gotten really, really big. When we took him to the vet at the beginning of the month, he weighed almost 150 pounds and the vet said his growth would continue for a while. We all liked going to the farmer's market on Sundays and for a while we took the big puppy along. Everybody loved coming up and petting him and he really loved the attention. Unfortunately, one Sunday, someone else's dog bit a little kid and the people who ran the market banned all dogs after that.

Bummer.

—•••—

June 10

School was over and Gary and I were getting ready for a busy summer. We had 12 houses signed up for mowing every other week. We were charging $35 per mow. Heck, that was $840 for the month, $420 for each of us.

We scheduled 4 mows per day, Monday thru Wednesday. It only took us a little more than an hour to finish each.

Dad got us a bike cart to carry the lawn mower and other equipment. At first I thought it was going to be really hard to pull something like that, but it actually was easy. Well, it was easy except for one house that sat up on a hill, where it was just too steep to pull the equipment up with a bike. Unfortunately, we had to tell the people we couldn't do the mowing for them and the reason why. They were nice about it.

Even though we didn't get that job, the next week we picked up two more lawns on nice flat, non-hilly streets.

We probably could have picked up more, but there were things we wanted to do during the weeks we weren't mowing, like camping.

— ••• —

Dad decided we would go down to Durango and then head over to Mesa Verde National Park. It sounded great and we asked if we could take Rascal along. Dad said we could but there was so much to see that we would miss because no furry friends were allowed.

Mom and Anna didn't want to go, so it was just us guys, like on our ski trip for Gary's birthday.

Gary was a little worried about his Mom being left out of the fun.

"She never got to go anywhere when my Dad was around." he said. "There was never enough money or enough time. I don't want her to be left out."

"Didn't she say she didn't want to go?" I asked, knowing that was actually what she had said.

"Yes, but she probably doesn't want you guys paying for everything like usual. So, she just said she didn't want to go."

Well, that wasn't the case at all. We decided to ask her again.

— ••• —

Mom and Anna were in the living room watching something weird on tv. The kitties were happily curled up in their laps.

They smiled when we came in and sat down on the couch next to my Mom.

Anna spoke first.

"Hi guys. What's going on?"

Gary answered. "Mom, we just want to know why you don't want to go on this camping trip. Is it because of money?"

Gary looked pretty serious when he asked that question.

Anna laughed. "Nope, that's not the reason. Kim can't go because of work obligations and I actually, have other plans."

"Plans? What kind of plans, Mom? You never told me about any other plans." Gary looked kind of aggravated that his Mom hadn't shared what she was planning on doing.

"Well, I'm going to a concert in Denver the Saturday you'll be camping, if you must know."

"What? What concert?"

"Bruce Springsteen."

"Wow! Are you going with Kim?"

"No."

"No?"

She smiled. "That's what I said...No."

"So, where did you get the tickets? Weren't they pretty expensive?"

"Ken Grossman had them, but he's still limping around and didn't feel like going. So...he gave them to Jimmy."

"Jimmy?"

"Yes, Jimmy. The Sarge. That is ok with you, isn't it?"

Gary shook his head yes.

"I was just worried you were going to be left out. Are you sure you don't want to go? It's going to be fun."

Anna laughed again. "I'm sure it is, but I wouldn't go without Kim and she can't go. Plus, then there was the concert. Gary, there'll be other times in the future we can go on a road trip like that. Plus, someone has to watch Rascal and the kitties. Right?"

"Right. I guess so. Sorry. I was just a little concerned."

Anna got up and came over to where we were sitting, the put her arms around Gary and gave him a hug.

"Best son, EVER!" she said. "I'm glad you worry about me."

I guess that made Gary relax a little. After all, we liked Jimmy Hughes alot and if Ken Grossman liked him, too...well, all was cool.

—•••—

We were leaving for Durango on Thursday morning. We packed a bunch of camping stuff in our popup trailer. Dad said not to overpack. We were not going anywhere special, so shorts and t-shirts and of course some underwear, plus a toothbrush, toothpaste, and a bar of soap. We did take jackets in case it got cold, but not our bombers. We didn't want them to get too dirty, plus it was really too hot for coats that heavy.

It took us a little over 6 hours to get to Durango, not including the hour we stopped for a late breakfast or early lunch in Monte Vista, Colorado. Dad had reserved a campsite at a KOA camp. It wasn't as rustic as me and Gary were thinking, but there was a swimming pool and other kids our age to hang out with later in the evening, if we wanted to.

Dad surprised us with a late horseback trail ride and that was a lot of fun. Gary had never been, but the horse people walked him through everything and gave him a really gentle horse to ride, named Pokey. I kind of told the people that I had experienc riding (I had ridden several times over the years) and so they game me Spunky. It was ok, because Spunky was as pokey as Pokey.

We rode in a group with other people who were on vacation. There were two really cute girls on the ride and interestingly, they were staying at the KOA camp also.

Cindy and Anne Myers were from Illinois. Their parents had rented a mobile home and were going to neat places in Colorado. Once they got done in Mesa Verde, they were heading up to Rocky Mountain National Park and then over to Devil's Tower before heading back to Chicago.

You do know where Devil's Tower is? Sure you do. It's the place where Close Encounters of the Third Kind happened. Well, the movie, at least.

I had been to Wyoming lots of times. We camped at Devil's Tower. It was pretty cool watching for aliens. The park showed the Close Encounters movie every night. Cool. That's pretty much all I remember about the place, except that the bugs were gigantic. They came out at night and buzzed around your campfire. I mean, these bugs were maybe 3 or 5 inches long. That is a big bug.

They never botherd us when we slept, because we were in our camper.

Anyway, the girls we met were about our age and after horsback riding and dinner down in Durango, we hung out at the KOA pool with them. Dad is a talker and spent his time chatting with the girl's Mom and Dad.

When it was time to turn in for the evening, Anne put her phone number in Gary's phone and told him to text her sometime. Gary didn't mention he had a girlfriend and when I asked him why, he just shrugged his shoulders and said he didn't want to sound standoffish. Ok, I believe him. He really never lies about anything, which can be a good thing or bad, depending on who he's talking to. Actually, he would probably lie if he felt what he said would hurt somebody, but, most of the time, he's a straight up truth teller.

— ••• —

We got on the road a little after 7 and it took us just over an hour to reach Mesa Verde. Stopping at one of the restaurants right outside the park that sat high up in the hills, , we had a great breakfast. All the tables had fabulous views of the area below.

Did you know Mesa Verde means green table? I was kind of surprised because the area looked a bit like a dry plains area.

Mesa Verde is about an hour from the Four Corners. This is where 4 states come together to meet...Colorado, Arizona, Utah, and New Mexico. There's a monument and everything. Dad said we would drive there after we spent a couple days touring the Pueblo ruins. Puebloans were the people who lived in the Four Corners region over 1000 years ago.

Dad had booked two different tours for us and we were able to see a lot of the places where those people used to live. I had brought a camera to take pictures, but Gary only had his phone. That was ok because it took really good snaps.

The tour guide talked about the people who lived in the area and about how they disappeared. Scientists thought that a really bad drought made living here almost impossible for them, so moving was the only way that they could survive.

Ruins of a lot of their villages and homes are left all over in the park. It used to be that you could explore everything yourself, but I guess that changed years ago when some of the ruins were vandalized. Why do some people think it's ok to damage stuff? What is their problem?

Anyway, Mesa Verde is really most famous for houses built into some of the cliffs.

The places where the Pueblo people lived started as caves under rocks that stuck out in different spots. There are more than 600 cliff dwellings. Scientists or really, I should say archeologists, thought that they built their towns there because it was a great defense against invaders that would try and raid their villages. Because of where they lived, they could just pull the ladders up and nobody could attack them. Pretty smart.

— ••• —

We camped in a campground just outside the park. It was pretty rustic. Each site had a fire pit and a gravel area, so if it rained, you weren't tracking mud into your camper.

Because Gary and I wanted to cook over the campfire, Dad had brought hot dogs and stuff in a Coleman Cooler that even had wheels so you could pull it and not have to carry it. He filled it with dry ice and everything stayed fresh, including the cream he had to have for his coffee. Me and Gary haven't really gotten into drinking stuff like that, although, it really smells great when you make it when you're camping.

After we had our dinner (hot dogs soda and smores), we sat out and looked at the stars. It gets really, really dark there and you can see just a ton of things in the sky, including a few shooting stars. Neat!!

— ••• —

In the morning, we went on another really fun excursion. This time we got to raft down the Animas river and see ruins that you couldn't see unless you were on the water.

I think maybe, if the school offers some sort of class in stuff like this, I'll take it.

Anyway, we spent one more night at the campground and the next morning, we packed up and headed for the Four Corners. It wasn't as interesting as Mesa Verde, but at least we could say we'd been there.

As we drove, we saw stores or trading posts with Native American gifts and jewelry.

"Do you think we can stop at a couple?" Gary asked Dad.

"Sure. Were you looking for something special?"

"I wanted to get my Mom something. She like turquoise."

"Maybe we should get something for Mom, too." I said to Dad.

He agreed, but said we could stop on the way back from the Four Corners.

—•••—

Did you know...you can stand in four Different states at once in the Town of Teec Nos Pos, Arizona!

There's a place called Four Corners Monument at the intersection of Arizona, Colorado, New Mexico, and Utah, and it's the only spot in America where you can stand in four different states.

Back in 1912, to commemorate the end of territorial disagreements between those states, an official monument was erected to mark the intersection of all four of them.

Now, of course, it's a tourist destination and we had to go there for our camping trip!

—•••—

There were a lot of shops there and after we had done the standing in four states stuff and took some pictures, we did a little browsing.

I didn't buy anything there, but Dad bought Mom some earrings and Gary bought a cool turquoise bracelet. It wasn't real expensive or anything, but it was nice. I'm pretty sure it was not for his Mom—it was probably for Debbie, bcause he still wanted to stop at a couple of the other places we had passed when we were driving here.

That was ok with Dad, because he likes to browse and I liked looking around, too.

I had thought of buying Lori a little something, but it wasn't Christmas or anything and then, if I did, she would know I liked her. I didn't want that to happen...yet.

Gary seemd to think she already knew.

"Davey, don't be so worried. It's just a gift for a friend. You can buy something for Eddie, too, or maybe for Dana?"

"If I bought something for Dana, she would think I liked her a lot more than I do. I mean, I like her, but more as a friend."

"OK, fine, then buy Eddie something and then you can get something small for Lori."

Gary's plan sounded like it would work, so I took the time to look at all the stuff girls like Lori might like. She loved that old jeans jacket she wore all the time...i.e. the one with the rhinestones. It had a kind of Indian pattern on it. One of the shops we looked in had some bling like the purse stuff I had given her for xmas.

There were little messages on each item, telling what the meaning of the piece was. There was one tiny bling thingy that had a teeny feather and what looked like a tooth of some sort, plus a piece of turquoise, all hanging down with thin pieces of leather. The note attached said that particular item brought luck and happiness to the person who wore it It was only $13, so I bought it for her.

— ••• —

Just a note...at the last minute, after we got home, I got scared and decided against giving it to her. Worthless, I am.

Of course, all Gary did was laugh at how ridiculous I was being.

— ••• —

We took our time heading toward home, stopping at a couple more places to look at Native American gifts and jewelry. Gary bought his Mom a silver and turquoise pendant that you could either wear as a necklace or take off the chain and pin it to your shirt or dress. It was nice, a lot more expensive than the little bracelet he had bought first. He also bought another vest, this one was a lighter leather, with a woven leather edge. It was nice.

I almost bought a t-shirt, but then, didn't, only because I couldn't find one I really liked. Most of the clothes said made in China, not the vest Gary bought, but the t-shirts and stuff.

In the end, I saved my money, except for a pair of silver and turquoise earrings that looked like little turtles. I figured Mom would like them (and she did).

— ••• —

We made it home late Sunday night. Everybody was happy to see us, especially Rascal, who yipped and jumped up on us, almost knocking us over. The Moms wanted to know how everything went and if we had pictures. Of course, we told them yes and would get them onto the computer so we could do a kind of picture presentation by hooking up the computer to the tv in the living room. We planned to show all of them tomorrow after dinner.

We gave the presents to the Moms after we had gotten everything out of the camper. They loved the stuff we had gotten them. Anna was really happy with the necklace and Dad, being the kind of Dad that doesn't want to leave anybody out, got her a pair of earrings so she would be getting two presents like Mom was. All cool.

I was a little tired, even though we hadn't done anything really strenuous, but I decided to go up to my room and hit the sack. Gary had gone up to his room too, but a minute later there was a loud yell and a sound like something had been dropped. Of course, I immediately went up to see what was going on.

Gary's door was open and I saw Gary on his hands and knees, holding a box down on the floor.

"What are you doing, Gary? What was that noise?"

"Guess what I have under this box?" he said.

I had no idea. I saw that his chair had been knocked over, which was probably the sound I had heard from downstairs.

"Ok, so what's in the box?"

"It's a Scorpian, Davey. I was starting to unpack my stuff and all of a sudden, this Scorpian fell out of my backpack. It scared the heck out of me and I knocked the chair over when it dropped down on the floor in front of me."

"Wow! How big is it?"

"Not big. You want to help me try and get it into a container or something?"

"Sure. I'll go get something from the kitchen. Just keep holding it in the box."

I ran downstairs immediately and went to the kitchen to see if there was anything we could get the Scorpian into. Dad came into the kitchen and asked what I was up to. When I told him that a Scorpian was in Gary's backpack, he immediately went upstairs and told Gary he would take care of it.

Dad got a piece of cardboard, like the back of a paper tablet, and carefully pushed it under the box. Dad had told me to get a plastic kitchen garbage bag and I held it as he picked the box and cardboard up off the floor and put it in the bag, then tied it off and took it down and out to the trash.

I'm pretty sure he squished it, but I don't know.

— ••• —

We carefully went through all our stuff to make sure there were no other creepy crawly things lurking in sleeves or a sock or whereever. We were all surprised that one had actually gotten in, because we were careful not to put anything down on the ground. Everything was either in the camper or the Jeep.

Still, somehow, it managed to get in. I was glad we were able to catch it without anybody getting stung. I guess it was just a little more excitement to finish off an already fun trip.

— ••• —

During the few days we were gone, Dad's friend Frank at the hardware store called Dad to see if Gary and I wanted to do more inventory stuff. Dad didn't tell us he called until after we got home. Of course, we said yes. Gary and I were going to be the richest kids in 8th grade. Thanks Dad's friend!

July

July was starting out pretty well. Gary and I were making extra money by working on Fridays at Frank's hardware store, plus, of course we were still doing our mowing. We would do that until school started at the end of August and then, we would either do the lawns after school or on Saturday or Sunday, depending on when the families wanted them done.

Mowing usually stopped middle or end of October, which was perfect. By then, we would have bunches of money and wouldn't have to worry about buying Christmas presents.

Dad was still giving us a little for doing chores around the house and Gary and me put it all away. Some of it went into a bank account, but a lot of it got stashed in our rooms.

It was cool not to have to ask for money if we wanted to buy something or go somewhere that cost more than usual. Sure, we still asked permission when there was something special we wanted to do, but we didn't have to ask the parents to pay. It felt good.

— ••• —

The Fourth snuck up on us really fast. I didn't know much about Lori's house, but Mom said we were to bring our swimming suits because they had a pool.

A day or so before the party, Mom took us over to the mall. I needed new swim trunks and Gary just needed them, because he didn't have any. As I was browsing in Kohls, there was a tap on my shoulder. Turning, I saw it was Dana and with her was this kid I didn't know.

"Hi Davey!. What's going on?"

"Shopping for a new swim suit for a party."

"You mean Lori's parent's party? Me and Jacque here are going to be there. Oh ya, this is Jacque. He just moved here from France. This is my friend Davey."

Jacque stuck his hand out to shake mine. His other arm was wrapped around Dana's shoulder and a kind of odd feeling came over me...jealousy maybe? I didn't know why I would start feeling like that. After all, I was only interested in Lori. Still...

"Nice to meet you." I said, then pointed over a few aisles toward Gary. "That kid over there is my friend Gary. We're both going to be at the party."

"Cool. You guys want to go down to the food court with us?"

"Can't. We're with my Mom and we're heading home as soon as I find some swim trunks."

Dana smiled. "Ok, see you in a couple days!"

And off they went, with Jacque's arm around her shoulder and her hand on his back. When, exactly, did that happen? I'm not sure why it bothered me...but it did.

Just then, Gary came up carrying a bag from the store. He had managed to buy some trunks. I was still browsing, but finally, settled on some blue ones with a picture of a dolphin jumping from a wave in the ocean. They looked pretty neat.

Mom had given me her Kohl's card and told me to pay for both me and Gary, but Gary had insisted he pay for his own. I guess that was his choice. Still, I used the card because I wanted to save as much money as possible.

— •••—

Mom had gone over to some other store in the mall and told us she would meet us in front of Kohl's. We walked out just as she was coming back.

She was carrying two shopping bags and when we asked her what she had gotten, she said we would have to wait until we got home to find out.

Of course, we really curious. What had she bought that was so special that she was keeping it secret?

— ••• —

As we drove up to the house, we saw Anna standing on the porch with Rascal. Seeing us, she smiled and waved.

"Rascal really wanted out and it was such a beautiful day, I decided to take him for a short walk."

Looking at her, you really couldn't tell all the crap she had gone through just a few months before. She had gained enough weight to make her not look skinny and starving like she looked before. Now, she was just slender. Plus, her hair had been cut short and looked kind of like a pixie cut, at least that's what Mom called it. She was very pretty.

— ••• —

Anna had started heading out on her own, doing a bit of shopping or going occasionally to play bridge at a club, which she liked doing. Because she was making pretty good money working part time as a tutor, she started to pay for some of the expenses herself...her own and some of the house expenses.

Like Gary said...his Mom was independent and didn't like taking from people without giving something back. Anna had started to pay Mom and Dad back for things like the car registration and insurance. She also bought groceries for the family and paid for takeout and other stuff.

Mom had told her no, that it was not necessary, but Anna insisted, saying that she wanted to pull her own weight when it came to money.

Cool. That's what me and Gary also wanted to do, although, as I mentioned before, if my Mom wants to pay for something for me, I am definitely not saying no.

Anyway, once we got in, we stood in the kitchen waiting for Mom to tell us what was going on.

"So, you do remember you had an idea about helping people, David?" Mom stood at the counter, smiling.

"Sure, lots of them. Which one were you talking about?"

"The phone idea to help some of the low income and homeless people around our town."

I had almost forgotten about the idea. It had been a long time from when I thought of it to now. I should have known that they hadn't forgotten about it.

Mom pulled a box out of one of the shopping bags and it was a disposable phone.

She continued. "Well it took Aggie and I a little work to get these with enough minutes to make it worthwhile for the person who got one. Aggie...she has a gift. She convinced the owner of the electronics store in the mall to sell us these disposable phones for cost. She's really something, isn't she?"

Well, yes, and I wasn't telling Mom that she had a demon helping her. I mean, does a demon have to be bad? No. That was obvious from all the good stuff that has happened.

Anyway, Mom had picked up a bunch of the burners, with phone plans that would last the people that got them for a full year. There were 10 phones and she indicated that we would take them up to City of Mercy and give them to the people who could really use them. To get a plan that lasted a year was a bit expensive, but Mom and Aggie decided to do it.

When we had bought Mrs. Skriver the phone, we didn't do a year's worth of access, but Aggie and Mom got the plan for her as well. She had the phone, but now, it would be good for the minutes we had gotten her PLUS a full year more.

I know that they spent more than the money that was left over from the Thanksgiving dinner, but somehow, they had managed.

Mom said that they had wanted to get more phones, but thought it would be a lot better to buy fewer, but do the year of service.

Although I agreed, I was a little concerned that too many other people who needed one wouldn't get one, but Mom assured me that they were working on more money for more phones.

— ••• —

The plan was to take the phones up to City of Mercy the day before the fourth. Mom asked me and Gary if we wanted to go along and of course, we said yes.

About 10 in the morning, me, Gary, Mom, and Anna headed up to the charity center. It was a beautiful day, but hot. We decided to leave the top on the Jeep because the temperature was heading into the 90s.

When we got there, Mom phoned in and the gates opened. As we drove up, we could see some of the kids outside playing and two ladies watching them. They saw us coming and one of them, a tall red-headed woman with a slight limp, came over to greet us.

"Hi. You're here to see Hook?"

Mom nodded. "Yes, we've brought some disposable phones for a few of your guests."

Gloria DelRio smiled. "Oh, you're the phone ladies. Hook's expecting you. Follow me."

She waited while we got out of the car and then led us up the main pathway to one of the front entrances. Remember, this used to be a factory of sorts and there were plenty of places you could go in and out. Because of the kids, however, most of the doorways were locked from the inside. You could get out, but you couldn't open the door from the outside unless it was unlocked inside.

228 - Demon for Rent

The other times we came up we hadn't gone inside. This was interesting. There were rooms running all the way around the edges of the building and a large open area in the center. On the very far side was a cafeteria with windows all along the wall that looked out over mountains. There must have been 20 or 30 people in that room having breakfast. Hook told us later that they continued to serve some breakfast stuff all day because the kids liked it the most.

Some of the people staying at the center worked in the kitchen and in other places. This was a way to pay the charity back for helping them. They never had to do the work full time. Part of their day was spent doing resumes and trying to find jobs in the surrounding towns. They had a resource center to help them do that.

The lenth of time single people or families spent at City of Mercy actually varied quite a bit. Many individuals, who were there by themselves, were able to leave after a few weeks. For families, however, it tended to be more like months.

The thought crossed my mind that this place would have been perfect to help Gary and his Mom. I wasn't really sure why they had not reached out for the help, but then I remembered what Gary had said about his Mom being proud and not wanting handouts from anyone. I guess the only reason she came to stay with us was because she was so sick she had no other choice.

Then, of course, Mom was there to convince her it was the right thing to do. Boy, I'm glad that happened...no, not that she got really sick...just the part where they came to stay with us.

— ••• —

We stood at the entrance to the cafeteria and waited for Gloria to get Hook. When he came out of the kitchen he was wearing an apron and a chef's hat that kind of flopped over to one side of his head.

Seeing us he waved and smiling greeted us.

"Kim, it's nice to see you again and these are your kids?"

"One of them. You met both of them before when we were doing the Halloween Charity event."

"Ah yes, I remember. Say you do remember how to greet me, don't you, David?"

Of course I did.

"Yes sir, Lieutennant Hook."

He laughed. "You did remember. Good job! So, Hook is fine or, if you want to get fancy, just call me Jack. And...the other young'un... Gary, correct?"

"Yes sir!"

"Well, come on. Follow me to my office and we'll discuss "the plan."

The plan was the phone stuff and the discussing, I guess was to decide who needed one the most.

— ••• —

Jack Davis turned out to be the general manager of the facility. We just thought he may have been some homeless guy who decided to work all the time for the charity, but that was not the case.

He had graduated from Stanford in Economics and went on to get his Masters, which I think was in social work. There were diplomas on the wall behind his desk, but because I hadn't worn my glasses (and I should have), the little print was blurry.

There were enough chairs for all of us to sit and after we did, he leaned back in his chair and folded his arms.

"So, you and Aggie have been up to a lot of good. Am I right, Kim? What's this about phones?"

"Jack, I have to tell you that this idea came from the kids here— David and Gary. Aggie and I just did a little work to help make it happen.."

"Is that so? The Lieutenant smiled, stood, and went to a big, old filing cabinet that was sitting in the corner of the office. He went through each drawer, pulling out manilla folders, some of which had a ton of papers and others, you couldn't tell if there was anything in them.

After he had gone through the entire cabinet, he brought the stack back to his desk. There were maybe 25 folders in the pile.

"So, if I'm not mistaken," he began, "you got disposable phones to pass out to some of the people here, correct?"

Kim nodded. "We don't have enought to give to everyone in that stack of folders, Jack. We can supply 10 phones to the most needy and the rest...well, we're working on getting the funds for more."

Jack nodded. You know that these people won't have enough money to buy minutes to use with the phones. Some of them have come here with absolutely nothing. They have no disposable money for anything,

Mom smiled. "We know that. Each phone has a year of usage paid for. By the end of a year, we're hoping that they'll be back on their feet and can buy more minutes themselves. Does that work for you, Jack?

"Damn, you ladies are good. I should have known you'd have a plan and it would be the right one. So, guys, let's make some decisions about who to give them to."

With that, he pushed the pile of folder to the middle of his desk and told us all to take one, read the person or family's situation, then make a mental note of what we each considered the neediest.

— ••• —

We each looked through every folder and when we were done, we discussed each possible recipient. In the end, we had whittled the group down to 11.

Obviously, that was one too many for the phones we had, but Mom said not to worry about it, because we would get another one as soon as possible.

The people and families we had picked were all pretty bad off. Gary and his mom were bad, I had thought, but some of these people were worse than them.

I supposed you're wondering how we picked. It was tough. So much need. I knew Mom and Aggie would get busy to get more phones for them and maybe for some of the people living in poverty in the area.

I'm still surprised about that...I mean the number of people who live in poverty. It doesn't make sense in a country this rich. .

— ••• —

We didn't entirely agree on who should get the phones. There was a woman with 4 kids and they had been living in their car. She was still working, but the money she was making wasn't close to enough to take care of her family. City of Mercy was helping her train for something better (right now she was working at a fast food place for minimum wage). She would work all day and then take classes in computer work at night.

The kids were bussed to school and when they were out, someone at the charity would watch them until their Mom got back amd when she took the classes, which were held down at one of the community colleges in our area.

Gary was the first to speak up about her.

"I think this family should be the first to get a phone," he said. "The Mom is doing everything in her power to get back on her feet, but to do it, she has to be gone a lot of the time. Without communication, how is she going to know if the kids are ok or if anything is happening at this place? I think she should get one of the phones."

Jack David took the folder with her info and separated it from the pile.

Anna was next to make a recommendation. As she had looked through everything, tears ran down her face. She understood, personally, what a lot of these people were going through.and I guess it hurt just thinking there were other people that had bad experiences like her and Gary.

As each person spoke up, Jack took the folder and put it in the hold pile. When we were all done, as I said before, we had 11 candidates for the phones. Mom had said no problem and for 11, I'm sure it wasn't. The big issue was that so many other people needed help.

Like I just said, how can a country so rich have so many people who are poor?

— ••• —

We left before the phones were being passed out. Later, Jack Davis let us know that everyone who got one was really happy and grateful for the kindness. I wish I were a trillionaire so I could help everybody! Maybe the demon can make that happen...probably not, but it was a great thought.

— ••• —

Lori's house was on the very western edge of our town. They had what seemed like a ranch, although Aggie said it was only 30 acres. Only? That's huge! Anyway, there were lots of trees and a pond where you could fish in the summer. There was also a barn or maybe it was a stable. I don't really know the difference except that horses are in a stable and there were some I could see in a fenced area nearby.

The land was pretty flat, but sat up kind of on a hill where you could look down on the town and see the foothills and mountains in the distance. Lori said that sometimes, in the summer, she would wake up and see snow on the peaks. Neat!

I had never though of Lori being a rich kid, but I guess she was. She didn't act rich. I mean a lot of rich kids are stuck up and act like you are lower class citizens. Not Lori. She always treated everyone with respect and picked her friends without thinking whether they had a lot of money. She is really something special. I've told you that before, right?

— ••• —

Looking at her house from a distance, it looked like a mansion. She told us later that they had 7 bedrooms, each with a bathroom. That is definitely a mansion.

Anyway, her Dad had inherited the property from his parents when Lori was just a baby. They had lived there ever since.

Just to let you know, Lori's Dad was the CEO of some big financial company. I wondered why he never seemed to be around when there were parties and stuff like that, but I guess it was because he traveled all over the world to the various locations where his company was. So, he was never home.

Well, today he was.

When we drove up to the front of the house, there were two guys parking cars. They looked like college kids. Valets for a barbeque?

Yup, Lori's parents were rich.

— ••• —

Aggie was in the front greeting people as they arrived. When she saw us she waved and came over to the car as we got out, hugging Mom.

"I am so glad you guys could make it." she said. "It looks like everyone we invited is showing up. I'm staying out here to greet people and then, Kim, we need to discuss some things."

She was probably talking about the phone stuff, but with Aggie and Mom, it could be anything.

Aggie told us to go in the front door and walk straight through to the back where the party was.

As we walked through the house to the back, I was surprised to see how fancy it was. The entryway was all marble and a spiral staircase swept upward to a second floor. Lori told us later that they even had an elevator. Geez..an elevator? Can I really call it a house? No. I don't think so.

Anyway, we walked thru the house to the back and came out on a beautiful stone patio that went all the way down to a huge swimming pool. When I say huge...well, it seemed bigger than that.

There must have been at least 100 people there already. Most of the kids were at the pool. When Lori spotted us, she waved and came over, pointing us to a bath house where we could change. A bath house, too? Oh my.

Gary had been pretty silent, but when we were changing he did comment.

"I'm pretty uncomfortable with this, Davey." he said, placing his clothes in one of the empty lockers. "I hope this doesn't upset my Mom."

I knew what he was talking about. Living in an old dilapidated trailer for so long and then coming out here to all this...yup, I could understand why he was concerned about his Mom.

"It'll be ok, Gary. We can check on her as soon as we change."

Gary said fine and as we started back to where all the adults were, he saw his Mom talking to a group of people near the food. One of them was Jimmy Hughes and he had his arm around her shoulder. She was laughing and it looked like everything was cool.

We went back over to the pool where our friends were and even though Gary's Mom seemed to be having a good time, he kept and eye on her the whole time we were there.

— •••—

The party went really well. All the food was super and later, after we had finished swimming and eating, they played music for dancing. Gary danced mostly with Debbie and of course, Lori danced with that kid. I danced with a couple of girls I didn't know. I was hoping that Lori would ask me like at the Valentine's dance...but she didn't.

It was ok. I still had a good time.

After it got dark, they shot fireworks off. We always worried about fire and starting one, but Lori's parents had hired a professional to come in and do it. All went off without a hitch.

Then, before we left for the evening, I got the greatest news I had ever heard. It was mind-blowing. Yes, yes, yes...the demon is still around and is probably listening to my thoughts.

I suppose you're wondering what that news could be. Well....

— ••• —

Lori's boyfriend's Dad got transferred to Boston. Yay!!!!!

August 2

I guess I am the luckiest kid in the universe...well, at least in 7th grade. It was August and almost time to go back to school. 8th grade! Can you believe it?

I was getting older and taller and skinnier. Mom and Anna made Gary and me go buy new stuff for school. It was always cool and we did a lot of shopping at Kohl's, because both Moms liked their Kohl's cash. Of course, we shopped for pens and notebooks and other stuff that you gotta have for classes.

Mom paid for me and Anna paid for Gary. I think it made her feel really good that she could now take care of her son comfortably. She was doing really well tutoring and now that she would be teaching at the new elementary school...well, everything was working out great for them.

—•••—

Gary and I had made a lot of money, which would go for presents and all sorts of other stuff. We were really rich...well not rich like Lori's parents, but rich in the sense that it was the most money either of us had ever had...for 7th graders that is.

My birthday came up on the 14th and of course, we had a party with all our friends. They held it at Splitzies, a newish bowling alley kind of near the event center where we had done Thanksgiving. I had mentioned liking to bowl and of course, my parents remembered.

Splitzies did not just having bowling. There were pool tables and an arcade with a lot of fun games. They also had really good food, with stuff that you probably wouldn't get normally in a bowling alley. That was because the owner also owned a bakery and so all the bread and rolls were fresh and yummy. Everything was perfect.

I got a lot of neat presents, but the best was that my parents decided to let me get contacts.

Gary got me a kit to build a racing car and him and me spent hours putting it together. When we were done, we took it out to run it on the sidewalk, but somehow, we had done something wrong and it veered off the path and crashed into a tree. We ended up taking it apart and reading the directions again (thoroughly this time) and rebuilding it.

There was a competition up at one of the ski resorts during the fall and we did take it there to compete. We came in 3rd. Not too shabby for building it ourselves and then having to rebuild it.

Lori gave me new ski gloves. I didn't even know she skied and had no idea that she knew I did. No, it wasn't the demon who told her. I'm pretty sure she just asked my Mom.

Anyway, everything for my birthday was perfect. Life was good and...it got better.

—•••—

School was starting toward the end of August, but the weekend before, my phone rang and it was Lori.

"Davey, a bunch of us are going to a movie on Saturday. Do you and Gary want to go with us?"

My heart skipped a beat.

"Sure. Who's going?"

"Well, it'll be you and me and Gary and Debbie and then, a few of our other friends."

What??? Did I hear her correctly? Me and her? I had to be cool about this.

"Sounds great, Lori. Should we meet you there?"

"No, my Mom will pick you guys up. Oh yah...you do know there's a back-to-school dance middle of September. Are you planning on going?"

YIKES...

"I hadn't thought about it. Did you have something in mind?"

"Oh, well I figured that maybe we could go together?"

"Uhh...is this one of those Sadie Hawkins dances?"

"Nope. I just thought it would be fun if we went together. Of course, if you don't want to, I would understand."

"No, I'd love to go with you."

"Great! It's going to be a really good year. Don't you think so, Davey?"

"Oh yes...a really good one."

— ••• —

A really, really, really, REALLY good year.

www.ingramcontent.com/pod-product-compliance
Lightning Source LLC
LaVergne TN
LVHW091637070526
838199LV00044B/1109